MW01286061

Shall you not rest in peace...

HELL NIGHT SERIES
ALEX GRAYSON

prologue

JW
The Past

TONIGHT IS HELL NIGHT. *The one night a month that I, my brothers, and all the other kids in Sweet Haven walk through Hell and come out on the other side broken and feeling lost. It's a night that the adults change from sweet and loving parents, to the monstrous evil that normally lays dormant.*

Tonight isn't the usual Hell Night though. It's not the kids who are suffering the horrors and pain of being forced to do things they don't want to do. It's the adults who are screaming and crying in fear. It's the adults who are begging and fighting against the hands that are holding them down. Tonight, the adults are walking through Hell.

It's late. Like after four in the morning. The official Hell Night, or what the adults call The Gathering, ended a couple of hours ago. I'm sore all over. My brother was rough earlier. More so than normal.

Only wearing a t-shirt and boxers, my hair still wet from my shower, and barefoot, I creep along the side of my house. I make sure to stay in the shadows.

My heart pounds in my chest and nerves make my stomach feel queasy. I whip my head around when I hear a scream a few houses down. It's an adult. A woman. I briefly wonder who it is. I push the thought to

1

the back of my head because I don't have time to think about it. I need to get to my brothers. We're all supposed to meet Mae and Dale behind The Hill.

I round the front side of my house, but come to a stop when I see dark figures, a bunch of them, stalk up the steps onto my porch. I back up and dart behind our neighbor's, Mr. and Mrs. Sanders', house.

I'm just rounding the corner when I hear a loud bang and shouts come from inside my house. I pant as I start running, looking behind me to make sure no one's spotted me and is following.

The night opens up to more screams and yells. Suddenly, I'm falling, and my hands go in front of me to catch myself before my face smashes into the ground. The grass is wet with dew and my nails dig into the blades as I push myself up. I turn and slowly walk back to what I tripped over. It's a body. Bending down, I notice it's Mr. Sanders. Something dark is on the front of his shirt just below the collar. I can't see the color, but from the way his eyes are open and sightlessly staring up at the sky, I've no doubt it's blood. He's dead.

A thrill rushes through me. I'm glad he's dead. I just wish I was the one brave enough to have killed him.

My feet squish in the cool wet grass as I leave Mr. Sanders on the ground. I stop behind a shed when I see a short figure up ahead hunched over behind a tree. The figure turns their head, and I recognize the face from the moonlight. Bending low, I jog over to my brother, Judge.

"Where're the others?" I whisper once I'm at his side.

Without turning his head, he answers in a low voice. "I'm not sure, but I've got a guess." Reaching back, he grabs my shirt. "Come on."

He pulls me behind him, but there's no need. I'd follow him anyway.

We're forced to stop again when someone comes barreling out of the shadows in front of us and runs toward a car. They get the door open before a deep voice rings out.

"Halt! This is the FBI! Put your hands behind your head and get on your knees!"

The light from inside the car reveals Noah Vincent's face. He's one of the younger adults, and a friend of my brother, Trey. I remember when he used to fight Hell Night. A couple years ago, that changed. Now he willingly joins in. Whatever happens to him, I hope it hurts.

I don't get a chance to see if he does as the FBI orders, because Judge and I are sprinting again. Instead of heading toward The Hill like we should be, we're running the opposite way. Judge doesn't have to tell me where we're going. There's only one reason we would be going this way. To get Emo and Trouble.

Emo has been acting more volatile than usual lately, and I know it's because he's still torn up over the death of Rella, Trouble's sister. He told us he thought he heard her scream last night. That's not possible. We saw her ghostly-white body. We saw the blood soaking into the wood of the gazebo beneath her. There's no way anyone could live with the amount of blood she lost.

We're only a couple of houses away from Trouble's when a familiar scream has me halting in my tracks. It's my mother's. A moment later, I hear my father bellow. I don't stop because I'm concerned with what's happening to them. I stop because I want to take a minute to relish in their pain. I want to soak up the sound of their fear and helplessness, because they've been the cause of mine for as long as I can remember. Nothing that they're going through could come even close to what I've endured.

"JW," Judge hisses a few feet away from me. "We gotta go."

We run in the opposite direction of where my parents are, but their sounds of torment follow me. It's a sound I hope I will always carry with me. Even after my brothers and I leave this place of Hell behind.

chapter one

JW

TOSSING MY PHONE IN THE passenger seat, I flip my lights on, pull out of the access road, and haul ass after the cherry red convertible that's going sixty-eight in a fifty-five zone.

Damn crazy idiots.

I gain on the car, and either they haven't spotted me behind them or they just don't give a fuck, because their lead foot is still very much on the gas pedal. Irritation has my hands choking the steering wheel when they don't slow down once we hit Malus's outer limits. What in the hell is so Goddamn important that they couldn't get to where they're going a minute or two later?

Thinking about the people walking the streets and the kids playing on the sidewalks only a mile away makes me want to kick the dickhead's face in, *then* issue them a ticket. Or better yet, toss their ass in a cell and let them stew for a night or two.

They have a Texas license plate, but I don't recognize the car, so they can't be from around here. Which is a whole other potential problem.

Outsiders aren't welcome in Malus.

Flipping the switch on the control box on my dashboard, I blip my siren a couple of times, just in case the person hasn't spotted me behind them. Their head pops up, and I can barely make out a pair of sunglasses in their rearview mirror.

Thankfully, and wisely, they begin to slow down. I cruise to a stop behind the car just a few blocks away from the sheriff's office, which is convenient if things happen to go sour.

Climbing out of my truck, I approach the car slowly. Once I'm at the back fender, I notice the small hands gripping the steering wheel. Feminine hands. Ones with fingernails painted a bright red. The woman's head is facing forward, but she tilts her head to the side once I'm at her door.

Huge black sunglasses that cover half of her face stare up at me. Her lips match the color of her nails. Her hair is in a scarf, but I still see red strands peeking out of the edges of the silky material.

"License and registration, please," I request, an irritated bite to my tone.

After blowing out an aggravated sigh, she digs in her purse and produces a small wallet.

"Is there a problem, officer?" she asks, handing over her license.

"It's Sheriff. You were goin' thirteen over the speed limit and didn't slow down once you reached the town limits. I'd say yes, there's a problem." I glance up from looking at her license. "Registration?" I remind her, arching a brow behind my aviators.

"Oh, right," she mutters and reaches for the glove compartment. I look back down at the license.

Eden Delmont. Lives is San Antonio, Texas. Born December 15th, 1987. I look at the picture displayed. Red hair and green eyes. Because I'm a man first and a sheriff second, I note how pretty she is, even though she's not smiling in the picture.

Something white is shoved in my line of sight, and I realize it's her registration. I snatch it from her hand, because if she wants to play the bitch role, I can certainly play the asshole. She faces the windshield again and her hands go back to the steering wheel, her thumbs tap rapidly and her knee bounces.

People get nervous when they get pulled over. It's to be expected. But this is more than simple edginess.

"Is there a problem?" I ask.

She doesn't turn her head when she mumbles. "No."

"You mind telling me why you were in such a hurry?" When she keeps her lips sealed stubbornly shut, I point to the town ahead with the hand holding her license. "You see those houses and buildings?" I don't give her time to answer. "There are kids playing along the streets. People walking their dogs. What in the hell was so important for you to put their lives in danger?"

Her lips purse and she white-knuckles the steering wheel, staying silent. What in the fuck is wrong with this woman? Is she high, drunk, or just a cunt?

I release a tired breath and take a step back. "I need you to step out of the car."

This time, I get a response. She whips her head around. "Why?"

"Because I'm going to run your license and registration, and I get the feeling as soon as I turn my back, you're going to flee."

"You can't!" she blurts. Her hands fly to the door handle. Had I not already taken a step back, my balls would have been flattened to pancakes. She jumps out of the car and slams the door shut. Her hand flies to her ribs, just below her left breast. I can't see her eyes because of the sunglasses, but from the scrunch of her nose, she just winced.

"Please don't run my license," she begs and leans back against her car, her hand still holding her side.

"Why?" I ask suspiciously. "You got somethin' to hide?"

As she bites her bottom lip, avoiding my question, I take in her appearance behind my sunglasses. She has on some kind of flowy-type skirt that goes all the way down to her feet, which are encased in sandals. Her shirt is a deep-red silk, sleeveless, with a V that cuts low, showing off her creamy white cleavage. The bottom of the shirt stops just before it hits the low waistband of her skirt, giving just a hint of her stomach. The scarf around her head is long, stopping at her waist, and hiding her hair. A shit ton of skinny metal bracelets loop around her wrists and long silver dangly earrings hang from her ears. She looks like a glorified gypsy. A gorgeous glorified gypsy.

"No, no. Nothing like that," she finally answers, interrupting my perusal of her body. I lift my eyes back to hers.

She exhales heavily and slouches back more against the door. I tip my chin to her ribs.

"Are you injured?" I ask.

"What?" She looks down at her hand, then straightens from the car, her hand falling away. "I ran into the banister at home."

She's lying through her fucking teeth. Suspicion forms in my mind. You can tell a lot about a person by looking into their eyes.

"Remove your glasses," I order.

"No."

My brows jump up in surprise. "Excuse me?"

"Why do you want me to remove them?"

This chick is really starting to piss me off. I take a step toward her.

"Because I said so," I grit. "And because I'll be able to tell if you're on drugs or drunk by seeing your eyes."

My answer shocks her. She sputters out a breath and her hand jerks, like she wants to grab her ribs again. "I'm not drunk or high."

I wait her out, crossing my arms over my chest.

It takes her a couple of minutes, but she finally sucks her teeth and rips her glasses away, carelessly tossing them over her shoulder into the car. "You happy now?" she spews.

I notice two things once I get a good view of her face. One, is that her license didn't do her one bit of justice. She's fucking stunning and her eyes are the prettiest green I've ever seen. They remind me of emeralds.

The second thing I notice is that one of her eyes is slightly swollen with the skin around it an ugly purplish-green. My blood runs hot, because I know what a black eye from a fist looks like. My teeth creak as I grind my molars together. If there's one thing I hate most in the world, it's abuse against women and children.

"Who did that to you?" I growl the words, not even attempting to hide the rage simmering inside me.

It's her turn to cross her arms over her chest. She adds a cocked hip to her stance.

"No one," she mutters, her eyes skittering away from me. "I hit a table when I fell after running into the banister.

"Bullshit," I state, my words a deep rumble. Her eyes jump back to mine. "You ain't foolin' anyone with that lame ass story, sugar. Now why don't you try again." I step closer. "Who fuckin' gave you that black eye and busted ribs?"

Her shoulders droop and her arm wraps around her middle, as if she knows her tough girl act isn't working, so there's no need to keep trying. Her head swivels to the left, looking down the road past my car, before she swings her eyes back to me.

"An ex-lover of mine," she admits reluctantly.

"Where is he now?"

Her brows knit together as she again looks behind my car. "I thought he was following me, but I guess I was wrong."

I tense. "That why you were speeding?"

Her earrings sway when she nods. "Look," she starts, looking down at her feet before lifting her head again. "Can you just give me a warning or something and let me go? If my ex finds me, it won't end pretty. Running a license through the system will leave a trail he'll easily be able to follow."

"What makes you think he'll be privy to that information? It's not exactly made public anytime law enforcement runs a driver's license."

She tucks her hands into her long skirt, her bracelets jiggling. "Because he has connections with the San Antonio Police Department and they'll notify him if my name turns up in the system."

"Your license says you live in San Antonio. Why are you all the way out here?"

"Because that's where he lives too."

"Where're you headed?"

She shrugs one shoulder. "I don't know. Just away."

I look to the right, toward town, as I contemplate my next words. The citizens of Malus don't welcome new people, unless we specifically invite them. There are things we do that most people wouldn't agree with. To keep our secrets safe, we keep to ourselves and never let in outsiders that could potentially cause problems. Under normal circumstances, I'd let this woman go on her way. For some reason, that thought doesn't sit well with me. I feel like if I let her leave, I'll be sending her to her death bed. My conscience and morals won't let that happen. I may not know this woman, but there's no way in hell I'll let her go knowing there's someone out there wanting to hurt her.

I flip up my aviators to rest on top of my head then scrub my hand over my jaw. Silently cursing myself up one way and down the other, and hope that Judge won't have my hide, I make a suggestion.

"Why don't you follow me into town and stay for a few days to make sure this ex-lover of yours hasn't followed you.

Her eyes widen. A moment later, the perplexed look is gone and one of stubbornness replaces it.

"I'd rather just be on my way, if it's okay with you. The more distance I put between me and San Antonio, the better, and I'm still way too close."

"Well, you see, that's not okay with me. I can't just let you leave knowing you'll be in danger."

She huffs out a breath on a humorless laugh. "I know my rights. You can't keep me here."

I flash her my teeth. "Your tag's expired."

"Damn it," she mutters and tips her head back to the sky. The slender column of her neck mesmerizes me. All too soon, she brings her head back down.

I hand over her license and registration. "Give me a couple of minutes, then follow me into town. I just need to make arrangements for a place for you to stay."

"Whatever." She snatches the papers from my hand, yanks open her door, and drops down into the seat. That's a big fucking mistake for someone with sore ribs. She sucks in a sharp breath and rests her head back against the headrest.

I close her door for her and lean my hands on the edge. She opens her eyes to slits and glares at me.

"We're having your ribs looked at too." I hold my hand up when she opens her mouth to spew whatever shit she's come up with. "Not up for discussion. You're obviously in pain. You need to make sure there aren't any broken or cracked."

"Fine," she grumbles and snags her glasses from the middle console and slides them back over her eyes.

I pin her with a look. "Two minutes and then follow me." I push off from the door. "The name is JW, in case you were wondering."

Without waiting for a reply, I stalk back to my car, climb behind the wheel, and pull up Judge's name on my phone. He answers on the third ring.

"What?" he grunts.

"I need a favor."

There's a couple of taps on his end then he grunts again, "What?"

"I'm bringing in a woman. She's in trouble and needs a place to stay. I need you to call Jenny to see if she minds having company for a few days."

"Who is this woman?" he asks, a hard edge in his tone.

My jaw tenses, but I unsnap my teeth. He's going to be pissed, but fuck if it'll make a difference. Eden will be staying in Malus for a few days whether he likes it or not.

"Someone I caught speeding just outside of town. Before you get bent out of shape, she's staying here, so you'll just have to deal. Her ex has already done a number on her. Apparently, he's looking for her and she has nowhere to go. I'm going to look into the situation."

There's a loud bang, and I can just imagine his fist hitting his desk. Next comes his muttered curse. Judge takes the protection of Malus and its citizens very seriously. My brothers and I do as well, but Judge takes it to another level. Nothing and no one are more important. While that's the case for Trouble, Emo, and myself most of the time, we also recognize there may be situations where risks need to be taken. Most of the time we're just an ordinary town, so the chances of our special brand of justice coming to light are extremely slim.

"Find out whatever you can quickly so this shit gets taken care of in a timely manner," he grinds out. "I'll give Jenny a call."

I slip my aviators back on and turn over the ignition, my eyes on the back of Eden's car. "Got it. And thanks."

He doesn't bother to say goodbye before the line goes dead. Not that I expected it. Judge is a man of few words.

As I roll past the red convertible, my eyes slide to Eden, who's sitting stiffly in her car. My gaze moves to the rearview mirror, and my body relaxes back in the seat when I see her pull away from the side of the road. It wouldn't have surprised me if she had whipped a u-ey as soon as I rolled past her and hauled ass in the opposite direction. I'm just glad I didn't have to chase her down.

Because I would have.

Eden Delmont may not want my help, but that's exactly what she's going to get.

chapter two

EDEN

I SIT RIGIDLY ON THE BUTTERY soft leather sofa with my hands buried in my deep blue skirt as the sheriff who pulled me over speaks to a blonde-haired woman. She was introduced as Jenny. Her eyes keep flickering to me, a look of concern bringing a frown to her face. It irritates the hell out of me to have them talking about me like I'm not even here. It also irks me for some bizarre reason how close he's standing to the pretty blonde. And that only pisses me off even more, because, really, why would him being close to her bother me? I mean, yeah, he's gorgeous. And I admit, his voice is deliciously deep and gravelly. Not to mention he's got a killer body made for a woman to do sinful things to. But I don't know this guy from Adam. And anyway, none of that should matter in my current situation. I'm literally running for my life, for God's sake.

The woman faces JW again and gives him a nod. He smiles, and damn it, it only adds to his appeal. Especially the dimple that dents his cheek. I've always been a sucker for dimples.

Stupid, Eden. So stupid.

How stunning this man looks isn't something I should be thinking about right now. I've got more important things to worry about. Like why I'm even in this town; in this stranger's house. I shouldn't be here. I need to keep moving. The longer I'm in one place, the more of a chance he'll find me. I've no doubt once he does, he won't let me live. I've seen too much.

I should be concentrating on how I'm going to avoid kicking the bucket.

JW and Jenny walk back into the living room. Jenny smiles and takes a seat on the love seat, while JW comes to sit on the couch with me, keeping one of the cushions between us.

"Jenny's going to let you stay here for a few days to let you lie low while I check over a few things."

"You really don't have to do that." I look to Jenny. "Your offer is very generous, but it's probably best for me to move on."

"And what happens the next time you get pulled over?" I slide my eyes back to JW. "I guarantee they'll run your license with your expired tag."

I close my eyes and silently curse myself for the dumb oversight of my tag. My birthday was last month, and I had every intention to renew it before the end of the month, but then my life went to crap and it slipped my mind. I could kick my own ass for being so stupid.

"It's no problem," Jenny says, her tone soft. I open my eyes. Understanding and compassion flashes in her eyes. "You can stay as long as you need."

"Neither of you understand what you're asking. You don't want Diego to find me here. He's a mean son-of-a-bitch, and he won't be alone. He'll have his friends with him." Or at least I think he will.

JW and Jenny share a look, something passing between the two, before he brings his gaze back to me.

"You let me worry about that. If he comes here, he'll be taken care of," he says cryptically. "Diego is his first name?" I nod. "And his last?"

I tug on my lip with my teeth for a moment before spitting out, "Tomas."

JW's eyes narrow in recognition. "As in *the* Tomases?"

"Yes."

"Fuck," he mutters and rakes his hand through his hair.

Yeah, it's not as cut and dry as he thought it was going to be.

"I'm lost," Jenny remarks with a frown. "Who're the Tomases?"

"Up and coming Spanish cartel. They've been trying to take over the west side of San Antonio for a couple years. They're currently at war with the Santiagos. They're mean, violent, and don't give a shit who they hurt in their endeavors." His head swivels my way. "You sure know how to pick the wrong family to get involved with."

My back straightens and my eyes narrow into slits. "I didn't do it on purpose, asshole. He lied about who he was when I met him. What gives you the right to judge me?"

He leans forward, his elbows on his knees, and puts his face closer to mine. His pine scent swirls around me.

"Because I'm the guy trying to save your ass." His hands ball into fists. "If I remember correctly, Diego is Emiliano's son, correct?"

"Yes."

His nod is so stiff I'm surprised it didn't pop a tendon in his neck.

"Why is he after you? This seems more than just an abusive ex."

My nails pinch into my palms. "I saw him murder a woman. Although there's something strange he asked for when he gave me this." I point to my black eye. "He wanted to know where I hid the microchip."

"Where *did* you hide it?"

I shake my head. "That's just it. I don't have it. I have no clue what he's talking about."

"Are you sure?"

"Yes, I'm sure. You think I would keep something that could get me killed? Sorry, but I want to live."

He sits up and rubs his hands down his jean-clad legs. "Okay. Tell me exactly what happened."

I look away and out the window in front of us, gathering my

thoughts and remembering the fear that gripped me when I witnessed something so vile.

"A week ago, Diego and I spent the night at his house. I woke up late and he wasn't in bed. I had an appointment, so I got up, dressed, and went to look for him to let him know I had to leave. The house was huge. I went to each room looking for him. When I opened the last door, I had no clue what I was walking into. Diego had a girl chained to a wall. She was naked, and he was beating her with a whip."

I close my eyes and swallow down the bile trying to force its way up my throat.

"Her body was covered in lacerations," I continue, my voice just above a whisper. "I froze in shock. All I could do was stand there and watch. I don't know if the girl was alive. But I know she couldn't have survived it when he grabbed a knife and sliced her from her pubic bone up to her sternum. Her guts spilt from her body and landed at his feet."

I turn back to JW and see a scary mask over his face.

"I don't know how I managed it, but I left without making a noise. He never knew I was standing there. Or at least, I thought he didn't. I went home to think before going to the police, but then he showed up. Apparently, one of his staff saw me at the door and told him. After I fell to the floor with the hit to my face, he demanded to know where the disk was. When I told him I didn't know what he was talking about, his boot landed against my ribs. The only thing that saved me is one of my neighbors heard his screams and called the cops. The sirens scared him off, but he gave me a warning before he left. He told me his real name and said I had a week to come up with the chip. Today makes a week. Once he told me his name, I knew there was no way I could go to the police. Everyone knows the Tomases have connections in the department."

JW springs up from the couch and begins pacing the room, muttering to himself so low I can't understand him. His hands are propped on his hips and he looks irate. I can practically feel the pissed off vibes coming from him.

He spins back, his eyes piercing me where I sit. "You said you don't have this chip. You don't have any idea what he's speaking of?"

I throw my hands in the air in frustration and let them fall heavily back in my lap. "I've already told you," I say in exasperation. "I don't know anything about a chip."

A knock at the front door stops whatever he's about to say. With a muted growl, he stalks out of the room. My eyes move to Jenny. She smiles faintly at me.

"You have to excuse JW. He's normally not so hot with his temper. He's typically pretty laid back."

"Guess I just bring out the worst in him. Which is telling because I just met the guy an hour ago."

Her hair bounces when she shakes her head.

"That's not it. Violence against women and children is a very sore subject for him."

I tilt my head and regard her. "Are you two… together?"

Why does the thought of that sour my stomach?

She laughs lightly. "No. I'm with Judge."

I inwardly release a sigh. "Judge?"

She nods. "Yes. Although that's not his real name, it's what we all call him."

JW comes storming back in the room. His expression is still flat, but not quite as dark as it was a moment ago. Another man is on his heels. I mentally roll my eyes when I notice his good looks. Why is it that hot guys always hang out with other hot guys? Thick black hair and stunning blue eyes makes him almost as good-looking at JW.

"This is Dr. Trayce. He's going to check over your ribs," JW states before walking behind the bar in the corner. Once there, he grabs a glass from under the bar, pulls the stopper off a decanter, and pours a healthy amount of the amber liquid in the glass. His throat bobs as he tosses it back.

The new man, Dr. Trayce, steps forward and offers his hand. His eyes assess me with curiosity. When his gaze lands on my nice shiny black eye, the muscles in his jaw twitches.

"You can call me Trouble."

I frown, look down at his hand, before slipping mine into his. "Eden."

"Which side is injured?"

It takes me a moment to realize what he's referring to. "The left."

He takes a seat on my left side. "You mind lifting your shirt?"

I lift my left arm over my head, and using my right hand, pull my shirt up to just below my breast. Instead of paying attention to what the doctor's doing, I look back over to JW. He has one hand leaning on the bar, while the other holds a freshly poured glass. His gaze is locked on me. I lose his eyes just long enough for him to tip the glass back and drain it.

I have no idea what he's thinking, but whatever it is sends a light thrill through me. Goosebumps appear on my arms, and I don't for the life of me understand why.

I break my gaze away when Trouble presses against a sore spot. I hiss out a breath and look down to where his fingers are. The skin is a light-purple but doesn't look too bad. My eye looks much worse.

"I don't think they're cracked. And they're obviously not broken. You're breathing fine and there's no inflammation in the area. I pressed pretty hard. Had they been broken or cracked you would have been withering on the floor." He stands. "Only thing you can really do is ice the area and don't sit still for longs periods at a time. You want to stay mobile to keep from becoming stiff. If there's any problems, let Jenny know and she'll call me."

"Thank you."

He tips his chin, then turns to Jenny. "Remi wanted me to pass along that Elijah likes the teether you bought him."

Jenny's eyes light up and a stunning smile takes over her entire face. She claps her hands excitedly. "Really? That makes me so happy!" she gushes. "Tell her I'm coming by tomorrow."

He quirts a brow. "She already knows."

Jenny giggles, and it reminds me of a school girl bubbly giggle. The sound is sickenly endearing, and I can't help the small smile that plays on my lips.

"Walk me out," Trouble tells JW in more of a demand than a request.

JW walks over to me and holds out his hand. "Phone." I give it to him and a second later, his phone chimes. I toss mine in my purse when he hands it back to me.

"I'll be by tomorrow," he says before walking out of the room.

Jenny gets to her feet. "Come on. I'll show you to the room you'll be using."

"I really appreciate you doing this," I say, following her out of the room. "I mean, you don't even know me. Why would you let a stranger in your home like this?"

She looks at me over her shoulder as she ascends a set of stairs. "Because violence against women and children is a sore topic for me as well."

I frown. I get the feeling she's intimate with the subject. Has she been in an abusive relationship? I push away that thought for now and continue to trail behind her.

At the top of the landing is a huge sitting area with a banister looking out over the foyer below. There are several closed doors on both sides of the hallway we walk into next. She stops at the second door and pushes it open. The room isn't big, but it's not small by any standards. I take in the queen bed, night stands on either side, the dresser with a huge mirror, and a comfortable looking chair in the corner.

I turn back to Jenny. "This place is huge. Are you and… Judge the only ones who live here?"

She walks over to the window and pulls the curtains open, letting in the natural light.

"Judge isn't here all the time, and when he's not, it's just me. I like the big space though."

I toss my purse on the bed and take a seat on the edge. "Well, thank you for letting me stay."

She smiles brightly. "It's no worry. I'm glad to have you." She walks toward the door. "I had plans to heat up some leftover lasagna. I can heat up a plate for you as well if you'd like?"

"That would be great. Thank you. I need to call my parents to let them know I'm okay before they send out a search party. I'll be down once I'm finished."

"Take your time," she says and closes the door behind her, leaving me alone.

I blow out a breath and fall back on the bed. I stare at the ceiling, but I don't really see it. My mind keeps going back over the last hour. Everything happened so fast. I was driving with one eye on the road and one on the rearview mirror. I couldn't be sure, but I could have sworn there was a car following me.

Today was the deadline Diego gave me to hand over this mysterious chip. I left yesterday because I had no other idea of what to do. Like I told JW, I couldn't go to the police. There's no telling how many people there are in the Tomas's pockets. If the wrong person heard I went to the police, they'd hand me over to him.

I shudder when I think about the woman in chains. Who was she? Did she have family looking for her? Shame drops like lead in my stomach, because maybe she has a mother and father who're looking for her. What if she was a wife and mother? Are her kids crying for her?

Guilt for not reporting her murder brings tears to my eyes. I haven't given myself time to really think about the ramifications of me not going to the authorities. Unless her body is found, no one will know what happened to her. I can't imagine what her family must be going through, wondering what happened to her.

I angrily swipe my tears away and sit up. As much as it makes me feel like a selfish bitch, I just can't report her murder. Not yet anyway. Once this is all over—if it ever is—then I can tell the police what I witnessed. I just hope they can find her body and give peace to her family.

I blindly reach out for my purse and dig out my phone. Bringing the screen to life, it opens up to my recent calls and my eyes land on JW's name. I back out of my recent calls to my phonebook. My guilt grows when I find Mom's number and press the little green phone icon. I push the thought away and close my eyes as I hear one, two, three rings.

"Oh, dear Lord, Eden, is that you?" mom says in a rush.

I open my eyes and smile faintly. "Hey, Mom."

Her breath fans across the line. "Thank goodness. You had your Dad and me so worried with the message you left us yesterday. Where in the world are you?"

I fold my hand in the material of my skirt. "I'm just… away. I'll be back as soon as I can."

"You listen here, Eden Marie," she says, her voice stern. "You tell your Mama what's going on right this minute."

I can just imagine her standing on the other end of the line with her hand on her hip and a scowl pulling at the skin around her lips and eyes. What I wouldn't give to see that expression on her face instead of sitting in some strange woman's bedroom.

"I can't, Mom."

"Eden—"

"No," I interrupt her. "You know I would tell you if I could. I never keep things from you or Daddy, but this one time I've got no choice. I promise I'll be back as soon as I can and will tell you everything. In the meantime, you're just going to have to trust I'm doing what's best."

"Are you in danger?" Her voice drops, giving away her worry.

"No," I lie. If they knew I was in danger, there's no way they wouldn't call the police. "I just needed to get out of town for a while. I swear I'll explain soon."

She's quiet for a moment, and I fidget on the bed. Melanie Delmont is a force to be reckoned with. She's head strong, independent, can be very stubborn, brave, and loves her family fiercely. You step between her and her daughter or husband, you better watch out. She may be short and stalky, but she's not above fighting dirty to get to her family.

"Okay, Eden. We'll do this your way for a while, but you keep in touch. If I don't hear from you at least once a day, I'm calling the cops, you hear me?"

I release a silent breath. "I got it, Mama. Thank you. I love you."

"Love you too. Whatever's going on, please be careful. And call me tomorrow."

"I will. Give Daddy a hug for me, will you?"

"Okay, honey."

After we hang up, I drop my phone by my hip and dig my fingers in my eyes. I'm relieved to have my parents taken care of. I've been stressing on how they would take me leaving town. My parents and I have always been really close. We never keep secrets from each other, so for me to do that now, I know is hard on them. Thankfully, Mom is giving me time to work out my problems. I just hope she gives me enough time.

With a tired sigh, I get up from the bed. As soon as I'm on my feet, my stomach rumbles, reminding me I haven't eaten since yesterday afternoon. Lasagna, even reheated, sounds really damn good right now. Afterward, a nice long hot shower, followed by a good night's sleep, something I haven't had since the day I witnessed that woman's murder.

Opening the bedroom door, I'm immediately met with a delicious smell. As I descend the stairs, my thoughts move to JW and the crazy way my body reacts to him. You'd think after sleeping with Diego and then finding out what his extracurricular activities entailed, I'd be turned off by men for a while. Apparently, I'm way off base thinking that, because I was most definitely turned on.

Especially when he looked at me with his enticingly gorgeous baby blue eyes.

chapter three

JW

I DROP DOWN INTO MY OFFICE chair at work and swivel around to face my desk and the three men who walk through the door. Trouble and I just left Jenny's place. Instead of having to repeat myself, I held off on telling him what's going on until I called Judge and Emo to set up this meeting.

Once Emo closes the door behind him, he stands in front of it with his tattooed arms crossed over his hard chest, his black soulless eyes staring at me.

Both Judge and Trouble occupy the seats across from my desk, watching me expectantly as well, waiting for my explanation of bringing an unknown to Malus.

I lace my fingers and place them on the desk in front of me, ready to get down to business.

"Her name is Eden Delmont. She's from San Antonio and has a bastard of an ex after her. He's already got his hands on her once." I move my gaze to Trouble. "As you've already seen." He gives me a tight nod. "Her time was up today. The next time he won't leave her alive."

"What do you mean her time is up?" Judge asks, his jaw ticking.

"He thinks she has some microchip. She claims she doesn't and has no idea what he's referring to," I answer.

"And you believe her?"

I look at Trouble. "Yes. I do."

"Why? You know nothing about this woman."

I swing back to Judge. "Because my instincts tell me to and they've never steered me wrong before."

After a moment, he nods, trusting my judgement.

"I still don't like that she's here. We need to take care of this shit fast and get her gone."

Judge's words have my fingers biting into my skin. Yes, we normally don't invite random people to stay in Malus, but the thought of Eden being kicked out has me wanting to put my fist through a wall. The feeling is unreasonable and unwelcome, so I force it away.

"She also saw him murder a woman." I let that sink in, because I know that'll change Judge's tune. After all, that's what we do. Take out bastards who harm women and children.

Pure hatred settles over Judge's and Trouble's faces.

"As soon as the problem is taken care of, she'll be gone," I reassure Judge, then tack on because he needs to know I'm not budging on this, "But not a minute before."

He doesn't acknowledge my statement and continues, "What do we know about this guy?"

I unlace my fingers and lean back in my chair.

"It's Emiliano Tomas' son, Diego."

Trouble whistles then rubs his hands down his face at this news. Just as expected, Judge snarls out a curse.

"Son-of-a-bitch! Really, JW? Diego fuckin' Tomas? Do you have any clue what kind of guy he is?"

I nod tightly. "The kind who puts his hands on women. Exactly the kind of person we fight against and take out."

"Fuck!" He stands and starts pacing the room. "We're just asking to bring heat to Malus with this. You sure you want that?"

I shrug. "It won't come to that."

"You don't know that," he counters.

I get up from my chair and lean my fists on my desk. "It doesn't fuckin' matter, Judge. We've never let shit like that stop us before. He's already killed one woman. Eden needs our help. If we don't, we're sending her to her death bed. You know that as well as I do. I'll do some digging and we'll keep this under the radar."

He spins away and grabs the back of his neck. I give him the few minutes he needs to get over his snit.

Normally, when we come across situations where we need to step in, we simply hunt the person down and take them out, leaving no trail of us behind. The situation is more complicated because of who the guy is and who he's connected to. It would be hard to get to Diego undetected because he has body guards and tight security. It's not an easy in and out. We'll get the job done, but there has to be more of a strategic plan set in place. And it would be better if he comes here, versus us going to him.

"We'll get it done. Just be careful and keep me posted."

I barely restrain the need to bare my teeth at Judge. Never have I ever put the town in jeopardy, and it pisses me off that he thinks I would start now.

Without another word, he turns on his heel toward the door. Before he can open it, I give him a warning.

"She's staying with Jenny until this is taken care of. I expect you to show her respect and not make her feel unwelcome."

I know how Judge can be sometimes. He has a straightforward personality and can come off as an asshole with his bluntness. Eden seems like she can hold her own and won't be intimidated easily, but I still don't want her to feel blackballed because Judge is angry at me.

He doesn't respond, but I know he'll heed my warning. He jerks the door open and stalks out of the room. Trouble comes to his feet.

"Let me know when the time comes and when you need me," he says.

If anyone can understand the current situation, it'd be Trouble. A little over six months ago, his now wife came to town and ended up needing refuge from the man who raped her. He went head to head with Judge because Judge wanted the woman gone, even though she was eight months pregnant.

It's not that Judge isn't sympathetic—he's actually very compassionate when it comes to violence against another person, he just doesn't like not being in control of the situation. He's always been in control. Even as kids, he looked after Trouble, Emo, and me. That's how he got his nickname Judge.

I thank Trouble and he leaves. I move my eyes to Emo, who's now standing beside the opened door. His arms lay at his sides, one hand balled into a fist, no doubt letting the key in his grip rip through his skin. It's what he does in tense moments. That key is never out of his sight, and it's been the cause of all of the scars on his hands and arms.

Without a word, he gives me a silent nod, his way of letting me know he's in with my plan and will help when needed. Emo lives for violence against those who harm innocent people.

A moment later, I'm alone in my office. Pulling open my bottom desk drawer, I pull out the bottle of whiskey and lowball glass I keep stashed there. Pouring a couple of inches in the glass, I toss it back and grit my teeth at the burn.

After putting the bottle and glass back, I get up from my chair, ready to get the hell out of here, just as my office phone rings.

"JW," I bark into the receiver.

"Mrs. Baker called. Sunshine is in a tree again," Rita, the station's secretary and dispatcher says.

Just hearing the name Mrs. Baker, causes my head to pound.

"Have Sanchez or Williams do it. I'm headin' home."

"They're on a call out at the Wilkins's farm."

I work my jaw back and forth, trying to relieve some of the tension in my temples.

"Fire and rescue then," I grind out.

"They're responding to a kitchen fire at the Laymen's," Rita responds.

"Fuck my life," I mutter. "Fine." I snatch up my keys and cell phone and stride to the door. "I'll hit her place before going home. And Rita. Don't call me with stupid shit like this for the rest of the day. I'm done until tomorrow, unless it's a true emergency."

"Got it, Sheriff."

I bypass the front of the office and opt to go out the back door. I parked on the side of the building this afternoon to avoid anyone stopping me on the street to chat. It's already bad enough that I have to stop by Mrs. Baker's to get her beast of a cat out of the tree. This is the third time this week and probably the millionth time this year. The old woman needs to get rid of the damn cat because all he does is cause trouble, but he was attached to her late husband and now she's attached to him.

A hot shower and a beer are calling my name, and I'm only too eager to answer.

FOURTY MINUTES LATER, I'm pushing through my front door. I slam my keys and phone down on the table beside the couch and angrily yank off my boots, wincing when my boot grazes across the deep scrapes on my palms.

Goddamn cat. I damn near strangled the fucker when I finally got my hands around the scruff of his neck. The stupid furball kept inching higher up the tree. I'm not a light guy and the branches got thinner and thinner the higher I went. I'm lucky my ass didn't fall from the tree. As it was, one of the branches I stepped on snapped and the only thing that kept me from plunging to my death were my hands scrambling for purchase and sliding down the rough bark until I got a good hold. I left several good chunks of skin behind.

The next time Mrs. Baker calls, she can go after the devil cat herself or leave him up there, because I sure ain't doing it. The asshole will come down when he's hungry.

Ripping off my shirt, I toss it toward the kitchen and start working on my pants as I head to the bedroom. I don't wait for the water to warm up before stepping under the spray. I groan when the water hits me. That feels fucking fantastic.

I drop my head and close my eyes and let the water do its work on alleviating the tension in my shoulders. An image of Eden pops in my head and there's a new tension in my body. My eyes spring open when my dick twitches and starts to fill with blood. One thought. One damn thought of the woman and my dick perks up as if it's begging me to let my mind run wild. She's just a woman. One I know nothing about, except for what she's told me about what happened with Diego, but apparently, my body doesn't give two fucks about that. That's fine, because I don't need to know anything more about her to get under her long skirt. Single, attractive women are in short supply in Malus, and I haven't been to the neighboring towns on the hunt for one. It's been too long since I've gotten laid. Maybe Eden will be up for a little fun to take her mind off the shit storm she's in.

Giving into my body's demands, I grip my cock and squeeze the head while I conjure up just what I'd do to Eden if given the chance. The first thing I'd do is kiss that bright ass lipstick off her lips. Once I've succeeded with that task, I'd skim my lips down her neck, between the valley of her breasts, yank the material down that covers the plump mounds and take her nipples between my teeth. They'd be a dusty pink, hard as diamonds, and taste like cherries.

I jerk my cock, making sure my fingers run across the underside of the head.

The image transforms into Eden on her hands and knees on my bed. Her ass in the air, her little cunt and rosebud peeking at me. Her head is turned to the side as she watches me approach. I grip her hips and drag her to the end of the bed, then bury my face in her sweet pussy. She tastes like peaches and cream. So damn delicious. I run my tongue from her clit, up her slit, to her hidden entrance, then do it all over again.

She withers and moans, all the while bucking her hips, but I hold her still with a firm grip on her thighs. I devour her until she screams and claws at the sheets. Only when her tight walls stop pulsing do I get to my knees behind her and shove every inch of my cock inside her warm depths.

"Shit," I grit and pump my hand harder. My knees begin to shake like I'm some Goddamn school boy having his first orgasm.

Blindly, I reach out with my other hand and place it on the wall. My balls tense up and my dick swells even more. Intense pleasure races down my spine as my orgasm hits me so hard I become lightheaded.

"Fuckin' hell," I groan and tip my head back, letting the water hit my face.

I don't remember the last time I've come that damn hard. It's sure as shit's been too long. And that was just from a fantasy.

Once my bones are no longer made of jelly, I quickly wash my hair and body, then get out of the shower. Half-assedly drying off, I pull on a pair of sweatpants and go to the room next to mine. As soon as I open the door a chattering squeak greets my ears. Piper, my black ferret, races excitedly back and forth in her cage. Releasing the latch and opening the door, she darts from the cage. She makes it to the door before turning around and scurrying back to me. Her claws dig into the material of my sweats and she crawls her way up my leg. I scoop her up when she gets to my waist and put her on my shoulders where I know she wants to be.

"Hey, girl." I run my hand along her head and she burrows her face in my hair.

Chuckling, I take her back with me to the living room to grab my phone then go back to the bedroom. Normally, anytime I'm at home, I let Piper run free. She's a little shit sometimes when she finds something to chew on that she's not supposed to, and she likes to horde my socks, but she's typically a good ferret and she's litter trained.

Once I'm close enough to the bed, she jumps from my shoulders onto the mattress. She runs around, rooting under my pillow, only to pop out on the other side, looking at me as if seeking approval. I've had Piper for three years. One of the boys in town got him for his birthday. Three days later, they found out he was allergic to pet hair. No one else wanted her, and since I've always had a soft spot for furry creatures, she ended up with me.

Putting my phone on the bedside table and flipping the switch off on the lamp, I get in bed. It's still early, but I've been up since four this morning when I got a call from Lucy about a noise she heard outside her house. She thought someone was breaking in, but it ended up being a raccoon digging in her trash. I love my job, but fuck if it isn't a pain in the ass at times.

Piper comes to rest on the pillow beside my head. Yes, my ferret sleeps with me. No, I don't give a fuck if someone thinks it's weird.

I close my eyes and my thoughts once again drift to Eden and the clusterfuck I have to fix for her. Well, I don't have to fix it, but I find that I want to. Not only because she saw Diego kill a girl, but especially because he laid his hands on Eden.

The world doesn't need bastards like Diego running free. Unfortunately, there are more like him than most people realize. I don't like hurting anyone; I'm sheriff of Malus because I like to prevent shit like that from happening, but when it comes to scum such as Diego, I can't help the little thrill I get when we wipe the ground with their dirty faces.

When I find Diego, he better pray like hell I'm having a good day, because only that will determine how gruesome I am when I slaughter him.

chapter four

EDEN

I'M ON THE COUCH IN SOME other stranger's house with Jenny sitting beside me holding a cute little baby boy. Hysterical giggles fill the space in the living room, and I can't help the smile from spreading on my face. Remi, the woman's house we're in, glances over at her and the baby, her own smile making her already beautiful face even more stunning. Jenny has him lying on her legs while she gently tickles his sides.

We got here ten minutes ago, and as soon as we stepped foot through the door, Jenny was across the room and scooping Elijah up.

"So," Remi begins, plopping down on a recliner. "Are you getting the Malus look yet?"

I look at her in confusion, which makes her laugh.

"I assume you didn't see anyone on the way over here?"

Unsure if it was meant as a question or not, I answer anyway. "No."

She nods. "Figured. Be prepared to get ugly looks from people around town."

"Umm…. Why?"

Smiling, she grabs her long brown hair to pull it over one shoulder and starts braiding it.

"People around here don't take too kindly to strangers. When I first got here, I got some pretty unwelcome looks. I've dubbed it The Malus Look."

"Hmm… Why don't they like strangers?" I ask, intrigued.

Her eyes skitter to Jenny for a moment and they share a strange look before hers settles back on mine. "They just don't. Malus is a very tight-knit community, and everyone prefers to stay with their own. It's a protective mechanism toward the outside world."

I guess I can understand that. Especially for the folks who've been here for years. When you live in a small place like Malus, where everyone knows everyone, you become close. People become more than friends and consider everyone family. When someone new arrives who could potentially harm a member of the town, it's understandable to be leery.

Even so, I get the feeling there may be more that she's not telling me. I decide to keep my mouth shut though. What people do here is none of my business. I won't be here long enough for it to *become* my business.

"Would you like to hold him?" Jenny asks, surprising me.

"Oh, umm…." My gaze darts to Remi. She smiles at me in encouragement. "Sure." It's not that I don't want to. I just haven't had a lot of experience handling babies. I have no siblings and none of the few friends I have has any kids.

Awkwardly, I hold my arms out. I obviously do it wrong, because Jenny snickers and adjusts my arms the way they should be and gently settles Elijah against my chest.

"He's pretty good with holding his head steady, but just in case, keep your hand behind it."

I nod absentmindedly as I look down at the little baby in my arms. I've only ever held one baby in my life, and that was years ago. He's so much lighter than I expected him to be. I mean, he's small, so he can't weigh that much, but he almost seems lighter than a pillow. And his smell… Fresh baby powder and lavender lotion. He smells like comfort and home. A weird combination for a baby, but those are the two words that first popped in my head.

He's looking up at me with a pair of innocent blue eyes. Not the plain blue most people have, but a deep blue. It reminds me of the ocean. His tiny button nose and little pink lips are just too adorable to ignore.

"He's precious, isn't he?" Jenny's voice barely registers, because I'm too focused on Elijah.

Yes, he is precious. Probably the most precious thing I've ever seen. Having a baby of my own has never been big on my list of things I want to accomplish in life. But looking at this little person, a small voice in the back of my mind has me wondering if maybe I should shift some of those things around to make room for a baby.

"He really is," I murmur lightly.

When he smiles, that's all it takes for my heart to melt into a puddle. I don't know this baby, and I don't know his mother, but one thing's for sure, this little tiny human has captured my heart with one toothless grin. My own smile curves up my lips so big, my cheeks hurt.

I break my eyes away from Elijah and look at Remi. She's watching the two of us with her own smile.

"I never really understood the whole hoopla of having a baby, but I get it now. He's absolutely adorable."

Her smile grows. "I'm bias because he's mine, but I think so too. Even so, thank you."

My eyes fall back to Elijah. The little guy is so cute I could probably watch him for hours. Unfortunately, my baby watching is interrupted when the front door opens and JW and Trouble walk in. A flutter forms in my stomach when JW's eyes land on me. Something dark and potent settles in their gorgeous blue depths. The look makes my heart pitter patter strangely.

Trouble walks to Remi, who stands to greet her husband. My gaze moves to them, but I immediately skirt them away when he wraps one arm around her waist and he hauls her to his chest, planting a kiss so hot against her lips I feel the heat from it. I look back to JW to find him with his hands stuffed in his jean pockets, his eyes still locked on me. They slowly run down my camisole, over my long willowy skirt, and back up again. Warmth spreads in my stomach at the intense look in his eyes.

"Sorry to take him away, but I need to steal my son from you," Trouble remarks, stepping up beside me.

I snatch my eyes away from the man across the room and hand over the charming Elijah to his father. The look on Trouble's face as he looks down at his son shows his absolute adoration he holds for his child. Trouble is a very good-looking man, but looking at him as he stares down at Elijah and seeing the expression on his face makes him ten times hotter. I'm sure he's melted plenty of panties since he became a father.

"I thought you had a full day today?" Remi asks as she smooths Elijah's hair with a gentle hand.

"I'm not staying. I just came by to get a patient file I left here. Met JW on the way over. He needs to speak with Eden."

I look back at JW with a raised brow.

He juts his chin toward the door. "Take a walk with me?"

I nod and gather my purse.

"I'll stay here until you get back," Jenny says.

I feel JW's hand at my back when I pass by him and it sends chills over my arms. Before I get a chance to open the door, he reaches past me and opens it himself. A gentleman. Such a rare thing these days.

It's quiet for the first few minutes as we walk down the sidewalk. I take a look around since we're heading in the opposite direction of where Jenny and I came from. The town, or what I've seen of it so far, is cute and quaint. Businesses seem to be in the middle of town with houses on the outside. I hear kids' laughter somewhere, but I can't see them. Dogs bark off in the distance and someone is playing soft music.

"Is everything okay?" I ask, wondering what he wanted to talk with me about.

"So far. I just wanted to let you know I've done a bit of digging."

I stop and my head snaps in his direction. "What?" I ask, then wince when my voice rings out too loudly.

"Settle down," he says calmly, like he didn't just tell me something that could lead Diego right to the doorstep of where I'm hiding out. Or at the very least the town I'm in.

"I haven't dropped your name anywhere. I did some digging on Diego to find out where he is. Besides, there are ways of finding out information where it doesn't leave a trail."

I breathe a sigh of relief, happy my whereabouts are still hidden. For now, at least. I have no doubt Diego could still find me if he looked hard enough. I'm hoping whatever JW has planned will stop him before he has a chance to get to me.

We start walking again.

"Did you find anything?"

JW exhales heavily. "Nothing I didn't already know. Diego is a hothead and unpredictable. His father's been trying to rein him in for years with no success. The Tomases are harsh and very dirty with their business dealings, but Diego is the worst of the lot." He stops and rubs the back of his head. "I'm thinking about calling a meeting with Emiliano to see what can be done about Diego. It's a long shot, but worth a try."

This news sends a knot of dread straight to my stomach. I can't see anything good coming from this meeting, except putting JW and this town on the Tomas radar.

"Are you sure that's wise? From what I've heard of the Tomas family, they protect their own no matter the circumstances."

The thought of harm coming to him really unsettles my stomach.

"I'm not really seeing a choice here," he answers as we walk by an ice cream store.

An ice cream store? What a strange thing to have in a town this size. They either can't have much business, or the people of Malus *really* like ice cream.

"I checked Diego's bank account. He used his card at a gas station in a town about an hour and a half east of here, which is an hour away from San Antonio. That's the only purchase, so we don't know where he's moving next. Could be he's heading this way, or it was just a coincidence. Either way, I've got people keeping an eye out for him in case he strolls into town."

His jaw is locked tight when he finishes, and the look in his eye is telling. He's pissed.

"Why are you doing this?" I ask the question that's been bothering me since he led me into Malus yesterday.

His jaw gets tighter and his brows slant into a scowl.

"Because I'm an officer of the law. It's my duty to protect people."

I shake my head, not letting him off the hook. "It's more than that. If that were the only reason, you would have advised me to go back to San Antonio to file a report. You haven't done that. You're wanting to take care of this personally. Why?"

His steps halt and he turns to face me, his expression serious.

"People like Diego make me sick. He deserves whatever justice is brought to him. I just happen to be the guy who wants to make sure he gets it."

His lips are in a straight line and the muscle in his jaw twitches. Glancing down, I notice his hands balled into fists. His words and posture have me wondering if something happened in his past to make him so passionate about the current subject. Maybe he was close with someone who was abused.

"Come on. I'll take you back to Trouble's," he grunts and spins on his heel.

"What's up with Trouble's name?" I inquire, falling into step beside him. "I can't imagine that's his real name."

"It's not."

He doesn't offer more. I try another approach.

"What does JW stand for?"

He's quiet for so long I think he's not going to answer.

"John Wayne."

A laugh escapes my lips before I can stop it. "Really?"

His mouth quirks. "Really."

"Did your parents name you after the actor or is it a family name?"

The air around us changes, and I look over to find he's tense again. "No. John Wayne isn't my real name. It's a nickname my brothers and I came up with when I was younger because I was a John Wayne fanatic."

I hold my tongue for a moment, then decide to just spit out my next question. It's obvious this is a touchy subject for him, so if he doesn't want to answer, I won't take offense.

"What's your real name?" I ask quietly.

Again, he's silent for so long I think I'm shit out of luck on getting an answer. I'm surprised when he finally does speak.

"Liam." His eyes cut to me. "But no one calls me that." His voice is stern, no doubt warning me against using his given name. "All of my brothers go by nicknames instead of the names we were given by our parents."

I nod and say no more. Whatever their reason is for not using their real names is none of my business, but I can tell from the shift in his body this subject makes him uncomfortable.

A few minutes later, we're walking up Remi and Trouble's driveway. Just as we reach the steps, the door opens and Trouble steps outside with Remi behind him.

"I'll keep you updated on the Diego issue," JW says, turning to me. "In the meantime, I'd advise you not to use your credit or debit cards. Do you have cash?"

"Yes. I pulled my savings out the day I left."

"Good."

"You ready?" Trouble asks, walking down the steps.

"Yes."

Remi and I go back in the house for a while longer. The whole time, Jenny has Elijah in her arms. You can plainly see the love she holds for the baby. She'd make a great mom one day.

The sky is turning cloudy as we make the short trek back to her house an hour later. My eyes catch on a man and woman across the street, and my feet pause when I notice the look they're casting our way. It's not an all-together inhospitable look, but it for sure isn't a friendly one either. Several yards further down the sidewalk, there's a woman sitting in a rocking chair giving me the same adverse look. *Me*. Not Jenny.

"The Malus look," I murmur and resume walking.

"What?" Jenny asks, then follows my line of sight. "Oh. Just ignore them." She snorts derisively. "So, tell me what you think of JW."

I arch a brow and glance at her. "Why?"

She shrugs, but I see a small smile playing on her lips. "Just wondering what you thought of him."

Now it's my turn to snort, because she isn't fooling me. She's fishing for information.

"Not that it matters, but he seems nice," I answer evasively.

She laughs. "Nice isn't the word I was searching for."

"I know, but that's all you get right now." I flash her a grin.

We walk by a house that has a woman backed up against a car by a man in the driveway. The kiss he's giving her isn't so hot that it would be considered too scandalous for public, but there's still plenty of feeling behind it. When his lips leave hers, he murmurs something to the woman. Jenny giggles beside me and his eyes lift to hers, one brow curving upward playfully. When his eyes meet mine, the look disappears and turns flat, turning into the Malus look. I sigh and shift my gaze away from him. The woman glances over just as we walk by.

"Hey, Jamie," Jenny chirps.

The woman smiles and gives a little wave. "We still on for dinner this weekend?"

Before she can answer, the man says something to Jamie so low we can't hear him. She laughs and Jenny snickers.

"Call me tonight!" she calls out to Jamie, who gives her a thumbs-up.

A few minutes later, we're back at Jenny's. I head to the

bedroom to grab my phone charger, while Jenny goes to the kitchen to find something for dinner. Walking back out to the living room, I find Jenny by the sliding glass door leading to the back yard. The look of horror on her pale face has me rushing to her.

"What's wrong?" I demand.

Instead of answering, she throws her hand up to cover her mouth, spins, and sprints away. I look out the glass and nearly lose the contents of my stomach as well.

There's a small dog lying on the deck with his neck twisted at an odd angle, his tongue hanging out the side of his mouth. Most of his hair is no longer white from the blood coating him. It's not the blood that's revolting though. It's the gory mess of the dog's entrails spread out beside him.

chapter five

JW
The Past

DREAD FILLS MY STOMACH as I'm led into the great hall of Hell. Mom and Dad are behind me and my brother, Trey, walks beside me. He's older than me by thirteen years. Mom says I was a miracle her and Dad never thought would happen. I often wish I hadn't.

Older brothers are supposed to protect their younger siblings, but Trey has never protected me. He's the cause of the pain I go through during Hell Night.

Hell Night is what my brothers and I call the once-a-month activities all the adults take part in. The activities they force the kids to go through. Most kids anyway. I've never known a time when Trey was forced to do the disgusting things he does to me. He's always done them willingly and without mercy. Even going so far as sneaking in my room at night during other times of the month. Mom and Dad made him stop after he got too rough one night and I came down stairs the next morning, barely able to walk. They said these activities are sacred and only meant for once a month. Like it matters.

Sickening sounds reach my ears when we enter the large room. I'm always paired with my brother. There's only been a couple of times *someone else has taken me, and that was only because Trey was too sick to attend.*

"On the bed," Trey's deep voice commands.

I want to turn around, spit in his face, and tell him no, but that's never gotten me anywhere, except a punch to the stomach. I still end up on my hands and knees for him. Mom and Dad never help me. They just watch as they take their own child they chose for the night. Hell Night is the only night a month that my family turns evil. Any other time they are sweet and loving parents.

I get on the bed and sit back on my heels, facing away from my brother. I try to ignore the sounds around me, but it's hard to do when the cries, grunts, and screams become louder. I spot my friend Judge lying on his stomach with Mr. Portland on top of him. Judge's face is red and he's squeezing his eyes shut.

I next look to Trouble, who's bent over a table with Mr. Leland behind him. Mr. Leland has Trouble's arms wrenched behind his back. Trouble's head just hangs, and it looks like he might be passed out.

My eyes move across the room to Emo. He's in a chair with little Rella, Trouble's sister, on his lap. Emo's dad is behind Rella with his hands on her shoulders, pushing her down. Emo's eyes look dead as he stares off into space. His jaw is tense though, so I know he feels more than he's letting on.

"Assume the position, you little shit," Trey growls behind me.

Before I get a chance to do as he says, my head is shoved forward, and I barely catch myself with my hands before my face plants into the mattress. The sheets are silk and feel cool against my skin. The smell on the sheets reminds me of what my clothes smell like after Mom's washed them.

I look to my left and see Mom on her back on a bed with a girl named Katie lying the opposite way on top of her. Dad is behind Katie holding her hips. I turn my head away when he does something that makes Katie scream.

As my pants are yanked down to my knees, I'm reminded of what's about to happen. I wonder what I've ever done to my brother to make him do these things to me. Why does he hate me so much? How can he hurt his little brother? I know if I had a little brother or sister, I'd do all I could to protect them. Just like Trouble does for his sister. He's not always able to protect her from the evil of Hell Night, but there's been a few times he did.

Pain enters my backside and the base of my spine. I drop my forehead to my crossed arms in front of me and suck in a sharp breath, then blow it out through the piercing pain. Tears pool in my eyes but I refuse to let them fall. Trey knows he's hurting me, but I won't let him see how much. It seems to spur him on more if I do.

I squeeze my eyes shut and block out what's going on around me. As much as I try to push away the pain though, nothing works. I still feel it in every part of my body. Even the parts Trey doesn't touch.

I dig my nails into my arms, hoping that will override the pain in my lower half. It doesn't work. I stifle a cry when my hips are yanked back, and agonizing pinpricks radiate through my bowels. Blood coats my mouth, and I realize I've bitten my lip. It's weird because I don't feel it.

Holding my breath, I send up a silent prayer that I'll pass out from not breathing, but just as I become lightheaded, my body's instincts take over and I suck in air.

There's nothing I can do to make the terror of what's happening to me go away. There never is.

All I can do, all I can ever do, is endure it and wait for the hours to pass....

chapter six

JW

T HE CALL COMES IN RIGHT as my ass hits the seat of my truck. Sometimes when things are slow in Malus, which is pretty much always, I make a few rounds around town to check things over. I also like to hit the farms on the outskirts.

Grabbing my phone, I expect the call to be from the station, so I'm surprised when I see Eden's number flash across the screen. I close my door and start my truck as I swipe and accept the call.

"Sheriff Ward."

"Hey. This is Eden," she starts. My hackles rise when I note the tremble in her voice. "Can you come to Jenny's?"

"What's wrong?" I ask. Checking my mirror, I pull away from the curb and whip a U-turn.

"It's not really something I want to describe over the phone. It's better if you see it."

Concern seeps in my blood, causing my foot to press harder on the gas pedal. "Two minutes. I'll be there in two minutes. Is everyone okay?"

Her breath fans across the line. "Yes. It's just…." She trails off. "Just get here quickly."

"I'm only a few blocks away."

I toss my phone on the dash, my mind whirling with what could be wrong. I only saw her not even two hours ago. What could possibly go wrong in that short time? And does it have to do with Diego? At that thought, I accelerate, going too fast for the center of town, but unable to slow down.

A minute later, I'm breaking in front of Judge and Jenny's house and jumping from my truck. Not bothering to knock, I open the door and stalk inside. My eyes light on Eden and Jenny on the sofa. They're sitting close, huddled together. They both turn at my entrance and Eden gets to her feet, a look of relief sagging her shoulders.

"What's happened?" I demand, striding across the living room.

"Come look." She gestures to the door leading to the back yard.

When I step up to the door, the sight that greets me turns even my stomach, and I've seen some gruesome shit in my life, even being the cause of it a few times.

"Damn." I mutter. It's not uncommon for a wild animal to hunt pets and their carcasses to end up on someone's property. We are in the wilds of Texas, after all.

Turning, I find Eden right behind me, her eyes leveled on the poor dog. "Go back and sit with Jenny. I'll take care of this."

Her eyes flit away and meet mine. Sadness lurks in their green depths. "I wanted to wait for you, but I need a closer look at him."

I scowl. "What the fuck for?"

Her eyes glisten with unshed tears. "Because I think he's my dog, Sampson."

My brows shoot up, and I glance at the dog over my shoulder before looking back at her.

"You didn't have a dog with you in the car when I pulled you over," I remark.

She nods and her throat bobs when she swallows. "I know. I left him behind and a co-worker was supposed to check in on him. If I wasn't back in a few days, she was going to take him for me."

Fucking hell. This shit just got messier.

I grab her hand and push open the door. I don't know how long Eden and Jenny were at Remi's house, but the dog had to have been left while they were gone, or they would have noticed it before now. The dog couldn't have been out here long, but even so, with the heat of the Texas sun blaring down on the carcass, the flies have already started their feast. It won't be long before it begins to smell.

Eden's fingers tighten in my hand and her breath hitches the closer we get. Her bracelets jingle when she throws her other hand over her mouth and releases a choked sound. I step in front of her, blocking her view. She's seen enough.

I grab her hand from her mouth and place it on my chest. "Is it him?"

From her reaction, I already know the answer, but I need her to confirm it.

"Yes," she croaks. Her head falls forward and her forehead lands against my chest. "Even without recognizing the nametag I bought him, I'd know it was him."

My jaw tenses in anger. I manage to unlock my fingers from a fist and gently rub up and down her back. I've no doubt she can feel the tightening of my muscles though.

"It was him. Diego did this. He had to have."

Damn straight it was Diego, and he'll fucking pay even more for what he's done.

"Yes," I answer tersely.

Eden lifts her head and wipes away her tears, but her eyes are still sad. "I need to go call Marian. She's the one who was watching him. I need to make sure she's okay."

I nod, but before she can walk away, I grab her chin and make her look at me. "We'll get him, Gypsy. I promise."

She looks at me strangely for a moment, her brows puckered. I'm sure it's from me calling her Gypsy. She's in another one of her long flowy skirts, loose spaghetti strap shirt, with her hair in a silk scarf, hiding the flaming red hair. Once again, she reminds me of a gypsy.

After several seconds, she nods and turns away, walking back into the house. I close the door behind her and pull out my phone.

"I need you at Jenny's house," I tell Emo once he answers.

"Got it. Be there in ten."

Just as I hang up, the door opens behind me. Judge steps up beside me as I look down at the remains.

"Motherfuckin' hell," he snarls, throwing his hands in his slack pockets. "Any clue who did this?"

"Has to be Diego. The dog is Eden's."

His head snaps my way. "She sure?"

I jerk my chin up. "She left the dog at home for someone to watch while she was gone. That means he's already here. That or he's sent someone in his place. I don't think that's the case though. The day I brought her into town, I pulled her over for speeding. She said she thought she saw him following her. I didn't see anyone, but that doesn't mean he didn't stop somewhere close by out of sight."

"What kind of sick fuck decimates a dog like this?"

"The same kind who beats the shit out of women or kills them," I answer his rhetorical question. "Diego's unstable at best and a psycho at worst. That's why he can't get his hands on Eden. There's no telling what he'll do to her."

"I want a piece of him when he's found," Judge remarks darkly.

"Not until I'm done with him. And I ain't promising there'll be much left."

It turns quiet before Judge says something that has my molars grinding together and more anger slamming into me.

"Right before Jenny called me, I got an email about Richard. He's been located."

I hiss out a breath and lock down the violent need to smash my fist against something. Richard Panelly is one of the men on our list from our past. Any time one of them is mentioned, my temper skyrockets, just as my brothers' do.

"You want in? Or do you want one of us to take care of it?"

Fuck yes, I want in. Apart from certain names, we all share

taking out the people from our pasts. This is supposed to be my turn. Except.... I turn and look through the glass of the back door. I spot Eden sitting on one of the stools at the bar, her head in her hand as she talks on the phone.

The thought of leaving her when someone like Diego is close by sends a sharp pain to my sternum. I know my brothers will protect her, but it's not the same as doing it myself. There's something about her that draws me in, and I've yet to figure out what that something is. I just know if something happens to her, Hell will reign and there will be no stopping my wrath.

"Where," I grunt my question and look over to Judge.

"Southern Cal."

"Damn it to hell," I grit out. Too fucking far for a day trip. No way am I taking a chance and leaving Eden for that long. As much as it pisses me off, I'm going to have to pass this one onto the others.

"One of you guys go. I'll catch the next one."

Judge's brows lift in surprise. Yeah, join the club. I'm still trying to figure out what in the hell I'm doing too. None of us has ever given up our opportunity to slay someone from our past.

"Any update on Trey and my mother?"

It's a useless question, because the answer's always the same. We've had a few clues come in on the whereabouts of my brother and mother, but none of them ever pan out. If there's one thing in life I want to do more than anything else, it's find them and see their faces when they realize death has come for them.

That is a meeting I plan to relish in and take great enjoyment from. If we can ever fucking locate them.

Judge's face is grim when he gives me the same answer as always. "No."

The door opens behind us, and I don't need to turn to know it's Emo. He always brings ominous vibes with him, and I feel them now. Like slivers of ice sliding down my spine.

His silent form appears between Judge and I, and I glance over at him. His haunting eyes, so dark you can't see the pupils, settle on the mangled mess of Eden's dog. Something flickers in their depths. Fascination and enchantment. Blood has always been an enticement for Emo. Hunting the ones who hurt others and torturing them is his foreplay.

"What do you see?" I ask him. Emo's the coroner of Malus. As such, he works mostly with human bodies, but I know he'll be able to tell what did this to the dog.

Quietly, he squats and regards the dog.

"A knife. Sharp one, because there's no jagged edges. Someone slit him from neck all the way to the groin."

I nod, already knowing it wasn't an animal attack, but needing to make sure. The layout of the entrails are too perfect. Besides, a person has more of a chance winning the lottery than Eden's dog showing up here on his own and being attacked by an animal.

"I need to get this shit cleaned up. Once I'm done, I'm going to do some more digging and put the word out around town to let one of us know if they see anyone new in town. You two do the same." I look to Judge. "When are you due back here?"

"Not until the weekend, but I'm changing my plans. I'll be here until this is taken care of."

"Good." With this new development, I really don't like the thought of Eden and Jenny being here alone. Judge is protective of each of his women, so I know he'll keep an eye out for anything out of the ordinary.

Judge goes back inside to check on the women and Emo leaves. I grab a shovel, some thick plastic, and some old chicken wire from the garage. After digging a four-feet deep hole, I gently place Sampson wrapped in the plastic inside. I replace the dirt until there's only about a foot left then place the chicken wire in the hole before putting the rest of the dirt on top. We often get wild animals in these parts. The depth and chicken wire will hopefully prevent them from digging up the grave. Next, I clean the porch with baking soda and bleach before hosing the wood down.

When I walk inside, I find Judge on the couch with Jenny sitting in his lap, talking quietly. Eden is still at the bar, no longer on the phone, watching Judge and Jenny with a perplexed expression. Her head swings my way when I close the door. Her shoulders sag and her eyes droop with sadness, her hands twisting in her lap. I hate the look as soon as I notice it.

I stop in front of her, so close her knees touch my abs. I put both hands on her knees.

"I buried him in the back yard by the flower bed. Are you okay?"

She nods, but I know it's bullshit. She just found her dog brutally murdered. She's not okay.

"Did you get in touch with your friend?"

"Yeah." She runs her hands up and down her arms, like she's trying to ward off a chill. It can't be any cooler than seventy-two in here, so I know it's from the situation and not the temperature. "She's fine. Freaked because Sampson was gone when she went to go check on him this morning and was worried about telling me. I'm just glad she wasn't there when Diego took him."

"Judge is going to stay here until all this is over. I'll do a bit more digging and put out an alert in town."

Her eyes flicker over to Judge and Jenny and she bites her lip. I know what's coming next when her questioning gaze meets mine again.

"Is there something going on between them?" She juts her chin their way. "Because I just saw him kissing another woman on our way back here from Remi's."

I move my hands on the outside of her legs and shift them upward a couple of inches. The temptation to spread her legs and step between them is great, but I force the desire away. Now's not the time for seduction

"That's something you'll have to ask them," I answer.

It's no big secret that Judge and his ladies share an open relationship, but it's still not my business to tell Eden about it. Besides, they're better at explaining the situation than I am.

She frowns, but drops the subject.

"I'm going to head out. You've got my number if you need me."

Her tongue darts out to wet her lips and my eyes follow the movement. Of course, my body plays the insensitive prick and twitches in my jeans. Eden is a beautiful woman, and I'd give my left nut to have her in my bed, but that'll have to come later. When her emotions aren't so fresh from losing her dog in such a horrific way.

I give her leg a squeeze before turning for the door, giving Judge a chin lift on my way. Before walking out, I cast my eyes to Eden one more time and find her watching me, an inquisitive look in her eyes. Breaking my eyes away, I walk out and close the door behind me.

chapter seven

EDEN

STRETCHING AND THEN GROANING at the ache in my ribs, I get out of bed. The stress of yesterday has left me with a bitch of a headache. I grab some clothes and my travel bathroom bag and carry them to the bathroom. After doing my morning business and downing a couple of pain pills and my birth control, I get dressed in a black ankle-length skirt, a pale-blue off-the-shoulder peasant top, and toss my long hair into a half ponytail before tying a scarf around it.

Leaving the bathroom, I drop my bag just inside my bedroom doorway and walk out to the living room. The delicious smells of coffee and bacon greets me and my mouth waters. I lost my appetite yesterday, so I skipped dinner, opting to go to bed early.

Expecting to see Jenny in the kitchen, I'm surprised when it's Judge I find instead. He's standing at the stove, clad in dark-grey slacks, a light purple dress shirt, and dress shoes. He turns and looks at me over his shoulder, his expression cool, but not quite as much as yesterday.

After seeing him kissing the woman in the driveway and then him with Jenny on the couch, I'm unsure how I feel about the man. I'm leaning toward dirt bag at the moment though.

"Morning," I mutter and walk over to the coffee machine. "You mind?" I gesture to the machine.

"Help yourself." His voice is rich and deep, gravelly.

I pour myself a cup, keeping it black, and carry it with me to the bar. If my memory serves me correctly, Jenny said Judge lives here sometimes, something I find very strange after seeing him kiss another woman. I haven't spoken with him yet. Might as well get to know the man since we'll both be under the same roof for a while.

"Where's Jenny?" I inquire, then take a sip of my coffee.

"Still in bed," he throws over his shoulder.

Switching the burner off, he lays strips of bacon on a plate already piled high with scrambled eggs. He grabs more plates from the cabinet and starts divvying up the food. Picking up two of the plates, he sets one in front of me and carries the other one out of the kitchen. A moment later, he's back, sans plate, which I'm sure he gave to Jenny. Leaning against the counter, he picks up a third one. His eyes bore into me as he lifts his fork and shoves eggs in his mouth.

"Just spit it out," he says calmly after swallowing.

I set my fork down and regard him warily. I've always considered myself a straight forward person, and now will be no different. I'm new to this town, new to everyone here. I've got no ties to anyone and no one owes me a thing. The answers are none of my business, but I still find myself wanting to know. Jenny's been nice to me, so the thought of her being hurt in anyway, doesn't sit well with me.

"I don't get it. Jenny and I both saw you kissing another woman yesterday, then you showed up and she literally crawled in your lap."

He shrugs. "Maybe I'm her concerned brother and we're close."

I level him with a look that says I'm not an idiot. "Unless you're kissing siblings, don't try to bullshit me. I saw the way she looked at you and you her. It was an intimate look only lovers share."

He sets his plate down and picks up his coffee, his Adam's

apple bobbing as he downs the rest of it before depositing it in the sink.

"I'm only explaining this to you because you might be here for a while and see it for yourself. Jenny seems to like you, and if she does, then the others will as well. I don't want you thinking ill thoughts toward any of them." He pauses. "I'm a man who likes… variety. I don't settle for one certain type, because I like many different ones. I like options and I like change."

"Jesus," I mutter, disgust lacing my voice. "You make it sound like your speaking about a tie or a watch."

His eyes harden and the muscle in his jaw jumps. "And you sound like a judgmental bitch who has no fucking clue of the situation she's casting judgement on."

I narrow my eyes but clamp my mouth shut. He continues, his voice severe and cold.

"Jenny and Jamie are two of the four women I take as my lovers. Gillian and Layla are the other two. They aren't just lovers though, they're my companions. I care for them physically and emotionally, just as they do me. It's an arrangement we all enjoy. I spend time with them equally and separately, and I treat them fairly."

"Fairly?" I almost laugh, because I'm so stunned he would think what he's doing is fair to any of the women. "How can what you're doing be fair? You leave these women to be with another, as if they alone aren't good enough for you."

"They're more than good enough," he barks. "They're better than me. It's not them who's lacking, it's me. *I* would never be good enough for *them*."

His answer shocks me, and all I can do is stare at him for several long seconds before I get my bearings back.

"And are they allowed to take other lovers? Do you love them?"

He crosses his arms over his chest and sets one ankle over the other. "Yes. They can take other lovers if they choose, but only if it doesn't interfere with our arrangement. *They* choose not to. And yes, I love each of them, but I'm not *in* love with them. Just like they aren't in love with me."

"How do you know they aren't?" I snark and shove my plate away. I've only eaten a few bites, but suddenly I'm no longer hungry.

"Because they know it would be pointless. I don't do love, and I have no desire to give it a try."

I laugh at that, but it's humorless. He was right a moment ago. I have no right to cast judgement on these people. Just like my opinion on the circumstances shouldn't really matter to them. I should keep my mouth shut, but I just can't. I know what it feels like to love someone, hoping and praying they return the feelings, only for them to squash your heart. My college boyfriend hooked me line and sinker before throwing me back in the pond after I told him I loved him. He told me I was just a good time, that he was too young for anything serious. I knew he was a player when we got together, but my stupid heart thought I could change him.

"Love doesn't work that way. You can't just turn the emotion off. It grows whether you want it to or not."

He sighs and rubs his thumb across the crease between his eyes. After a moment, he settles his palms on the counter behind him.

"There's more shit to the situation than I'm willing to tell you. It's information you don't deserve to know. I may not be in love with them, but what I feel is the closest thing that I'll ever get to that emotion. Those women mean the world to me. I'd do anything for them. They know they'll never get more from me than what I've already given them. They're consenting adults and make their own decisions. If at any time, they need more, they can walk away. I'd never hold them back from a future they want. If that's a husband and kids, I'll be the first to pay for the wedding."

As he finishes his spiel, I almost feel sorry for him. To live a life so closed off from the prospect of love, must be a sad life. I may have been hurt in the past, but that doesn't mean I believe there isn't someone out there waiting for me. That I'll never find that special person I was meant to love until the day that I die. I firmly believe everyone has that certain person. You just have to open yourself up to the idea of it and grab a hold of it when it's presented to you.

I don't get a chance to reply to Judge, not that I could formulate a response anyway. As much as I still don't agree with his practices, I kind of understand it better. And again, he was right. Jenny and the others are adults, and as long as he's been completely truthful with them on where he stands, they have every right to make their own decisions. Who am I to agree or disagree? I'm just someone passing through town. I mean nothing to these people.

Light footsteps tap on the floor and we both look over to see Jenny carrying her empty plate into the kitchen. She still looks half asleep with her hair messily pulled back in a low ponytail and her eyes red. Yesterday was stressful on her as well. I'm sure it's not often she finds a butchered animal on her back porch.

Sadness creeps back in at remembering Sampson and the pain he must have went through. Diego is a bastard, and I hope like hell he pays dearly.

Judge meets Jenny before she can make it to the sink and takes the plate from her. After setting it down, he wraps his arms around her waist, tugging her closer, then leans down and kisses her. I watch him closely. He looks down at her tenderly, his expression softer than I've seen it the whole time we talked. He really does care about her. There's no mistaking that.

"Morning," he says low. "Sleep well?"

She yawns, throwing her hand over her mouth to cover it, and nods. "Yes. Thank you for staying."

He tucks a loose piece of hair behind her ear. "I'll be here until all this is over. I've already let the other women know."

Jenny's eyes slide to mine, and she gives me a soft smile. "Hey."

"Good morning."

She looks back to Judge. "You should be at work already," she remarks.

"I'm working from home for a while. Trouble and I don't think it's a good idea for the two of you to be left alone until this Diego is caught and dealt with. I'll be in my office for the next few hours, but my door will be open should either of you need anything."

She nods and leans up on her toes to kiss Judge. I decide to give them a bit of privacy and get up from my stool, slipping my phone in my pocket.

"I've got a phone call to make," I mumble, unsure if they'll even hear me.

Jenny apparently does, because she turns in Judge's arms and smiles.

Before I turn to leave the room, I glance at Judge. His expression is still icy, but it seems to have thawed some.

Once in my room, I plop down on the bed and blow out a breath. I'm not looking forward to this phone call. In fact, the thought of it has my chest feeling tight, like a band is slowly constricting around my sternum.

Pursing my lips and steeling my resolve, I swipe my screen to life, find the name I need, and bring the phone to my ear.

"Hello?" Millie, one of my best friends, answers sleepily.

"Hey, Mills."

There's a pause and a shuffling sound on her end, as I'm sure she gets out of the bed, not wanting to wake up her husband, Justin.

"Jesus, Eden," she hisses quietly. "Where are you?"

I lean back against the head board and stare up at the ceiling. "A small town northwest of San Antonio."

She huffs out a breath. "You were supposed to call me a couple days ago. I've been calling and texting. Why haven't you answered?" I inwardly wince when her voice rises, and guilt weights my shoulders down at the reminder of all the missed calls from Millie I've gotten over the last couple of days. "You had me worried sick. I almost called your mom."

My stomach bottoms out. "Please tell me you didn't," I beg.

"I didn't," she answers with frustration. "But I was going to today if I hadn't heard from you by tonight."

"I'm fine, okay? I just needed a couple days to adjust."

"Are you safe?" Worry laces her voice.

I think about her question. Am I safe here in Malus? It may be foolish of me, but my first instinct is to say yes. JW has no reason to want to protect me, other than his civic duty as a sheriff. But there's more to it than that. I feel it in my gut. It almost seems like it's personal to him, which is ludicrous, because I've never met the guy before in my life.

I tuck my knees to my chest and wrap one arm around my legs.

"Yes, I'm safe," I answer with the truth that I believe.

There's static in my ear as Millie blows out a breath. "Good. What are you going to do? You can't hide forever."

Millie is the only one who knows the truth about why I left, and that's only because she was at my house when I came barreling home, freaking out. I'm glad she knows because it means I have someone I can talk to about it. I've thanked God several times she wasn't there when Diego came by hours later.

"I'm not sure yet, but the sheriff here is helping me. I need you to do me a favor and talk with Clayton and Hannah. Just tell them I had a family emergency. I don't want them to think I've abandoned them."

Clayton and Hannah are siblings who visit the homeless shelter where Millie and I volunteer three days a week. Technically, we're only supposed to offer the shelter to people who are actually homeless. Clayton and Hannah aren't, but where they live is awful. They mainly come to the shelter to get away from home and to eat. They haven't outright admitted to being abused, but I've seen the bruises. They always play them off as being clumsy accidents, but I'm no fool. I've contemplated calling the authorities, but the two have already been in the foster system and are deathly afraid of going back. They were separated the last time, and both were sexually abused. I'm not sure how they managed it, but their parents were somehow able to get them back.

"They asked where you were yesterday," Millie states solemnly. "I told them you were sick."

A ball of anger forms in my stomach. I wish I could find Diego and beat the shit out of him.

I clear my throat and try to sound like I'm not on the verge of murder.

"Tell them I miss them, and I'll be back as soon as I can."

"I will." Millie turns quiet for a moment. "Justin still thinks you should report Diego and what he did to that girl, and what he did to you."

I shake my head, even though she can't see it. "It wouldn't do any good. If anything, it'll piss him off more."

"Keep me posted, okay? And for goodness sake, answer your phone when I call," she finishes, exasperated.

"I'm sorry." I hate that she worried so much. "Just don't call my parents. They'll call the police, and it'll put them on Diego's radar."

Diego's never met my parents, and the short time we were together, I never mentioned them. To him, it probably seems like we're not close. I'm grateful I never brought him home to meet them.

"I've got to go. I'll call you in a couple days."

"Alright. Just be careful."

"You know I will."

We hang up, and I drop my phone by my hip at the same time I suck in a deep breath.

Diego's taken so much from me. More than he probably realizes. He deserves to rot in prison for the rest of his stinking life.

I can't wait for this to be over, so I can get back to *my* life.

chapter eight

JW

"STOP STRUGGLING, YOU OLD bastard," I grunt to Cliff, keeping my grip light on his frail bicep so I don't bruise him.

"Then lemme go. I ain't done nothin' wrong," he whines.

"Dorothy wouldn't agree with you."

He spits on the sidewalk, almost falling over as he does so. I grab his shoulder and steady him.

"That old biddy don't know shit. She needs to keep her damn leaves on her property."

"Cliff, it's a fuckin' tree. She can't help the wind from blowing the leaves into your yard."

He grumbles and clumsily stumbles up the steps to the sheriff's office. This is the second time I've had to bring Cliff in this week for dumping leaves from his yard into Dorothy's. Next week we'll do this all over again. She has a tree close to their property line and he has a fit when the leaves fall into his yard. This only happens when he's drunk. Unfortunately, that's far too often. When he's sober, he's a completely different person. Nice and sane. His attitude toward Dorothy is flirtatious. The old man likes her, but he doesn't want to admit it, especially when he's drunk. He lost his wife of

59

fifty years, six years ago. He didn't take the loss very well, and I suspect he hates himself for caring about another woman.

I happened to come across Cliff yelling at Dorothy while I was driving by. The little old lady had her broom in her hand, trying her best to smack Cliff with it as he dumped a pile of leaves in her yard. The transformation between the two elderly people is amazing when Cliff hasn't been drinking. Tomorrow, Cliff will go over to Dorothy's house, apologize, and she'll make him some coffee. They'll chat, be friendly, and act like nothing ever happened. Until the next time Cliff decides to break out a whiskey bottle.

"Hey, Mr. Levins. How's it going today?" Rita asks as we approach her desk.

"It'd be better if this fool—" he throws his thumb over his shoulder toward me, "—would let me go so I could go on about my business."

"Not if your business consists of throwing shit in Dorothy's yard," I retort and propel him forward.

"It's just leaves."

I chuckle. "Exactly so, which makes me wonder why you're so insistent on throwing them in her yard. Know what I think?" I don't give him time to answer. "I think you like riling your neighbor."

"That's stupid," he mutters. "Why'd I want to do that?"

Rounding the corner to where Malus's only two cells are, Sanchez spots us and gets up to open one.

"That's only something you can answer Cliff," I tell him as I march him over to the opened cell and deposit him on the bed, where he slumps. "I suggest you think about it while you're here for the next few hours. Once you figure it out, I bet you'd spend a lot less time in this cell."

He lays down and turns his back toward me. "Whatever. Just go and leave me be."

Two minutes tops and he'll be sawing logs in his sleep. Cliff hasn't been officially arrested. It's just time in the cell to sleep off his drink.

I shake my head as I leave the cell. Sanchez chuckles and resumes his seat at the small desk in the corner.

"One of these days he'll get a clue and figure out he likes old Mrs. Owens," he remarks, picking up a straw and puts it between his teeth to chew.

"That day can't come soon enough."

"Need me to stick around until he sobers?"

"Gimme a couple hours and I'll be back. I'm gonna run to The Hill and grab some lunch and take care of a couple things. I'll be back to take over."

"Sounds good."

"Want anything from The Hill?"

He kicks his feet up on the desk and gets comfortable. "I'll grab something when I leave here."

I tap the door on my way out. Rita's on the phone, so I stop by her desk to make sure it's not important. I continue on my way when she shakes her head.

The Hill is only a few blocks away, so I choose to walk instead of drive. I pass by a big open grassy area that has a huge playground for all the children in Malus. Picnic tables and benches surround the playground. I laugh when I see a boy chasing after a girl with what looks like a worm dangling from his hand. Several other kids are on the playset while their parents sit in the sun and watch them. One family is sitting at a picnic table having lunch.

The area is a lot happier than it was back when it was Sweet Haven. That's where the Hall sat. When my brothers and I moved back, one of the first things we did was burn down the offending building. Everyone left in town stood around the big ball of flames, each of us relishing watching the place that held so many painful memories burn to the ground. Afterward, my brothers and I felt the landscape left behind would be a good place to build a play area for the children. What once was a place that created nightmares is now a place that helps make good memories.

It's noon on a Friday, so several cars dot the parking lot of The Hill. The inside will be even fuller than it appears from the outside, because, like me, many people in town live so close to The Hill, they walk to the restaurant.

I'm surprised to see Mae behind the bar when I walk inside. Her and her late husband, Dale, owned The Hill back when the town was called Sweet Haven. The place was shut down after the town was raided twenty-three years ago. When she came back twenty-one years later, The Hill was still in her name. With her permission, Doris and Meryl had opened the place back up years ago and ran it. Instead of taking on the task by herself, Mae decided to offer half of The Hill to Doris and Meryl. They've pretty much taken over since Mae is getting on in years and it's harder for her to get around. She doesn't like not being a part of the restaurant anymore, but I think she's starting to understand that she needs to take it easy.

"Hey, Mae," I greet and lean over the bar to kiss her cheek.

"Hey, you." She smiles, throwing a towel over her shoulder. "How's your day going?"

I sit on a stool and lace my fingers on the scarred wood. "Just dropped Cliff off in a cell."

She sucks her teeth while rolling her eyes. "That man…. I tell ya. Why can't he just admit he has a thing for Dorothy?"

"My guess? Because it'll make all of our lives easier."

"Too right you are, son. Now," she slaps her hands on the bar, "what can I get you?"

"Why are you here? I thought you only came on Mondays and Wednesdays?"

Her cheeks carry a healthy flush and her smile is wide. As much as I don't like her being here on a Friday, one of the busiest days of the week, I have to admit, she looks more energized than I've seen in a while.

"Doris has come down with a stomach bug and Tina's baby is sick." She points her finger at me when I open my mouth, already knowing what I was going to say. "Don't you start with me. I've already heard it from Judge and Trouble. I'm only here for today. Tina's husband will be home tomorrow to watch the little one, so she'll be in then."

I cross my arms on the bar and lean toward her, not completely giving up on my argument.

"As long as you call one of us if you get too tired. We can cover your shift if we need to."

She scowls, but it's not a real one because her eyes are too soft. She knows my brothers and I only have her best interests at heart. After all, Mae and Dale were the ones to take us away from the hell we were living in as kids and were more parents to us than our actual parents.

"I know it and appreciate it, but I'll be fine. I'm only here until six anyway." She pulls a glass from under the bar and fills it with water before placing it in front of me. "You here for lunch?"

"Yes, ma'am. The usual."

As she walks away to put my order in, feminine laughter has me swiveling on my stool. I spot Remi and Grace in a booth, with a woman with red hair sitting across from them, her back facing me. At first, I don't recognize the red head, because I've only ever seen her with a scarf over her hair, but the minute her head turns, and I get a side glimpse of her face, I'm shocked to find out it's Eden. Only her head and shoulders can be seen over the back of the booth.

Before I know it, I'm getting up from the stool and walking over to them. Remi spots me when I'm a few feet away, and smiles.

"Hey there," she chirps.

I tip my chin. "Remi, Grace." My eyes move to Eden, and they catch on hers. "Eden."

"Hi."

My body reacts when she speaks. Not only because it likes her voice, but especially because she's fucking gorgeous with her hair braided and tossed over her shoulder. With it normally hidden behind a scarf, I didn't know it was so thick and long. The end of her braid rests in her lap, meaning it'll reach her ass when she stands.

An image of me wrapping the long length of hair around my

hand as I drill into her from behind pops in my mind. I try to will the image away, but it's already there and not going anywhere.

"You want to join us?" Grace asks, pulling my attention away from Eden.

"Sure."

With no other choice, not that I'm complaining, I take the only seat available; the one next to Eden. She scoots over to give me room. I want to haul her closer to me, but figured it's not a good idea. Her sweet scent hits my nose, and I pull in a deep breath, taking in more.

"How are you ladies today?"

Grace answers first. "Good, now that the holidays are almost over. I was going crazy sitting at home not working."

Grace is an elementary school teacher. School starts on Monday after having four weeks off for Christmas and the New Year.

"Isn't it usually the other way around?" I ask. "Aren't you supposed to dread when school starts back up?"

She laughs. "I suppose so, but not for me. I love my kids too much to be away from them for long."

Grace is a good woman who was dealt a shitty life. She came to live in Malus five years ago when her husband nearly beat her to death.

Don't worry. My brothers and I took care of him for her.

I glance over to Eden, who's fiddling with the end of her braid. "Where's Jenny? I figured she'd be here with you?"

She looks at me out the corner of her eye. "She's with Judge. He was going to drop us off and run some errands before coming back to get us, but Jenny had something she needed to do as well."

That explains why Eden is here without protection. No one in their right mind would come inside The Hill to get to her. And that's the only reason why I haven't called Judge to bitch him out about leaving her alone.

I toss my arm over the back of the booth, and I immediately feel the warmth of her body hit mine. I'm tempted to drop my arm to her shoulders, but I settle for my fingertips barely grazing the skin on her upper arm. She stiffens beside me, but after several seconds, she relaxes again.

"Any plans for the day?" I ask the women.

"Nothing except wait for Trouble to get home." Remi frowns as she says this. "Susan's watching Elijah for me because I was going crazy at home, worrying about him."

Her anxious gaze slides to Eden's before meeting mine again. There's a silent question in her eyes, one she can't ask with Eden at the table. She's worried about the task Trouble and Emo are on and wants me to find out what I can. The men left yesterday and are due back tomorrow morning. I have every bit of faith they'll be back in one piece with no one the wiser of what they did in Southern Cal, but Remi's new to what my brothers and I do. She'll always worry, no matter how many times Trouble's away taking care of shit, but over time, it'll get easier.

I give her a subtle nod, silently letting her know I'll make a phone call later, and she gives me a grateful smile in return.

"Is he away on business?" Eden asks the seemingly innocent question. If she only knew the true answer, she'd probably haul ass out of town and straight to the police in the nearest town.

"Yeah, he's uh, at a physician's conference," Remi supplies. I barely hold back my wince when her reply sounds only half convincing.

Luckily, Mae comes up to the table with our lunch. Mae may be getting on in her years, but she makes being a waitress look effortless. She's got three plates lining one arm and holding the last one with her other hand. Her memory is still sharp as she replays what everyone ordered and places the right plates in front of the correct person.

"Thanks, Mae. This looks delicious, as always."

Mae pats Grace's cheek and grins. "Thank you, dear."

Resting one hand on her hip, she regards me with something akin to curiosity in her eyes. "I didn't realize you knew Eden."

I take my arm from around Eden's shoulder and cock a brow. "And I didn't realize you knew her either."

Her eyes narrow when I avoid her question. "I didn't, until she walked in earlier. How do you know her?"

"Does it matter?"

Being evasive is the best course of action at the moment, or Mae'll be pulling out wedding magazines and asking what flavor cake Eden wants for the wedding reception. If it were up to her, my brothers and I would have been married off years ago and our wives would be popping out baby number five.

"It might," she answers, lifting both eyebrows, still waiting on my answer.

"I pulled her over just outside of town for speeding," I say bluntly. There's a sharp pinch on my side, so I tack on. "But she had a good reason. Nothing more than that."

Mae's arm drops to her side, and her lips purse, like she doesn't like my answer. She turns, and I swear, if I didn't know the woman better, I'd say she was sulking as she walks back to the bar.

"Thanks, ass," Eden mutters, and I can't help but chuckle.

"I'd say you got me back. Those damn nails of yours are killer."

The table is quiet, except for our muted voices. When I look over at Remi and Grace, I find them both watching us with unconcealed nosiness. I clear my throat and snatch up my burger. The last thing I need is for either woman to suspect something is going on between Eden and myself. I'm still trying to figure out the answer to that myself. Or rather, if I actually want anything to go on between us.

Do I want to fuck her? A big fucking hell yes. Should I fuck her? I'm not sure yet. Women are tricky. You fuck them once and they either treat the encounter as a casual fling or they cling to you like peanut butter in the roof of your mouth. I've got no desire to be like Trouble and marry and settle down. The stain of my past is too much a part of me. No way would I want to dump that baggage on a woman's lap.

"How's Emo doing?" Grace asks after a few minutes.

I drop the rest of my burger on my plate and wipe my mouth with my napkin. I lean back in the booth and drape my arm over the back again, this time keeping my fingertips away from Eden's shoulder. Getting more comfortable, I spread my legs under the table. When my thigh bumps hers, I decide to leave it there. I'm surprised when she doesn't move hers away either.

"He's doing alright. You know how he is."

She nods, her eyes looking doleful. The thing about Emo is that he enjoys pain. He uses it when the darkness inside him becomes overwhelming. It helps calm him in ways that nothing else can. Except for doling out death and sex. Not just any kind of sex though. Emo likes it rough, both for him and his partner. There're not too many women in Malus who could handle the kind of rawness Emo needs in the bedroom. Grace is one of the few and the woman he chooses to use the majority of the time.

I've suspected for a while that Grace has feelings for Emo, but the woman is smart. She knows Emo isn't capable of giving her what she ultimately wants; a man who could love her unconditionally and take her heart in return without squashing it. Emo isn't built that way. He's much too dark for a woman like Grace. Even so, she's still there for him any time he needs her, and for that, my brothers and I are eternally grateful to her.

"I was hoping he'd have contacted me recently. I haven't... heard from him in a while."

I keep my voice low when I tell her, "I'll let him know you asked about him."

She swallows and smiles tightly, reclaiming her fork and stabbing a fry.

No one speaks after that. Once everyone is done eating, I get up and pay for our meals. Mae's still looking at me with inquisitive eyes as she hands me my change, and I know her questions from earlier won't be the only ones she'll have for me. She's just biding her time and forming her attack. I have no doubt come Sunday, the day my brothers and I go to her house for dinner each week, she'll regale me with more questions.

When I make it back to the table, I overhear Eden tell the other women she just shot Judge a message that she's ready to go. I whip out my own phone and send my own message.

Me – Don't worry about picking Eden up. I'll walk her home and stay with her until you get back.

Judge – Got it. Shouldn't be much longer.

"Come." I offer Eden my hand. "I'll walk you home."

She takes my hand, scoots to the edge of the booth, and stands.

"Thanks. But there's no need. I've already messaged Judge. He should be on his way."

"He's not. I sent a message and told him I'll take care of it."

She pauses for a moment before nodding and slinging her purse over her shoulder. I was right; her hair does reach her ass.

As I walk behind the women and watch the sway of Eden's hips and the end of her thick braid bounce against her plump ass, I realize something.

I'm in big fucking trouble, because there's no way Eden's leaving here without me getting a very generous taste of her and have her in my bed. Over and over again.

AFTER LEAVING REMI AND GRACE at their places, which were on our way to Judge's, we walk up the steps to Judge and Jenny's house. All of Judge's women have a place of their own. Most times, he's with one of them, but every so often, he'll stay in his renovated childhood home. When my brothers and I came back to town ten years ago, we all had our homes gutted and refurbished, not wanting anything from our pasts to invade our futures.

Eden stops at the screen door and turns to face me.

"Thanks for walking me home."

Those metal bracelets she's always wearing clink together as she grabs her braid and twirls the end around her finger.

"It was my pleasure." I take the end of her braid from her hand and finger the strands myself. "You should go without the scarf more often. Your hair is gorgeous."

Her eyelids lower and her tongue darts out to swipe her bottom lip, tempting me to run my tongue along the same path and lick away the moisture she left behind.

Her voice drops when she speaks again. "It's a pain to take care of. I've been thinking about cutting it off."

"No," I growl before I can stop myself. Her brows shoot up, so I soften my tone. "It'd be a sin to cut off all this stunning hair."

She smirks. "I highly doubt God would fault me for cutting my hair."

"You're probably right. Let me rephrase. It would be an utter shame."

I step closer to her, my fingers still gripping her braid. I wrap it around my fist. She moves back a step and her ass meets the screen door. I twist the braid a couple more times.

"What are you doing?" she whispers, her eyes darkening to an emerald green.

I close the remaining gap between us. "Showing you the benefits of not cutting your hair."

Pulling gently on her braid until her head tips back, I dip down until my lips graze hers. They're soft and sweet. So much fucking better than I imagined.

Her mouth opens when she releases a breathy moan, and I take advantage, sweeping my tongue inside to explore better. My cock swells against the zipper of my jeans, and I want nothing more than to hoist her up and grind myself against her warm center. Preferably with her skirt lifted. Would she be bare beneath her skirt or would she have on a pair of cute little panties? Either would work for me.

Her small hands grip my shirt at my sides, and I wonder if she's going to push me away or pull me closer. I'd stop if she wanted me to, but I really fucking hope she doesn't.

When her grip tugs me closer and her tongue shyly meets mine, I groan in relief. I shift closer and encircle my arm around her waist, pressing her flush against me. My dick both weeps and rejoices at the intimate contact. Leaving her delicious lips behind, I trail wet

69

kisses down the side of her neck. The unique flavor of her skin is addicting, like heroine to a druggy.

"Want to know why I don't want you to cut your hair?" I murmur against her neck.

Her head tips back until it thumps against the door. "Why?" she breathes.

I nip the flesh where her neck meets her shoulder.

"Because I want to feel it trailing over my chest as you ride my cock."

She shudders out a breath, her nails digging into my sides. I nudge away the thin material of her shirt on her shoulder with my chin and run my tongue and lips over the exposed skin.

"I also want to wrap it around my fist and use it to tug you back as I fuck you from behind. I bet your pussy would strangle my cock when I do that, wouldn't it?"

Instead of answering verbally, she nods and presses her hips hard against mine. I wedge one of my legs between hers and press my thigh into her core. Surprise and pleasure force a growl from my lips when she wraps her calf around my leg and digs her pussy onto my thigh.

I'm fucking dying. Dying to flip her around, toss up her skirt, and give us the pleasure we both crave. I'm dying to drop to my knees and lick up every drop I know her body has produced. I'm Goddamn dying to have her delectable lips surround my cock and have her suck until she drains me. I'd grip her long hair and help guide her to the finish line.

A throat clearing behind us has Eden stiffening in my arms. I don't give a fuck who it is, I want to kill them. Eden lifts her head from the door and peers over my shoulder at the unwanted and untimely intruder. My grip on her hair tightens for a fraction of a second before I let her go. Red tints her cheeks, but I'm not sure if it's from what we were just doing or being caught by Judge and Jenny. Her eyes shoot to me, and she gently presses against my chest. I take a step back, missing her body against mine the second it's gone.

"Sorry!" Jenny squeaks from behind us.

I shoot Judge a glare over my shoulder. The bastard has the audacity to raise an eyebrow, like he doesn't care what he just interrupted. He meanders up the fucking stairs, as if cock-blocking me is an everyday occurrence, his hand entwined with Jenny's, pulling her behind him. At least she has the sense to look embarrassed and regretful for the interruption.

I step back from Eden and pull her to the side, so the two can go inside.

"Payback's a bitch," I inform Judge in low tones as he opens the screen door.

"This was payback. For the time you interrupted Layla and me in the back of The Hill."

"Fucker," I mutter, because he's right. That shit was hilarious at the time. It's not so funny now.

He laughs and lets the screen door slam behind him. "No fucking on my porch," he calls out.

Ignoring his demand, I look back to Eden. Her cheeks are still pink. The color matches her gorgeous red hair. My dick twitches, and I'd damn near give anything to be alone with her right now. Even now, with the haze of desire muted and reality seeping in, I want her more than my next breath.

"Have dinner with me tomorrow?" The words come out more a demand than a question, but I don't take them back.

I know her answer before she shakes her head. It's in her eyes. The hesitancy.

"I don't think that's a good idea."

"Why the hell not?"

"It'll just add more complications to an already thorny situation," she answers, throwing her arms across her chest in a defensive move.

"I disagree." I step forward until I'm crowding her. "I think it'll make this situation a lot more pleasurable. Why not take advantage and get something good out of it? After what we just did, you can't deny we would be damn good together."

She tugs her bottom lip between her teeth, her brow crunching as she thinks over my offer. If I knew it would help my case, I'd drop to my knees and beg. The notion makes me inwardly cringe. I've never begged a woman a day in my life, and for the thought to cross my mind to do so now, makes my asshole clench. The woman does some serious shit to my manhood. If I didn't want her so much, I'd forfeit the idea and be on my way. But there's this pull I feel toward her I can't seem to ignore. Hell, I don't even want to try to ignore it.

After several long seconds, she finally puts me out of my misery.

"Okay." My dick goes from half-mast to hard as granite with her answer. "But," she tacks on, "There's no guarantee on the sex part."

I give her a cocky grin. "Sure." There most definitely will be. I'll make damn sure she can't resist me.

She narrows her eyes, but keeps her mouth shut. Leaning down, I place a kiss against her closed lips. "See you tomorrow," I murmur.

Spinning on my heel, I whistle a happy tune as I descend the steps.

Eden has no fucking clue she'll be on her back come tomorrow night, whispering my name as she comes over and over again.

chapter nine

EDEN

W HAT IN THE HELL POSSESSED me to say yes to JW yesterday? My last relationship ended with me witnessing my ex kill another woman. While I don't think JW is the type to kill or beat women, I'm still fresh out of a relationship that ended horribly. I can't afford to start something new. Even if it is only temporary. Besides, something tells me temporary with JW won't be so simple. Yes, I've had casual relationships before, and I've even had a couple one-night stands—what can I say? I enjoy sex. If I had met JW when I wasn't running for my life and currently depending on him to *save* my life, I would have already snatched him up and seduced him. It's just sucky timing. I need to be concentrating on staying alive, not on how big JW's cock is and if he prefers doggy style over reverse cowgirl.

Even through all the reasons why I shouldn't have dinner with JW rush through my head, I'm still looking forward to it. I know myself enough to not make any mental promises on what can't happen during our time together. Especially after what happened yesterday on Jenny and Judge's porch. I was so turned on from my encounter with JW, that I was forced to change my panties when I came back into the house. I may have also gotten myself off in the shower before bed. No, I definitely got myself off, and with thoughts of JW, it took all of *maybe* two minutes.

Thinking about it even now has me wanting to clench my thighs together as I make my way out of the bedroom. It's late, just after eleven in the morning. I haven't slept this late in years, but it felt good to simply laze around and not have to be anywhere or have any pressing matters to attend to.

Back in San Antonio, I'm a shift manager at an Irish pub and grill. Before I left, I called my boss, Finn, and told him I had to take a leave of absence due to a family emergency, and I was unsure when I would be back. The awesome guy who Finn is, he accepted my explanation without question and told me my job was there when I returned. I knew he would understand. He's been an exceptional boss. It's one of the reasons why I've stayed working for him for six years.

When I walk out into the living room, I almost turn back around to go back to my room. As it is, I barely muffle the groan working its way up my throat. Jenny's on the couch, her back to the armrest, facing me. Her grin is big and telling.

"It's about time you got up," she says enthusiastically, nearly bouncing in her seat. "I've been waiting hours."

Yesterday, when I came inside after JW left, I found Jenny and Judge on the couch watching the news. He had his arm thrown over her shoulder and she was snuggled up to his side. As soon as the front door closed, she tried to pull away, but Judge tugged her back to him, murmuring something in her ear. Disappointment lit her face, but I was grateful he didn't let her go. I have no doubt she would have thrown question after question at me. The rest of the evening was spent with my eyes glued to the TV and Jenny's questioning gaze glued to me. I didn't need to know Jenny that well to know it was killing her not being able to interrogate me. It was almost laughable. It would have been if I wasn't the one who would have been questioned.

After we watched a couple of movies and had dinner, Judge forced Jenny from the couch and they retired to their bedroom. I don't know why Judge kept Jenny stuck to his side, but no matter the reason, I owe him my gratitude.

My reprieve is obviously over though. It's not that it bothers me to talk about what her and Judge interrupted on the porch. I'm just not sure what to say, because I'm unsure how I feel about the whole thing. My mind's a fucked-up mess right now. I want JW—really freaking badly—but I also know it's just not the right time. I have no doubt I'll be weak if I'm alone with him for any amount of time.

I give Jenny a lopsided grin. "Can I at least make a cup of coffee first?"

She blows out a dramatic breath and nods grimly. "If you must. Then get your butt back out here. I've waited long enough."

Shaking my head, I go into the kitchen straight to the coffee pot. I sigh when the smell hits my nose. Coffee, it's my vice. One I'll have until the day I die.

I carry my steaming mug back to the living room.

"Judge in his office?" I ask, casting my eyes toward the hallway. The office door is closed.

"Yep, and he said he'll be in there for a while, so we've got plenty of time." Her teeth flash as she taps the couch in front of her.

Taking a seat, I glance at her over the rim of my cup, hiding a smile. She's practically hyperventilating waiting on me. I take a couple of sips before deciding I better start speaking before she passes out.

"Alright, let's have it." I say, settling my cup on the coffee table and turning on the couch so I'm sitting like her with my back to the armrest.

She leans forward. "What's going on between you and JW?"

I shrug nonchalantly. "Nothing."

She snorts and rolls her eyes. "Sure didn't look like nothing to me. He was two seconds away from shoving your skirt up and delving inside your panties. Had Judge and I been a few minutes later, I'm sure I would have gotten a clear view of JW's ass as he fucked you against the door."

I choke out a laugh. The woman is loony and not afraid to tell it how she sees it. She also could very well be right. I was so far gone yesterday that I probably would have let JW strip me and take me on the porch where anyone could have seen.

I cross my legs on the cushion and tuck my skirt under my legs. "Okay. How about this? I don't know what's going on."

She hums and taps her bottom lip with her finger. "That's better, but still not very interesting. I need more."

I laugh again. "Sorry, but that's all I got; except that I shouldn't let anything happen. It's terrible timing, and I'll be leaving soon."

She looks at me slyly before grinning. "Yeah, but you could have some fun while you're here."

I tilt my head slightly. "Why do you care?" At her frown, I rush to add, "I mean no offense. It's just, you don't know me. Why would you care if I had fun or not?"

A small smile forms on her face. "I just like the people around me to be happy." The smile disappears. "And I know what that man did to you. You deserve to be happy."

"I'll be happy once Diego is no longer a problem, and I can go back to San Antonio."

"But why not enjoy your time while you're here? Why not have something you clearly want? And don't even try to deny it. I heard you in the shower last night."

My eyes widen in horror and she bursts out laughing. "You're lying!" I squeak. I was quiet last night while I got off to images of JW. I *know* I was. Wasn't I?

After she settles down, wiping away the tears in her eyes from laughing so hard, she admits, "Fine. I'm lying, but your face says your guilty. Admit it. You want JW."

I do. Even if my mind wants to claim otherwise, my body says, *"Fuck you. I want to get laid"*.

"You've seen him. I'd have to be deaf, dumb, and blind to not want him."

She nods, her expression serious.

"We'll see," is all I can promise her.

She pouts, but accepts my answer, which I'm glad, because I'm done talking about JW and what could possibly happen between us. Deep down, I know I'm going to sleep with him. Denying the inevitable is a waste of time. I'm just not ready to admit it out loud.

I spend the rest of my day doing… nothing. I can't remember the last time I've simply lounged around the house. Even my days off from the pub, I spent them at the homeless shelter, running errands, or catching up on house work. I've enjoyed having no responsibilities, but I know it won't last long. I'll become restless, needing something to occupy my time. Hopefully, before that happens, I'll be back home.

I call Mom and Dad as I promised I would, so they don't call the police. Not that it really matters anymore. Diego already knows where I am. I'd still prefer to keep them out of it until JW does whatever he plans to do to keep me safe. If the San Antonio PD gets involved, I'll be forced to go back, and I don't trust them to keep me safe.

It wasn't Mom who answered, but Dad. He was just as adamant as Mom that I tell him what's going on. I explained the best that I could without giving too much away that I couldn't go into details, but it was being taken care of.

Judge came out a little after noon and made meatball sandwiches for all of us for lunch. Just as we were finishing up with our meal, two women who I hadn't met before showed up. Both were stunningly gorgeous and were introduced as Layla and Gillian. Remembering Judge and my conversation about him being involved with several women, I knew these were his other lovers. I watched his interaction with them closely. Other than pecking a kiss on the cheek of both women in greeting, he didn't touch them intimately. He was, however, more intimate with Jenny. I wondered if it was out of respect for Jenny because they were in the house he shares with her or if there's another deeper reason. Regardless, none of the women sent off jealous vibes. Even after Judge left the room to go back to his office. In fact, all three women seemed to be close. I was amazed at how well they got along.

JW sent me a text message earlier saying he'd be by to pick me up at five. It's now ten 'til, and I'm a nervous wreck. I don't know why I'm so anxious. It's not like this is the first time I've made plans with a guy knowing we may end the night with me in his bed. It's not the situation but the man. JW makes me nervous because of the feelings he provokes in me. Feelings I don't dare give a name to.

Just as Jenny appears in the mouth of the hallway, the doorbell rings.

"I'll get it," she chirps, smoothly changing directions to the door.

I stand and brush my hands down my skirt. I turn right as JW enters the room. I decided to not wrap my hair in a scarf and opted for a loose braid down my back since JW seemed to like that style more. That's the first place his eyes land and his gaze darkens with lust.

He steps further in the room, not stopping until he's right in front of me.

"Hey, Gypsy," he murmurs, dipping his head low and presses his lips against mine. Zings of awareness spark through my limbs at both the kiss and him calling me Gypsy. You don't take the time to come up with a nickname for someone unless you care for them, meaning I'm not the only one who feels this thing building between us. I just seem to be the only one trying to fight it.

"Hi," I whisper when he pulls away.

His smile only tips up one corner of his mouth, but it's still one of the sexiest smiles I've ever seen.

You're in serious trouble, Eden, my mind whispers unnecessarily.

Yeah, no shit, I inwardly snark back to myself.

"You ready?" JW asks, and I nod.

Judge comes out of his office just as we get to the door. His eyes slide to our clasped hands before lifting them to JW, his face blank. "I've got an early morning meeting tomorrow I need to attend to. I'm dropping Jenny off at Trouble's since his appointments don't start until after lunch."

"Eden will stay with me tonight, so you don't have to worry about her."

I jerk my eyes to JW. Did he really just say what I think he did. That's a whole lot of assumption on his part. I narrow my eyes at him, willing him to look at me. He doesn't, even though I have a death grip on his hand. I decide to broach the subject when we leave and not in front of his friends.

Judge gives JW a tight nod, and we turn to leave. I ignore the ridiculously huge smile on Jenny's face.

"See you tomorrow," she says, all too happily. When we pass by her, she tacks on in a low voice only for me to hear, "Have fun."

I give her a stern look, but it loses it's muster when my lips twitch. No one in their right mind could stay annoyed with a person like Jenny. She's too friendly and bubbly.

Once we're seated in JW's truck on our way, I look over at him. "That was pretty presumptuous of you, wasn't it?"

He smiles devilishly. "I like to call it confident."

"In my book it's called conceited," I retort.

He chuckles and reaches over the middle console for my hand. His laughter dies away and his expression turns serious. He kisses the back of my hand.

"I have a spare bedroom if that's where you want to stay." He turns his head partially my way. I can't see his eyes from the sunglasses he's wearing, but I know the blue orbs are no longer a baby blue, but a stormy grey. "There's no pressure for anything more than dinner. As much as I'd love to fuck you into tomorrow, I'm not into forcing or coaxing." His jaw bunches before he continues. "I want you completely willing and as hot for it as I am. I figured since you'll be at my place anyway, and with Judge having an early meeting, you could just crash there."

"Okay," I say quietly. I keep my eyes trained out the windshield, even though I feel his surprised gaze on me at my easy acceptance. I'm no push over, and I certainly won't be bullied or persuaded into doing something I don't want to do. I accept his invitation because I want to. JW, for some unknown reason, makes me feel safe. Like he won't let anything or anyone touch me without my permission. Maybe it's because of the badge he wears, or maybe it's because I've seen the hatred on his face any time what Diego did to me and that other woman is brought up.

We turn silent after that, and I take in more of the town. It's small, with shops, businesses, and houses clustered throughout the mile or so that makes up the town. When I rode into town that first day, I noticed more houses lining the outskirts of the town limits.

We take a left down a dirt road with a thick line of trees on both sides. I expect to see a house up ahead, so I'm surprised when the trees clear and it's a lake that we pull to a stop in front of. Looking around, there are no buildings in sight, only the water and a dock up ahead.

Before I can question JW on why we're here, he's already out of the truck and walking around to my side. He pulls my door open and reaches toward me with his hand.

"Why are we here? I thought we were going to your house?" I ask and grab his hand for him to help me out of the truck.

"We are." He lets me go and walks to the bed of the truck, pulling the tailgate down. He hands me a thick blanket. "We're having dinner here first." He winks. "A picnic. On the dock." With that, he grabs a basket by the handle, snags my hand, and proceeds to pull me toward the dock.

"Why?" I ask dumbly.

He glances at me over his shoulder. "Because it's nice outside."

"Try again," I snort.

"Because it's romantic," he replies with laughter in his voice.

"You don't seem like you're much of the romantic type."

We reach the dock, and I watch as we pass by bed after bed of colorful flowers lining the edges in long planter boxes.

"Fine," he sighs, stopping just before we get to the end. "I'm trying to seduce you and figured something like this would help." His lips twitch.

"Now why is it that reason I believe so much more than the others?"

Putting down the basket, he grabs the end of the blanket I hand him and we both spread it out.

"Hey, I may be trying to seduce you, but it's still nice out here, and you can't say this isn't romantic."

Reluctantly, I have to agree with him. It is nice out today. The sun is starting to set, and the temperature is just beginning to cool down. This time of year can still be pretty hot some days, but in the evenings, it cools off. It's a nice change to the sweltering heat in the summer.

I also have to admit, this is romantic. Picnics, no matter the location, are romantic. And this one is especially so, because of the beautiful flowers surrounding us.

"So, is it working?" He takes a seat and starts pulling items out of the basket.

I sit beside him and smirk. "Maybe, but there's still hours left of the day. There's no telling what could happen in that time."

He chuckles and hands me a plate filled with small rolls of different kinds of sliced meat, tiny blocks of cheese, grapes, and strawberries with their leaves cut off.

"So tell me," I say around the block of cheese I just tossed in my mouth. "Did you prepare all this or did you grab an already prepared tray from the store?"

He sucks in a breath and clutches his chest dramatically. "You wound me, Gypsy. Don't you have faith in my food prep skills?"

Popping a grape in my mouth, I smile. "Nope. This just looks too perfect to be made by anyone other than someone who does it for a living."

His eyes twinkle. "You'd be right," he replies sheepishly. I can't help but laugh.

We sit and eat for a few minutes, the only sound is the lapping of the water against the deck, birds chirping, and the occasional splash of a fish.

I gesture with the tip of my water bottle toward a boat pulled up on the grass close to the edge of the water. "Do you ever go out onto the lake?"

"Not as much as I used to."

"That's a shame. My dad used to take me out on his boat every weekend when I was a kid. It was just me, him, and the fish we'd catch. We never left without enough fish for at least several meals."

"Sounds like you had a good time on those weekends."

"Some of the best." I smile, slipping another grape in my mouth. "What about you? Are you close with your dad?"

The look that comes across his face sends shivers racing down my spine. Never have I seen such animosity in a person's eyes before. A chunk of the grape gets stuck in my throat, and I cough to dislodge it. If that look were ever directed at me, I'd be scared down to my bones. Thankfully, it's not. It saddens me because I know the look stems from thinking of his father.

"No," he grunts. "My dad was a bastard from hell."

"Was?" I ask quietly.

His eyes lift to mine. "Yes. He's exactly where he should be. In Hell."

Reaching over, I place my hand on his. "I'm sorry."

"Why? It's a wasted emotion when it comes to that man."

I shake my head. "I'm sorry because whatever he did to you must have been awful for you to carry so much hatred inside you."

"It's not what he did, it's what he didn't do. Him and my mother."

My heart aches for JW. I want nothing more than to go to him, wrap my arms around him, and offer whatever comfort I can. His body is too stiff for something like that though. I want to ask him to elaborate. I'm curious what the two people did who were supposed to love and cherish their child, but I hold back my question. Something tells me whatever is was, it was horrendous.

Wanting the lighter conversation of before, I suggest playing Would You Rather. His lips twitch, and I'm glad to see some of the darkness leave his eyes. The game may sound childish, but it's a really good way to get to know someone. For instance, I now know JW would rather eat bugs than cottage cheese, go skydiving over bungee jumping, and his favorite holiday is Halloween. He thinks cold coffee is an abomination and the person who invented it should be hogtied and strung up, he'd rather hold a cobra than be within ten feet of a spider, and he likes Coke over Pepsi.

Of course, JW had to dirty the game up by giving naughty scenarios. Like which one I would choose between; being watched while I have sex or do the watching myself. I chose the latter. What can I say? There's just something so hot about watching a man and a woman go at it. He followed that question up with would I rather watch two men or two women. His lips curled in disgust when I said two men.

By the time we're done eating and playing our little game, the sun has set behind the trees on the other side of the lake. The temperature's dropped at least ten degrees. Goosebumps appear on my arms when there's a slight breeze. I'm reclining back on my hands with my eyes closed, when suddenly, there's a shadow hovering over me. I feel the warmth of his body before I open my eyes and see him right in front of me. He's sitting in the opposite direction of me with his arm across my lap and resting by my hip on the blanket. His other hand lifts and brings my braid over my shoulder.

"I love your hair," he remarks, his eyes on the bright red strands.

I laugh. "I can tell."

He leans closer until his breath fans across my lips. "I love your lips too. Sweet and soft."

I hum in the back of my throat when his mouth slowly presses over mine. I open to him immediately, desperately wanting the taste of him against my tongue. He tastes like the grapes he just ate.

Using my hair, he guides my head to the side for a better angle. I really like when he does that. I like that he uses my hair to control where he wants me.

He tips my head back and starts trailing his lips down my neck. The short stubble on his cheeks and chin scrapes erotically across my flesh, doubling the pleasure of what he's doing. My stomach tightens and a shot of lust shoots straight between my legs.

"Lie back," he murmurs huskily against my ear.

The thought to object doesn't even cross my mind as I lay back onto the blanket. What JW's making me feel overpowers any inhibitions I may have.

I open my eyes when I sense him moving above me. His eyes blaze a bright blue as he stares down at me and the look sends shock waves of pleasure coursing through my blood.

He straddles my waist and bends low to settle his lips over mine once again. Lacing my fingers through his thick hair, I moan deeply into his mouth. His answering groan ramps up my need, and I jerk my hips up. I can't go far before my body meets the heat of his. The position is all wrong. I want him between my legs, not straddling them.

Before I can voice my want, his lips leave mine, sliding down the column of my throat and across my collar bone. Shivers wrack my body and a needy moan leaves my lips.

"Mmm… you taste so good," he groans throatily. "Like dirty words and late-night sex."

His tongue delves between the valley of my breasts my loose shirt offers him.

"Ahh… God, that's nice," I say with a shuttered breath.

When his teeth tug at my nipple through my shirt, I swear stars begin to dance behind my closed eyelids. I grip the strands of his hair, begging him without words for more. His mouth leaves one nipple, only to move to the next. I scissor my legs, trying and failing to relieve the ache building between them. His teeth clamp down on my nipple harder than before, and I cry out at the pleasurable stinging pain.

"Stay still." My eyes snap open at the order, and I look at him. "Right now, your pleasure is mine. I give it to you. You don't take it for yourself."

I want to protest, to demand he shut the hell up and get on with it, but his eyes have left mine and he's already making his way down my body. His breath tickles the sliver of skin exposed from the bottom of my shirt and the top of my skirt. His nose nudges up the flimsy material of my shirt, and when he spots my belly button piercing, a deep groan leaves his lips.

"Fuck if that ain't Goddamn hot," he rumbles thickly before dipping down and running his tongue over the silver metal bar.

The sight of my piercing may be hot to him, but his tongue is scorching on my flesh. Scorching and wildly seductive.

His tongue leaves my piercing and moves to the edge of my skirt, dipping inside and teasing me mercilessly. Slipping his fingers inside, he tugs the material down inch by inch, until he stops just before he reaches my pubic bone. My breath comes out in frantic pants, anticipation making me lightheaded and on the edge of exploding. And he hasn't even touched my pussy yet.

"JW, please, I'm going crazy here," I whimper.

"What do you want, Gypsy? Tell me."

I fist the blanket at my sides and lift my head to look at him. "Touch me," I urge, not even caring the words make me sound like I'm begging.

I am begging. *God, I need his touch so much.*

"Where?" he asks, pressing his chin in the apex of my thighs and pressing down.

A cry forces its way past my lips. "There! Oh, God, right there."

Instead of giving me what I need, his weight is suddenly off me. I snap my head up, ready to growl and throw a fit if I have to, when I find him moving further down my legs. When he's on his knees at my feet, my legs thankfully no longer beneath him, he puts his palms flat on my shins under my skirt and slowly starts pushing it upward. My legs part, the further his hands go. His eyes lock with mine, the blue in his so vivid, it sends sizzling tingles across my skin. When they reach my lower thighs, I belatedly remember we're out in the open where anyone can come across us. I dart my head around, suddenly feeling very much on display.

"No one's here but us," JW says, sensing my unease. "And I'll hear if someone approaches."

After a moment of hesitation, I decide to trust his judgement, and give a jerky nod. I'm not entirely sure I'd care if the whole town showed up, so long as JW doesn't stop what he's doing.

His hands continue upward. My breath gets stuck in my throat, and I bite down on my lip, growing impatient. He scoots forward on his knees between my legs, forcing them further apart. Air glides across my center just as my skirt clears my upper thighs.

"Fuckin' hell," he groans, his gaze zeroing in on the place he just revealed. "No panties. And so damn pretty and wet."

He licks his lips and doesn't waste another minute before his head is dipping down. My stomach muscles quiver when I feel his breath on me. He inhales heavily before the first swipe of his tongue damn near catapults me off the blanket. The feeling is almost too intense. A hoarse cry explodes from my mouth, and I grip his hair. The vibrations of his growl against my heated flesh only adds fuel to the fire building inside me. I've had men go down on me before, but I've never been so close to coming so soon after just one lap of the tongue.

"More," I shout, lifting my hips and trying to get closer. Another lave of his tongue has me jerking and digging my heels into the blanket.

Distantly, a buzzing noise reaches my ears, but I'm so far past the point of caring at the moment. The only thing that matters is JW and his magical tongue. Latching his teeth around my clit, he sucks the nub into his mouth hard, flicking his tongue back and forth, and grinds his scruffy chin against my entrance.

I hear the buzzing again, trying to force its way into my subconscious. The noise is easily forgotten when fingers probe my hole and JW pushes them in a couple of inches. I thrash my head back and forth, nearly overcome with the sensations he's eliciting inside me. Every nerve is sensitized. A third finger pushes inside with the other two. Penetration is always better when it's a dick entering you, but his hands are doing just fine at the moment. Especially with what he's doing with his mouth.

My hands still have a firm grip on his hair and my legs clamp around his head when the first electrifying jolt hits me. A rumbling growl pulses against my clit and he shoves his fingers in further. The fit is tighter because my inner walls clench and unclench around his fingers. He angles his fingers and the pleasure intensifies when he reaches my g-spot. Tossing my head back, I release a scream.

Once I slowly climb down from my high, I shudder out a breath. Opening my eyes, I glance down at JW. His smile is full of satisfaction, as it should be. He's damn good with his mouth and hand. He pulls his fingers free of me and lifts them to his mouth. One by one, he sucks away my juices, eyes flaring with desire. His chin glistens with my arousal. I've never been particularly fond of seeing the evidence of my desire on a man's face, but it works really well on JW. The sight makes me want to lick it away.

"So good. Just as sweet as I thought you would be."

Damn, that's hot too.

Hearing the buzzing sound again, I frown and look around for the source. JW scowls before snapping up the phone from the blanket.

Oh, it was a phone. I probably would have known that if it weren't for the haze still fogging my brain.

"This better be fucking good," he barks into the phone.

I flip down my skirt as he listens to whoever's on the line. His expression darkens, and his eyes move to me. A bad feeling forms in the pit of my stomach.

"When?" A pause. "Shit." Another pause. "She's with me. We'll be there in a few minutes."

As soon as the words leave his lips, I start throwing things back in the basket. Anxiety has my hands shaking and my stomach in knots. This must be about Diego.

He hangs up a moment later and I turn to him. "What happened?" I ask shakily.

His jaw flexes as he grinds his teeth together.

"Diego's made another appearance. He attacked a man named Derek."

I suck in a breath and release it on a painful exhale. "Is he…." I can't even get the words out.

"No," he grunts. "But he'll need stitches to close the gash on his forehead." His lips tighten. "Come on. We're going to Trouble's office so I can question Derek."

We finish cleaning up our picnic and head back to the truck. My chest feels heavy with guilt on our drive over to Trouble's.

How many more people will Diego hurt before this is all over?

chapter ten

JW

AS I STARE AT DEREK, seeing the bruise on the side of his face and watching Trouble put a bandage over the six stitches he needed, fury simmers just below the surface. Derek and his wife, Misty, have two small children. Children they adopted six months ago when it was discovered their father had been sexually abusing them for years and was sentenced to The Expiration Penalty. Those children suffered enough to last a life time, and for Diego to almost put them through losing another parent, makes me blind with rage.

Feeling Eden at my side, her own anger making her tremble, oddly eases some of the heat rushing through my blood stream. I'm tempted to reach over for her hand, wanting to feel her skin against mine, but I withhold the desire and take a step toward Derek when Trouble moves away from him.

I hold my phone up for Derek to look at the screen. "This the man you saw?"

He nods, then winces with the movement. "Yeah. I only got a glimpse of him before he hit me over the head, but that's definitely him."

I shove my phone in my pocket, my eyes briefly landing on Eden's heated, but worried, gaze.

"Tell me exactly what happened." I say, crossing my arms over my chest.

Derek grabs his wife's hand, who's sitting beside him on the bed, and kisses the back of it before placing it in his lap.

"I went out to the shed to get a bucket to wash the car. As soon as I stepped through the door, a noise came from behind me. I turned just as the bastard swung a shovel at my head. It was lights out after that." His gaze moves to Misty and shame and regret shines in his eyes. "I'm just glad he left and didn't go after Misty and the kids." His eyes close for a moment before they open again, and he looks back at me. "I almost sent Brittney after the bucket."

Misty leans forward and kisses her husband's cheek, tears swimming in her eyes. "Don't do that to yourself, Derek. Even if you did, you couldn't have known that man was in the shed," she reassures her husband quietly.

He nods but doesn't look soothed. What good parent would be? Even if he didn't know the danger that laid waiting, the threat of your child being hurt is crippling.

"I wonder what he was doing in the shed," Eden muses curiously.

"My guess?" Derek offers. "He was hiding out. The shed is big with plenty of room. We have a mattress in there we had planned to use for Jacob when he grew too big for the toddler bed. It was thrown on the floor with a couple of blankets. There's also a lot of food wrappers lying around."

That explains why no one has seen Diego around. He couldn't simply walk into The Hill for a meal, so he came prepared. Even so, it's hard to imagine the likes of Diego slumming it in a dirty shed. The man's rich on his own. Add in his family's money and you had one loaded person. I bet it really busted his chops to have to live less than stellar for the last week. It also shows his desperation. Whatever he thinks Eden has must be really important.

"Keep a close eye on your family," I advise him. "I'm sure I don't need to tell you to not let the kids outside to play by themselves." He nods. "I doubt he'll go back to the shed, but it's better to be safe than sorry."

"You don't have to worry about that. I'm not letting any of them out of my sight."

I nod and turn to Trouble, who's leaning against a counter. "You mind taking Eden back to your place for the night? I want to take a ride around town and check out a few places. Not sure how long I'll be."

"I can do that." His eyes glitter with hatred. "You call me or one of the others if you find anything."

I tip my chin in acknowledgement, then face Eden. "You okay going with Trouble?"

Reluctance mars her features, and I wonder if it's because she won't be going home with me or from the prospect of staying with people she hardly knows.

I step up to her and tuck a piece of loose hair behind her ear. My finger lingers on her smooth cheek.

"I'm sorry our evening got cut short," I murmur quietly so the others can't hear. "But I'll make it up to you."

"Don't worry. I want Diego caught before he hurts anyone else." Her expression holds despondency, like she somehow feels responsible for what happened to Derek. She couldn't be further from the truth. The bastard's just a whacked-out asshole who enjoys hurting people he thinks is below him.

Leaning down, I press a quick kiss against her lips. "We'll get him. He'll show his face eventually."

And when he does, he'll pay dearly for everything he's done. Diego Tomas may be walking around Malus undetected, but he's a dead man walking. It's only a matter of time.

SEVERAL HOURS LATER, I toss my keys in the bowl on the kitchen counter. My gun, which is strapped to my side, gets set on the counter by the bowl. I'm tired, hungry, and very fucking pissed. I knew my chances of finding Diego were slim, but it still angers me no less that every place I checked was a dead end. I hit all the places he could be hiding out in—garages, a few abandoned houses, and even Emo's Dad's hunting lodge. No fucking luck. There has to be some place I'm missing.

Stopping by the fridge, I snag a beer, twist off the cap, and down half of it, turning over every possible avenue Diego could use. Even his car hasn't been spotted. The fucker's good, but he's not invisible. Someone will eventually spot him.

Remembering the blueprint of the town I found years ago that my parents had, I finish off my beer, toss it in the trash, and go to my bedroom. There's not much of my parent's belongings that I kept when I moved back to town, but I did keep the map and a few banker boxes full of papers. Good old Mom and Dad were part of the town council, so they had access to a lot of the town's records. Apparently, they kept a lot of them at home.

My jaw tightens when I remember the town's law book regarding Hell Night that was among the papers. The shit my brothers and I have found out about the town over the years never ceases to amaze me. Experiencing the depravities of the town's monthly rituals was hard enough as kids, but it was so much more than we thought.

Members of the same family are not permitted to create a child together. It's totally acceptable to fuck, and even rape, a family member, so long as a child isn't conceived.

Females are not allowed to participate during their menstrual cycle. Get this shit. It's considered sacrilegious to rape a female during her period, but any other time of the month it's okay.

Females are required to submit to an ovulation test the day before The Gathering. If the female is found to be ovulating, she is given a dose of Levonorgestrel the next morning following The Gathering. In other words, the morning after pill is shoved down her throat to prevent an unwanted pregnancy.

It is the sole discretion of the child's parents on whether they give permission to other members of the community to show affection to their child. Affection my ass. *Or they may choose to keep that luxury to themselves.*

Once a child reaches one year of age, the parents are required to initiate the child in The Gatherings. Final initiation will commence once the child reaches five years of age.

That last one had a red haze forming over my eyes, and I had to work to control my temper. Final initiation means penetration. Those sick fucks would allow a baby to be touched in any other way, except penetration. That was reserved for when they reached five years old.

Once I'm in my closet, I crouch down and pull out the black tote tucked underneath a shelf. Flipping the lid off, I rifle through the papers and pull out a tube buried at the bottom. I lay the engineering paper on the floor of my closet, using the tote and lid to hold it open. The entirety of the town is laid out before me. I know every nook and cranny of Malus, but I hope, as I gaze over the blueprint, that I'm missing something. Diego has to be somewhere, and there's not a single person in town who would hide him. Meaning he's holed up somewhere where I haven't looked or in some hidden place no one visits.

Nothing. There's not one Goddamn place on the chart I haven't looked, just as I suspected. So, where in the fuck is he?

Angrily, I roll up the blueprint, stuff it in the tube, and shove it back in the tote. I come to a stand and kick the tote back underneath the shelf, then frown when something on the wall knocks loose. Bending back down, I look under the shelf, surprised to find the bottom half of the drywall pushed in, revealing a hidden alcove behind it.

What in the fuck? How in the hell have I not known this was there? Most of the walls were torn down and replaced when I had the house gutted. Thinking back, the closets and bathroom walls were the only ones that weren't ripped out.

Shoving a couple of boxes aside, I yank the drywall away and spot a wooden box. I take the box out to the bar in the kitchen, grab another beer, and take a seat. Adrenaline rushes through me as I open the box. There's a thick expandable folder filled with papers. Beneath the folder are at least twenty compact VHS tapes. I disregard the tapes for the moment—it's not like I can view what's on them anyway without a compact reader. I'll give them to Emo to transfer to something that's readable.

Pulling out the folder, I'm shocked to see they're birth and death certificates. They can't be state issued, because no one who was born or had died in Sweet Haven was ever reported. The town didn't want to run the risk of being caught with what they were doing to the children. Apparently, The Council still kept their own records of every birth and death. Some of these are dated as far back as the early nineteen hundreds.

I look through the stack and stop when I come across my parents'. My paternal grandparents are listed on my father's birth certificate. I remember my grandparents. They never participated in Hell Night. Not because they didn't want to, but because they were too old. They had my dad in their early-fifties. My earliest memory of them they were already in their late seventies. Even though they couldn't physically participate, they were still at every Hell Night. I remember seeing them sitting in comfortable leather chairs off to the side as they watched what all the kids went through.

Flipping to the next page, I find my brother's certificate, and mine behind his. I locate Judge's, Trouble's, and Emo's as well. I pull Trouble's out of the stack, knowing he'll want it. He recently discovered that the people who raised him weren't his biological parents. They were murdered in cold blood when he was a baby because they refused to allow their children to be a part of Hell Night. Come to find out, both his biological parents and Mae and Dale—who he also recently discovered were his grandparents—kept their pregnancies a secret until they couldn't hide it anymore. His birth parents are listed on his birth certificate.

Snapping up my phone, I shoot Emo a message.

Me – I found some old compact VHS tapes I need you to make viewable as soon as you can.

His reply comes immediately.

Emo – How many?

Looking at the stack, I take a guess.

Me – Twenty or more.

Emo – It'll take time, but I'll get it done.

Me – I'll drop them by your place tomorrow.

I pull up Judge's number.

"What," he growls, sounding irritated and out a breath.

"Bad time?" I ask with a bit of amusement lacing my voice.

"I'm fucking Jenny. What do you think?"

"I think you probably shouldn't answer the phone when you're bangin' your woman," I answer bluntly.

"With the shit that's going on and the lateness of the hour, I figured it was something important. Now, you gonna to tell me why you interrupted me?"

I glance at the clock on the stove and realize I've been looking over the birth certificates for over an hour.

"I found a box in a hidden alcove in my closet. You'll be interested in what I found."

"What," he snaps.

"Compact VHS tapes. Emo's going to convert them. I also found certificates for every person born and died in Sweet Haven."

"That's not possible. The town never reported births or deaths here."

I take a long pull from my beer before setting it back down. "These aren't state issued. The design is similar, but I think The Council did these themselves as a way to keep a record of everyone."

A feminine moan comes across the line. The horny bastard can't even stop fucking Jenny long enough to talk on the phone.

"Wouldn't surprise me," he grunts with a strained voice. "They had to have had a filing system of some sort to keep records of the citizens. Bring them by the office in the morning, I'd like to take a look at them."

"Got it." I drop the folder back in the box on top of the tapes. "Now, get off the fuckin' phone and go satisfy your girl."

The line goes dead, and I chuckle. An image of Eden and me earlier by the lake filters through my mind. My phone went off four times while I was exploring her delectable body. Not once was I tempted to check it before I was done. I sure as hell wouldn't have answered had I been in Judge's shoes, and I was fucking Eden. There's not a damn thing on earth that'll pull me away from her tight heat once I have her beneath me.

Tipping my beer to my lips, I chug the rest before dumping the bottle in the trash. I make a quick sandwich, inhale it, then go for the shower, where I'll spend another night beneath the spray, rubbing one out to images of Eden.

THE NEXT DAY, AFTER DROPPING the birth certificates off with Judge at his office, I pull to a stop in front of Emo's house. He's the only one of us four who lives on the outskirts of town versus closer to the middle. The location fits Emo. If he's not in the company of one of my brother's or me, he'd rather be alone. His house is set off the road with no other houses around it.

Grabbing the box with the tapes, I get out of my truck. The door is already open when I walk up the steps. I find Emo in his office sitting behind his desk. There are three monitors in front of him with another two on a second desk beside him. I set the box down on the floor beside his chair.

"Beer?" I ask, making my way to the kitchen.

"Yes."

Grabbing Emo a beer and a water for myself, I carry both back to the office and sit in a chair in a corner.

"How long will it take you to put them on a thumb drive?" I twist the cap off my water and take a swallow.

Emo grabs one of the tapes and slides it inside the VHS adapter. "Depends on how much footage is on the tapes. I basically have to play every one and record it on my computer before transferring them to a thumb drive." He walks over to a closet and pulls out an old VHS player from the top shelf. Setting it on the desk, he connects a couple of wires to the back of the player before connecting them to the back of his CPU. "If the recorder used the SP mode then the tapes will hold thirty minutes max if they used the full tape. If they used the SLP or EP mode, they could be up to two to three hours in length. That's not including the transfer time."

"Shit," I mutter. That could take anywhere from ten to sixty hours or more.

Emo retakes his seat and puts the adapter in the VHS player. His dark eyes move to me. "We can view one right now so you at least have an idea of what you've got here."

Nodding, I get up and move behind his chair.

"Where did you find these?" he asks, his fingers flying over his keyboard. A window pops up on the screen.

"Behind the drywall in my closet. They have to be my parents."

Saying the words has a lead ball forming in my stomach. There's no fucking telling what's on these tapes, but I have an idea. I just hope I'm wrong. Seeing the muscle jump in Emo's cheek alerts me that his thoughts aren't far off from mine.

Without another word, he presses the spacebar on his computer and the video starts playing. At first, it's just a black screen. The sound comes first. Moans, grunts, and the soft wails of children. Seconds later, it looks like someone removes a cover from the lens, and what comes across the screen has bile churning in my stomach at the same time violent anger fills my blood stream. My knuckles protest as I ball my hands into fists so tight it's a damn near miracle I don't crush the bones.

Children of all ages are lying on various different surfaces as men and women surround them. Putting their dirty hands on them and creating a hell so dark there's no hope of escaping. Some children just lie there, tears soaking their cheeks and their expressions appearing dead. Some are crying and begging to be let go. Some are putting up a fight. A fight they have no chance of winning. Even if they were to get free of their tormentor, the other adults in the room would stop them from leaving.

A phantom feeling of my brother's hairy chest pressed to my back as he did the same thing these evil people are doing rushes through me. The pain of being raped repeatedly while my parents sat and watched and even had their pick of children to abuse.

My hand reaches for the back of Emo's chair, the disturbing video making me lightheaded. I briefly realize I recognize none of the children, which means this video must have been before my brothers and I were born. However, I do know some of the adults. Especially the ones lying on a bed with a little boy between them. The picture is grainy, but they're close enough to the camera for me to know they're my parents.

"Turn that fuckin' shit off," I snarl at Emo.

The video screen disappears, but I still hear the cries and see the images in my head. I turn away and hit the closest thing my eyes land on. A bookshelf. The books fall to the floor at my feet and the shelf beneath them is now in two pieces. The skin on my knuckles is torn, but I ignore the bloody mess as I roughly run my hands over the back of my head, trying and failing to calm my temper. Thoughts of my past always tempts me to fly into a rage, but seeing the evidence makes me blind with it.

It takes me a few minutes and several deep breaths before I manage to gain control. It's no surprise when I turn and find the same intense anger reddening Emo's face. He's facing the computer monitor, one hand still on the mouse with the other balled into a fist beside the keyboard. Smears of blood under his palm coats the surface of the desk, the key he's holding the weapon digging into his skin.

I thought the adults in Sweet Haven were sick before, but to know they actually recorded Hell Night, no doubt for the purpose to watch again later, makes me wish each and every person who willingly participated in the once a month ritual stood in front of me so I could shoot them point blank between the eyes. The action isn't nearly enough punishment for them, but it would do knowing they were headed straight to Hell to become the devil's bitch.

I put a hand on Emo's stiff shoulder. He tenses at the touch, but eventually settles. I unlock my jaw and force the words out between clenched teeth and a raw throat. "You gonna be able to handle recording these?"

No one in their right mind would enjoy what I'm asking of Emo. He's struggling just as much as I am, probably even more. My childhood, along with Judge and Trouble's, was horrific. Emo's was worse because he lived his hell day to day, whereas the rest of us only lived it once a month. I hate that I'm putting him in this situation, but he's the best man for the job and will get it done the quickest.

He gives me a tight nod.

"Take as much time as you need. I'm sure the other tapes are pretty much the same. And for God's sake, walk away if it gets to be too much."

The only response I get is an eye twitch.

I leave the room and go to the bathroom, where I find some alcohol, a rag, some gauze, and medical tape. Emo's not in his office when I come back. Switching direction, I go out into the hallway where I know he'll be. I find him standing in front of a closed door down at the end of the dark hallway. His head is bent down, black hair in his face, and his chest pumps crazily. I step in front of him, blocking his view of the door. A low growl emits from his throat. Ignoring it, I grip his chin and make him look up at me.

"Not now, Emo. Bathroom," I order.

The hiss that leaves his lips is an animalistic warning. It would scare the shit out of anyone else and make them turn tail and run, but to me, the sound is normal. Emo is a loose cannon on his best days, but he won't hurt me. We've been through too much shit. We're brothers. Besides, Emo only maims people who are guilty of hurting others.

The eyes that meet mine look wild and unhinged, like he's on the verge of losing control. His body shakes and the veins in his

99

neck bulge unnaturally. I hold his stare, unfazed by the dangerous vibes oozing off of him.

"Lock it down and go to the bathroom, Emo." I keep my voice hard, unwavering. When he gets in these moods, strength and persistence is the only thing that snaps him out of it.

After a moment, he jerks his chin away, gives the door behind me a hated stare, and stalks off toward the bathroom at the other end of the hallway. I follow behind him and set the items I collected on the counter. Emo's leaning against the sink, his arms lying lifeless at his side. Blood drips from one closed fist.

"Open," I demand, holding out my hand. With an iron set jaw, Emo opens his palm and drops the key in my hand. It's coated in blood and has chunks of skin in the grooves.

I stuff the key in his front pocket and turn him around so his hand is over the sink. Turning the faucet on, I rinse the fresh gash then pour alcohol over the wound. This may seem overboard, me caring for him like this, but if I don't, then he'll let it fester and become infected. It's not that he can't take care of himself, he just doesn't care enough to want to.

"Grace asked about you the other day," I say quietly, wrapping his hand in gauze. Tearing off a piece of tape, I secure it in place.

He grunts, his eyes focused on the sink where there's pink water around the rim of the drain.

"She wants you to call her. Might be a good idea to have her around for a while until you're done with the tapes."

His uninjured hand rubs against the key in his pocket. "I'll give her a call," he replies gruffly.

I put the first aid stuff back in the cabinet by the sink and turn to Emo. "You know that girl has it bad for you, right?"

"And you know I can't give her what she needs. The only thing I can offer is a twisted fuck."

"Well, it's a twisted fuck she obviously enjoys, or she wouldn't be coming back for more. Just let her be here for you over the next few days to help calm the darkness." I walk to the doorway, but stop and turn around. "There's no need for you to sit and watch the videos. Just play them and leave the room. Call one of us if you need help."

I don't leave until I get his nod of acceptance. Once in the hallway, my eyes move to the end and the closed door. The next few days are going to be tough on Emo, and it fucking kills me what he's about to go through. I advised him to not watch the videos as they recorded on his computer, but I know he won't listen. He'll watch every single fucking second, even if it is torture for him. He'll use it as another form of punishment he wrongfully feels he should bear. Emo blames himself for the death of Rella. He blames himself for the pain she went through, no matter how many times we've told him otherwise.

Closing the front door behind me, I find Grace's number and hit send.

"Emo should be calling you to come over," I say when she answers. "Watch over him for a few days. He's not going to be in a good place for a while."

"What's wrong?" she asks, concern edged in her voice.

"Nothing that can be discussed. Just be prepared, and call Judge, Trouble, or me if things get out of control."

There's not a chance in hell Emo would hurt her beyond the pleasurable pain Grace likes. No, what worries me is the pain he'll want her to inflict on him.

"One of us will be by tomorrow to check on him while you're at work."

Her breath crackles across the line when she says softly, "Okay."

Disconnecting the call, I climb in my truck and head to the sheriff's office.

chapter eleven

EDEN

I LOOK DOWN AT THE PRETTY shimmering midnight-blue color on my nails and wiggle my fingers. My eyes slide past them to my feet, which are encased in sandals. My toenails are painted the same color. The color looks surprisingly good against my pale skin. A pale moon against the dark starry sky.

The thought of what JW will think of them crosses my mind, before I inwardly berate myself. It doesn't matter what he thinks. That's what I tell myself anyway.

I finger one of the red curls that blows over my shoulder from the slight breeze. My hair feels softer than usual. I need to find out what shampoo the lady in the salon uses.

"I love your hair," Jenny sighs beside me.

We're in front of Trouble's doctor's office waiting for Remi to come back out. She went inside with Elijah to check in with her husband before we head to The Hill for lunch. We actually managed to get out of the house today without an escort. Not that I'm complaining about having protection with us with Diego God knows where in the area, but it's nice to be with just women. The only reason JW, Judge, and Trouble allowed it is because we're in the center of town, surrounded by a shit ton of people. Not to mention, we were made to promise we would check in at least once every thirty minutes. Ordinarily, I would balk at the demand, but not in this situation. I'm no dummy. I know the danger Diego presents. I don't want to die or get hurt, and I for sure don't want one of my newfound friends to get hurt either.

"Eh." I pinch the end of the curl and let it bounce back. "It looks fine now, but it's a pain to take care of. It normally takes me a good thirty minutes to brush after a shower, and I have to keep it pulled up or braided to keep it from tangling too much."

"Is that why you normally have it wrapped in a scarf?" she asks, petting my hair like it's an animal.

"That and I normally can't go anywhere without people commenting on it or trying to touch it." I laugh when she drops her hand with a contrite grimace. "I don't care if you do it because I know you. It's the complete strangers who come up to touch it with hands I don't know where they've been."

I've had long hair since I was a little girl, only trimming the dead ends. It's thick and reaches just below the curve of my butt. As much as I may bicker about taking care of it, I do love my hair. I've thought about cutting it over the years, but I know I'll probably feel naked without the long locks. It's as much a part of me as my hands and feet. I can't imagine not having long hair.

Jenny's nose wrinkles. "Eww… that's just nasty," she says with a shudder.

"Agreed."

She looks past me and tilts her head to the side, a frown pulling her brows down. "I wonder who that is. I've never seen him before."

I whirl around, half scared to see Diego behind me. I release a breath when it's not him I find, but another man I've never seen walking our way. He's about a block away, but there's no mistaking his extremely good looks. Dark hair, cut short, tanned, black cargo pants, tight white V-neck shirt stretched across a massive chest, and black boots. As he gets closer, and his eyes light on both Jenny and me watching him, dimples pop out on both cheeks.

"Hello, ladies," he says smoothly, his voice a delicious deep timbre.

"Hi," Jenny replies a bit breathless.

My reaction is only marginally better when I barely get out a "Hello" without a stutter.

"I was wondering if you might be able to help me."

Jenny snaps out of her stupor first and steps forward, offering her hand with a huge grin plastered on her face. "I've no doubt I could help you with something. I'm Jenny."

I scarcely hold back my choked laugh as he takes her hand. "I'm Ki." He introduces, his beautiful browns dancing in amusement. Releasing her hand, he turns it to me. "And you are?"

I place my hand in his. Warm and rough, just how a man's hand should feel. "Eden," I supply.

His eyes run over my hair, down my body, and back up, once again meeting my eyes. The look isn't lewd, just appreciative, earning him brownie points.

His eyes flick to Jenny's before coming back to mine. "Pretty names for such gorgeous women."

I flush from the compliment then realize he's still holding my hand. One corner of his full lips tips up when I gently pull my hand away and take a step back.

"I'm looking for—"

"Who in the fuck are you?"

The guy turns around quickly at the growled words, and I see JW barreling across the street. He doesn't stop until he's on the sidewalk and in the guy's face. He looks pissed. No, he looks livid. The easy going look on the new guy's face disappears, something hard replacing it.

"The name's Ki. And who in the hell are you?" Ki says, not backing down from the ire practically seeping out of JW's pours.

"The sheriff of this town and your worst fucking nightmare if you don't tell me what you're doing in Malus."

I step forward, getting ready to try and diffuse the situation, when JW's eyes snap to mine.

"Stay back, Gypsy," he grunts, before locking his eyes back on Ki. "You gonna answer me?"

I bristle at his tone and narrow my eyes, getting pissed myself.

"If you'll step the hell back, I'll be happy to answer. I don't take too kindly to people getting in my face and acting all growly and shit when I haven't done anything."

"My fist is going to meet that pretty face of yours if you don't answer my fucking question in the next three seconds."

My eyes widen, because I'm pretty sure JW's not exaggerating. The look in his eyes suggests he's ready to kill the guy if he doesn't answer.

"JW, that's enough!" I bark.

"Kian?"

We all turn and spot Remi standing behind us with Elijah in her arms. As soon as she sees Ki, a big grin forms on her face and she squeals. She rushes to Jenny and gently deposits Elijah in her arms before sprinting to Ki.

"Oh, my God! I can't believe you're here!" she yells, launching herself against him. He chuckles and wraps his arms around her in a tight hug.

"It's good to see you, little sis," he murmurs against her hair.

Realizing the man isn't a danger, JW takes a step back, but he doesn't lose the scowl. If anything, it deepens as he crosses his arms over his chest.

Remi pulls back but keeps her hands on Ki's chest and stares up at him with eyes full of love. "You were supposed to tell me when you were coming," she accuses good-naturedly.

He tweaks the end of her nose with the tip of his finger, his dimples popping out once again. "I wanted to surprise you."

"Well, you certainly managed that," she responds with a laugh.

"Someone better tell me who in the hell the guy is who has his arms wrapped around my wife."

Remi spins around just as Trouble walks into our small group. His hands are casually shoved into his pockets, but from the hard set of his jaw, the relaxed look is deceiving. He looks about ready to throw his own punch.

Remi leaves the curve of, who I'm guessing is her brother's arms, and walks over to grab Trouble's hand from his pocket. She tugs him with her.

"Trouble," she begins, her smile widening, "This is my big brother, Kian. Kian, I want you to meet my husband, Trouble."

Some of the displeasure leaves Trouble's face when Kian holds out his hand for him to shake. Once he lets go, he puts a possessive arm around Remi's waist, even though the act is wasted because the man is her brother, not potential competition.

Out the corner of my eye, I notice JW moving to my side. I cast him a contentious look to let him know I didn't care for his attitude of before.

Remi introduces her brother to each of us. When they turn to JW and me, his arm locks tighter around my waist, and I get tugged into his side. I think about shoving him away, but if I'm honest with myself, having his solid frame against me feels entirely way too good to move.

The lucky bastard.

Kian holds out his hand to JW, and at first, I don't think he'll take it, but after a slight hesitation, he does. However, the hostile look stays on his face, and I can't help but wonder about the reason behind it.

Remi takes Elijah from Jenny and turns to her brother. "And this little man is Elijah."

The look of awe and instant love on Kian's face as he stares down at his nephew would melt anyone's heart. There's nothing more beautiful than watching a tough-looking grown man fall in love with a baby.

"He's perfect, Remi," he says softly.

I think all three of us women blink several times to keep back the moisture in our eyes.

Judge walks up just then, and he's introduced to Kian as well. He interlocks his fingers with Jenny's, but I don't get the sense it's out of possessiveness, but more of a natural reaction of being close to her.

"I wanna talk to you," JW murmurs, interrupting my perusal of his family and friends.

Before I can answer, he's tugging me away from the group and around the corner of Trouble's office building. I open my mouth to ask what in the world he's doing, but I'm stopped short when I'm pressed to the brick building and his lips are devouring mine.

All thought escapes me as he attacks my mouth, demanding entry with the rough swipe of his tongue. I open immediately, because I'm weak and have no chance, let alone no desire, to deny him. JW can be very persuasive, especially with his talented tongue.

His arms band around my waist, tugging my chest against his, at the same time my hands lace through his hair, yanking his head closer to me. The man is impossibly addicting. I love his taste, and I love the way he makes me feel. Like I'm the only person in the world. Like I'm special.

His groan is deep and growly when he pulls away and begins trailing his lips over my chin and down my neck. I tilt my head to the side to give him easier access to the tender spot he's laving.

"You taste so fuckin' good," he whispers. "I could live forever just from the sweet taste of you."

I breathe out a sigh of pleasure. "JW."

His hand smoothly moves across my butt to the back of my thigh, where he pulls my skirt up to my knee, lifts my leg, and wraps it around his hip. Feeling the hard bulge behind the zipper of his jeans feels so good I shamelessly grind against it. All reason has fled my mind as soon as his lips touched mine again. There's nothing and no one who can make me feel as good as JW.

"We gotta stop," I whimper, both hoping he heeds my words and ignores them.

"In a minute," he mutters, gently biting down on my collar bone.

I bite my lip to keep back the pleasurable cry wanting to slip free. His face moves to my cleavage, where he buries it between my boobs. I toss my head back against the brick wall and nearly come undone when his hips press harder against my center. I'd give almost anything to have him pull up my skirt, slip his cock free, and take us both to heaven as he plunges his hardness inside me.

He lifts his head from my boobs and lays a biting kiss against my lips. "Wanna know something?"

I open my eyes and regard his through a lust-filled gaze. "What?" I gasp.

"I almost killed Remi's brother."

The seriousness of his tone says he's not joking.

"Why?" I ask through a dry throat.

"Because I had no clue who he was. He could have been one of Diego's men and could have hurt you."

This is something that crossed my mind as well. It could have been so easy for Kian to hurt me. Yes, he probably would've been caught with so many people around, but the damage would've already been done. Diego is just the kind of guy who would sacrifice one of his men to do his bidding.

"That wasn't the only reason though." He nips my lips once and pulls back, giving me his eyes. Ones that are grim and shining with intent. "He had his hand on you."

"It was just a simple handshake," I scoff.

"He had his hand on you and looked like he wanted to do a fuck of a lot more than shake your hand. No man touches what's mine or looks at you the way he did."

"I'm not yours," I retort irritably.

"Like fuck, you aren't. Every single Goddamn inch of you is mine. Deny it all you want, Gypsy. It won't change that fact."

I don't know if I should be offended or delighted at his barbaric words. Either way, I'd be lying if I said my panties didn't just get a little more wet with his caveman claiming.

What's it going to be next, Eden? my pesky inner voice chides. *Are you going to drop your drawers and beg him to take you if he starts drag-*

ging you around by your hair, beating his chest while he grunts "mine" to all the other cavemen in the area?

I ignore the crabby bitch in my head and lift my chin stubbornly. "And what about you? Are you mine?"

I want to slap away the smug look that comes across his face, but what he says next pushes the need away.

"For as long as you're in Malus, I'm all yours, baby."

He emphasizes this by tugging my leg up higher and pressing himself against me harder. I bite back a moan when he hits that perfect spot.

"JW!" someone yells, and I jerk my head around to look at the front of the building.

I just manage to pull my leg from his grasp and drop my foot to the ground when Judge walks around the corner. With cheeks blazing red, I turn my head away and brush down my skirt.

"What?" JW barks in irritation.

"Rita just called. She's been trying to get in touch with you." Amusement laces Judge's voice.

"Shit. I left my phone in my truck."

"Oscar and Frank are at it again."

He steps back from me and roughly rakes his hand through his hair. "Those old bastards are going to be the death of me. Seventy-year-old twins, and you'd think by now they'd learn to get along."

Without another word, Judge spins and walks off, leaving me alone with JW. A frustrated growl leaves his lips when he looks at me. "This isn't over."

"It is if it's up against a brick building," I reply, smoothing my hand down my skirt.

He steps into my space again, leaning one hand against the wall by my head and gently gripping my chin with the other, tipping my head back. "The next time I have your pussy pressed against me, we'll both be naked and in my bed."

I'm finding I'm more and more okay with the thought of being in JW's bed. In fact, I'm very much looking forward to it. Of course, I don't tell him this. The man's head seems to be big enough.

I smile sweetly at him. "We'll see." I pat his chest and roll to my toes to peck his lips. I slide from between him and the wall.

"Gypsy!" he calls when I'm just about to turn the corner. I look at him over my shoulder. "That wasn't just a simple statement. It was a promise."

I can't stop the small smile that curves my lips.

"Oh, and—" he begins, letting his hand fall from the wall and turning to me. "I love the hair and nails. I'll love it even more with your hair tickling my chest and seeing those blue tips wrapped around my cock."

chapter twelve

JW

ME – WHERE IN THE HELL ARE YOU?
 Emo – Home. Still not done with the tapes.
 Me – Get your ass to Trouble and Remi's. You've been at it for days. You need a break.

I pocket my phone and turn around to face the crowd in the backyard. Remi invited everyone to welcome her brother to Malus. Emo will show. He'll show, because he knows if he doesn't, one of my brothers or I will drag him here by his inky black hair.

When I stopped by to check on him yesterday, my worry over what he's been tasked to do grew. He looked haggard and half unhinged. Thankfully, Grace has been there as often as she can, and she's been giving us updates on his behavior.

Judge and Trouble know what's on the tapes and have been checking on him as well. Since I gave him the tapes three days ago, one of us has been by his house at least once a day. When I first told Trouble about them and what I asked of Emo, he about tore my head off. He and Emo have always had a special bond because of Rella. Judge and I loved Rella like a sister, but Emo was attached to her because of the pain they often shared together. Rella, the sweet and beautiful girl she was, never held what Emo had to do to her against him. She knew he was forced and had no other choice.

Soft laughter pulls me from my thoughts, and I look over to where Eden is standing with Remi, Trouble, Kian, and the Tanners. She has on a long white skirt with little powder blue flowers and a lavender tank top. I can't see her feet because the skirt covers them, but I know she's wearing a pair of white sandals. Her gorgeous red hair is pleated and tossed over her shoulder.

I scowl when I notice Kian standing too close to Eden.

The day I saw him with Eden and Jenny on the sidewalk outside of Trouble's office, my vision clouded with red, and I barreled across the road, thinking he was one of Diego's men. Once I found out who he was, I wanted to break every one of his fingers, slowly, and shove them up his ass. Jealously is an emotion I've never felt before, but I damn sure did then. Kian was touching something that was mine, and I'm a greedy bastard who doesn't share well with others. Especially when it comes to Eden.

Eden laughs at something he says and before I know it, I'm stalking down the stairs and across the yard. I place myself between her and the bastard, firmly securing her against my side with an arm around her waist. When I look down at her, she rolls her eyes. Leaning down, I plant a kiss against her lips, leaving Kian with no doubt who Eden belongs to.

"Behave," she whispers against my lips.

"As long as he stops fucking you with his eyes. I'm about ready to gouge them out with a dull knife."

"You're being ridiculous." Her voice is too low for anyone but me to hear.

I nip her bottom lip. "No, just letting him know you're off limits."

"You don't know me well enough to make that claim," she quips.

"I know all I need to to know you won't deny me when the time comes. Face it, Gypsy, you want me just as much."

She scoffs and rolls her eyes, but I see the secret thrill she's trying her best to hide. The woman likes me claiming her, even if she doesn't want to admit it.

"So, Kian," Amelia Tanner says, breaking into my hushed conversation with Eden, "How long do you plan to stay in Malus?"

"Only for a few days. I've got drills coming up soon, so I need to get back to the base for those."

My eyes slide to Trouble's. The sooner Kian is gone, the better. We don't welcome outsiders to Malus for a reason. There are secrets here that, if came to light, could tear the town and its people apart. It's already dangerous enough having Eden here. The chances of someone finding out our secrets are slim, but taking that risk is something my brothers and I don't like to do.

"Air Force, right?" Danny, Amelia's husband, asks. Kian nods. "My older brother's in the Air Force. He retires in five years. My sister's been in twelve years and plans to retire as well. Our father served thirty years."

"Did you enlist?"

Danny looks down at his wife, and though his eyes shine with love for the woman in his arms, there's a hint of hardness behind it. He looks back at Kian.

"No. It was always a possibility for me and my parents wanted me too, but I found something too important that I couldn't leave behind."

Amelia and Danny were high school sweethearts. On the night of their graduation, a week before he was set to ship out to basic training, Amelia, who grew up in shitty foster homes and lived in a shady part of town, was gang raped by four guys. They had her for three hours before the neighbors finally called the cops because they couldn't take her screams anymore. The guys who had her were known thugs and regular terrorizers of the neighborhood. Two of the four guys got away and were never found. Of course, they *would* have been found if Emo and I hadn't found them first and taken care of them. Their bones are in a bag at the bottom of the Mississippi River.

Just then, Sophia, Amelia and Danny's six-year old girl, comes barreling into her mom's leg. "Mama, I'm hungry," she complains, yanking on the bottom of her shirt.

I glance over to Judge, who's manning the grill, and see he's plating some of the burgers.

"Looks like you've got perfect timing, kid," I tell Sophia with a smile. "I bet you could talk Judge into giving you one he just pulled from the grill."

Her eyes light up and she starts tugging her mom's hand, struggling to pull her toward the food. "Come on, Mama. I wanna booger."

We chuckle at her butchered word use as Amelia is led away by her impatient daughter.

"Oh, shoot!" Remi turns to Trouble, Elijah in her arms as she feeds him a bottle. "I left the potato salad in the fridge. Would you mind grabbing it for me?"

Before he can answer, Eden's pulling away from me. I reluctantly let my arm fall away. "I'll grab it. I have to run inside for a minute anyway."

"Thanks." Remi smiles gratefully at her.

I watch her walk away, my dick twitching in my jeans at the way the material of her skirt swishes against the curve of her ass. An ass I want to squeeze and take bites out of.

Fuck! The woman is a temptation who I'm learning really quickly is bordering on obsession. Any time she's near, my eyes are glued to her. I smell her intoxicating scent, and I want to lick every delectable inch of her body.

When I look back to the others standing around, I've noticed they've dispersed. All except Kian, who has his eyes lasered on Eden as well. A snarl plays on the edge of my lips as I step in his line of sight. This guy is fucking with the wrong guy.

His brows lift in mocking amusement.

"She's yours, I take it?"

"Yes," I grind out. "If you want to make it back to Colorado in one piece, I'd advise you to keep your fucking eyes off her."

Lifting his hands, he lets out a chuckle. "Got it. Loud and clear. Can't blame a man for testing the waters."

He won't be testing the waters but drowning in them if he doesn't back the hell off.

Over his shoulder, I see Emo and Grace walking across the yard. I silently curse when I notice the condition he's in. His face is pale with dark circles under his eyes. He also looks like he's lost weight. The bandages wrapped around both hands and his upper forearms has a weight settling on my chest. There's no telling how many more wounds he has hidden underneath his clothes. Had Grace not been with him, I've no doubt he would have left the gashes without treating them.

It was a mistake asking him to transfer those tapes. I should have known it would be too much for him. The injuries on his arms are new, because they weren't there yesterday afternoon when I went to check on him.

I look over to the grill and find Judge and Trouble with the same pained expression I know my face holds. Feeling my eyes on them, they glance my way. Trouble's lips tighten, and I give him a chin lift.

I walk over to Emo, a tight smile in place as I look to Grace. Her expression is troubled as well. She may be into a bit of pain play, but she still hates hurting Emo.

"Give us a minute, Grace," I tell the woman at Emo's side.

She nods jerkily before walking off. Judge and Trouble walk up beside me.

"I'm coming by when I leave here to get the tapes. You've had enough. I'll find another way to transfer them."

Emo's eyes slide to mine. "No," he grunts harshly.

"Goddamn it, Emo," Trouble says, stepping toward him. "Look at you. You're fuckin' butchering yourself."

Blazing eyes flip to Trouble. "Doesn't matter. Other than the four of us, no one is watching those tapes." He bares his teeth. "Not one Goddamn minute, you hear me?"

"What tapes are you on?"

"Just leave it, Judge."

"Emo, what tapes are you on?" Trouble repeats the question thickly.

His eyes turn darker, the pupils nonexistent. "I said leave it." The snarled words curl his lips.

Trouble steps closer until he's in Emo's face. "Tell me what fuckin' tapes you're on."

Emo's jaw clenches and fire burns in his eyes now. A rage so potent, it's a wonder he doesn't incinerate everything within a one-mile radius.

"Ours," he growls, the words spitting from his lips. He looks at Judge and me before bringing desolate eyes back to Trouble. "All of ours." Pain twists his face gruesomely. "Mine and Rella's," he finishes the last words on a tortured whisper.

Trouble's head drops, and he takes a step back, his hand reaching back to grip his neck. My stomach bottoms out. We knew there was a good possibility that Emo would come across tapes that involved us. Watching children being tortured by people who are supposed to be family and friends is hard enough, but to see our younger selves, how weak we were, the utter helplessness, forcing those painful memories to the forefront of our minds, is something I'm not sure I can handle. For Emo to watch himself with Rella.... I'm surprised he's not in worse condition.

"No more," Trouble demands, his tone resolute. "You're fucking done with those tapes. We know what's on them. We don't need them all transferred."

"He's right," I insert. "There's no need for you to continue. We know what happened during Hell Night. There's no need to have those memories shoved in your face."

Emo's fists clench and unclench at his sides, blood appearing on the bandages. Had they not been covered with gauze, I imagine the key would be in his palm, cutting into his skin.

"No. I'll tell you when I finish. You can have them then."

"Jesus Christ, Emo," Trouble barks through gritted teeth, his control slipping. "Why? Why do you need to finish them?"

"Because it's the only way to see her," Emo discloses, further wedging the knife slicing through each of us. For the first time in a long time, Emo drops his mask, and what he exposes is a pain so deep, so all-consuming and devastating, it nearly cracks my soul. "I need to do this," he whispers raggedly. "Please, just let me have this. It's the least that I owe her."

"Emo." Trouble shakes his head "You've got to stop this. It wasn't your—"

"Let him be, Trouble," Judge grunts decisively. He places his hand on Trouble's shoulder, but his eyes are fixed on Emo. "Emo's strong. He'll stop when he needs to."

Trouble wants to argue, it's in the hard edge of his expression— hell, I want to argue as well—but Emo's a grown man and can make his own choices.

Instead of voicing his assertion, he steps forward, his hand going to the back of Emo's neck where he yanks him forward until their foreheads are almost touching.

"I'll leave it for now," he says in a low, rough tone. "But swear to me right now that you'll pull back before it destroys you. You may hold yourself accountable for what happened to Rella, but we don't. You're our brother and it fucking kills us knowing you're suffering for something you had no control over." He squeezes his neck. "Swear to me, Emo."

After a moment, Emo gives him a clipped nod. Before letting him go, Trouble pulls him into a tight hug. A few hushed words are murmured between the two that Judge and I can't hear before they pull apart.

"Where's Mae?" Emo asks, looking around the yard

"At The Hill. Doris came down with a migraine, so she's covering for her."

I glance around, looking for Eden, then frown when my search comes up empty. She should have been back with the potato salad by now. Worry slams in my chest.

"I'll be back. I'm going to check on Eden."

I stalk across the yard, up the porch steps, and through the back door. Walking down the hallway, I hear her voice before I find her in the bathroom.

"I'm okay, I swear." She pauses. "I trust him, Mills. I know he won't let anything happen to me."

Pride swells in my chest at her admission. In such a short time, Eden's come to mean more to me than an innocent person to protect. The connection I feel toward her grows with each day that passes. As crazy as it sounds, I'd give my life to ensure Diego doesn't get his hands on her again.

"How are Clayton and Hannah?"

Who are Clayton and Hannah?

Her shoulders droop at whatever answer she gets. "Please tell them I miss them too. Maybe the next time they stop by the shelter you can call me so I can talk to them."

I rest my shoulder against the door frame as she finishes her call. She's facing the sink, and I've got a side view of her. She hasn't noticed my presence yet and the angle of where I am, I'm not in view of the mirror.

"I need to go. I'll call you in a few days."

Warily, she places the phone on the counter and closes her eyes, her body sagging. Quietly, I walk up behind her. Her eyes spring open and she jumps when I slide my arms around her waist.

"Sweet Jesus, you scared me," she mumbles while lining her arms along mine, her eyes meeting mine in the mirror.

"Everything okay?" I lay my lips against the tender spot on the back of her neck.

"Yeah," she sighs.

"Who're Clayton and Hannah?"

She angles her head slightly to the side. "A couple of kids who come to the homeless shelter I volunteer at."

Why doesn't it surprise me that she offers her precious time at a homeless shelter?

"That's very charitable of you," I murmur and work my lips over the new spot she opened for me.

"Not charitable. I just enjoy giving something of myself to the community. Who needs it more than the people who have nothing?"

I kiss her shoulder and let my fingers slip underneath the edge of her shirt. "There should be more people like you."

She lets out a low moan, her hands gripping the counter in front of her. Her eyelids droop sexily as she continues to watch me in the mirror. "What are you doing?" Her voice is a breathless whisper. My cock reacts to the needy sound.

"Playing." I kick the door closed before slowly moving my hands up her toned stomach until they graze the bottom of her tits.

"I thought you said the next time I was pressed against you, I'd be in your bed?"

I tip my lips up as I continue to explore the soft skin on her shoulder. "Actually, I said the next time I had your pussy pressed against me, I'd have you in my bed," I correct her while pushing my cock against her ass. I'm so Goddamn hard, I could split wood.

"Oh." She moans and thrusts back into me.

Taking one hand from her shirt, I reach across her chest, grab the end of her braid, and bring it around her throat. Her eyes meet mine in the mirror again and she forces out a breath when the thick braid settles firmly against her neck. I let the length hang down the middle of her back.

"You're coming home with me tonight," I inform her.

"A-are you sure that's a good idea?"

"It's the best idea I've ever had."

Gripping her skirt at her thighs with both hands, I start lifting it. I may not be able to fuck Eden here in Trouble and Remi's spare bathroom, but I damn sure want to get a taste of what's to come.

As soon as the material clears her upper thighs, I dive my fingers between her legs.

Lord have mercy.

She's bare. No fuzz, no anything. She wasn't bare the other day on the dock.

"Motherfuckin' hell, baby," I groan at the first slide of my fingers against her smooth flesh. She's bare, not wearing panties, *and* she's soaked. So wet that she's dripping down her thighs. My mouth waters with the thought of licking up every single drop.

"Oh God." She grips my wrist, and at first, I think she's going to push me away. Thank Christ, she doesn't, and instead presses my hand closer. "That feels incredibly good."

Her eyes fall closed, so I grab the end of her braid and tug the noose I made around her neck tighter.

"Keep your eyes open," I order and her eyes snap open. "I want you to watch me as I fuck you with my fingers."

Her throat bobs as she swallows against the restraint of her hair. It's not tight enough to cut off her air supply, but it's enough for her to know it's there.

With my eyes pinned on hers, I rub my fingers between her pussy lips from her hole up to her clit. I pinch it between my fingers and she lets out a small cry, her eyes flaring wide. Releasing her little nub, I skate my fingers back down to her cunt and push a finger inside.

"So tight," I whisper. "I can't wait to have this wrapped around my dick."

"Yes," she hisses and clamps her walls around my finger.

I slip another in beside the first, and damned if I don't almost come in my jeans. Warm and soft and slippery. The best thing I've felt in a long time.

Inserting a third finger, I use the heel of my palm and press it against her clit. Her legs wobble, becoming weak, and I feel the weight of her body sagging. I hold her up by my fingers in her pussy and pushing my hips against her ass.

"Ahh... shit. It's too much," she whimpers. In the mirror, her eyes drift down to where she's impaled on my fingers.

"Not enough," I growl in return. I pull my fingers free then shove them back in, making sure my palm rubs against her clit. "I want you to come on my fingers. Come on, you can take it."

She shakes her head emphatically.

"Yes," I demand and pump my fingers faster. "Give me what I want, Gypsy."

She tosses her head back until it thumps back against my shoulder. I don't make her open her eyes when they fall shut. I do keep mine on her face though. She's mesmerizingly stunning in the throes of passion. It's a picture I know I'll keep with me forever.

Curling my fingers inward, I hit the spongy flesh inside. Her inner walls clamp down on me impossibly tight and she lets out a loud cry with her release. I cover her mouth with my other hand to muffle the sound. The last thing we need is for someone to hear her cries and come to investigate. Judge has already caught us twice. I'm not sure I'd be able to hold back from beating his ass a third time.

My cock hurts in its tight confinement. It takes iron will to force back the need to pull my cock free and plunge into her warm sheath. Later. Later, I'll know what it feels like to be surrounded by her.

Once her walls stop constricting, I slowly pull them free of her body. Her eyes open and meet mine. Bringing my fingers to my lips, I lick away her essence. The taste of her is damn near my undoing.

"My new favorite taste," I tell her huskily once I've sucked away all her juices.

Her cheeks, already flushed from her orgasm, pinken even more. "I can't believe we just did that."

"Why?" I turn her around to face me and unwind her hair around her neck. Her dress falls back down her legs.

"Because we're supposed to be outside at the barbeque. Had someone come in and heard…." She trails off.

"They would have turned around and went back out." I say, trying to appease her worry.

"Yeah, but they still would have known what we were doing. It's rude to make out in someone's house like we just did."

I chuckle and cup her cheek, rubbing my thumb across her bottom lip. Her mouth opens slightly, tempting me to shove my finger inside and demand she suck.

"What we did was more than make out, wouldn't you say? Besides, I can guarantee Trouble wouldn't have cared."

She frowns. "But I would have cared."

Smiling indulgently, I pull back from her. "Well, then, let's go back outside before they send a search party."

"Okay." She hesitates for a moment, her lip going between her teeth. "Do I look okay? I mean, do I look like—"

"You just rode my fingers and came all over my hand?"

She scowls and slaps my chest. "JW, I'm being serious. I can't go out there looking like we were just fooling around. These people are your friends, not mine. You can get away with it."

I laugh, but soon lose my mirth when I notice genuine worry in her eyes. I put both my hands on her cheeks and make her look at me. "You look absolutely gorgeous." I press a tender kiss to her lips. "And you may not have been here long, but in the short time you have been, many of those people out there consider you a friend. You don't have anything to worry about, Gypsy."

Her eyes move back and forth between mine, looking for the truth in my words. After a moment, she nods.

Kissing the tip of her nose, I unglue my hips from hers. "Come on. I've worked up a bit of an appetite. The sooner we eat, the sooner I can get you home."

She laughs and lets me tug her out of the bathroom. We stop by the kitchen and grab the potato salad from the fridge. As we walk across the yard to the two picnic tables where almost everyone is sitting, I spot Judge off to the side, well away from listening distance, his phone to his ear. He's facing the crowd, so I see the hard set to his jaw. When he spots me, he juts his chin up.

I stop Eden before we get to the table. "Save me a seat. I need to go talk to Judge for a minute."

"Sure."

Judge is just hanging up as I make it to him.

"That was Dax. He's got a situation in San Antonio. A father was found not guilty of raping and killing his fifteen-year-old son because the evidence they had was shitty. A video just came across his desk of the father committing both crimes. Double jeopardy law protects him. I figured you'd want in since you had to give up Richard."

I seek out Eden and find her sitting at one of the picnic tables beside Jenny. She throws her head back and laughs at something Gabby, one of the kids, says. All of the children are at a smaller picnic table in between the two big ones. She leans back so she can talk to the little girl, and whatever she says has Gabby giggling and clapping her hands.

I turn back to Judge. "I want in." I look straight into my brother's eyes and say with force, "She stays with you and Jenny. You watch her. You guard her with your life." He gives me a grim nod. "I mean it, Judge."

The only reason I'm agreeing to go is because it'll take me less than twenty-four hours to do what needs to be done, and I trust my brothers to keep Eden safe. It still pisses me off though that another night I had planned to spend with her is foiled.

"I hear you, brother."

I'm mildly surprised he doesn't give me shit on my obvious attachment to Eden, but push the thought away.

"Dax says it's time sensitive. He feels the guy will haul ass, even though he can't be charged twice."

"I'll leave tonight and be back by tomorrow afternoon. I'm going to make a stop to see Emiliano."

Judge's eyes narrow. "You sure that's a good idea?"

"Emiliano isn't stupid like his son. He knows how to choose his battles. I won't be coming in hot, but I will damn sure let him know his son is walking on dangerous grounds. We may have never dealt with him directly, but he knows our names just as well as we know his. He knows he's not the only one with people lining his pockets."

Judge grunts and stuffs his hands into his pants pockets. "Just be careful. Emiliano may not be stupid, but he can be reckless."

I tip my chin down. "I'm taking Emo with me. It's a good excuse to get him away from the tapes for a few hours."

"Good idea."

After giving me the details, we head to where the others are. As much as I try to rein in the anxious feeling of what tonight will bring, I know I do a shit job from the questioning looks Eden keeps giving me. I don't necessarily enjoy doing what Emo and I are setting out to do, but I can't help but feel a thrill knowing we'll rid the world of yet another piece of shit.

I grip Eden's hand underneath the table. If I'm lucky, I'll kill two birds with one stone and ensure Eden's safety. However, even if Emiliano does manage to get his son to back off, Diego's still very much living on borrowed time.

chapter thirteen

JW

I STEP INSIDE THE DIMLY lit dining room and lean against the wall, watching the man with his back to me, going through papers scattered on the table. I noticed the suitcases and duffel bag in the living room when I walked through the front door a few minutes ago, proving Dax's theory on the man taking off. Dax is a detective with the SAPD and one of the contacts my brothers and I use sometimes. Usually one to play by the book, Dax recognizes the fucked-up mess our judicial system is at times. When that happens, he calls us to take care of the problem.

The man, Alec Hallson, is oblivious of my presence, to the danger that awaits mere feet behind him. That is his second mistake. His first was leaving his door unlocked.

Stupid bastard. When you commit a crime such as the one he committed, you stay vigilant, no matter what. Even if you're found not guilty by a jury. You never know if an enraged family member of the victim will come seeking revenge. Or maybe just a couple of men whose sole purpose in life is to eradicate the world of sick people like him.

He mutters a low curse and bends to scoop up the papers he knocked to the floor.

"Going somewhere, Mr. Hallson?" I ask casually, making my presence known.

He spins in place, scattering more papers on the floor. His eyes widen as he takes in my relaxed stance against the wall.

"Who in the hell are you and what are you doing in my house?" Despite the vehemence in his voice, he can't hide the slight quiver.

"The name's JW," I offer. "And I'll give you one guess as to why I'm here."

His Adam's apple bobs as he swallows thickly. His eyes dart to the side toward the doorway that leads to the kitchen. "You want money? Are you here to rob me? Give me five minutes and I'll be gone, so you can take whatever you want. Hell, you can take the whole house."

I stand to my full height and flash him a grin. "Wrong guess, but nice try."

Beads of sweat break out on his forehead, the moisture gleaming in the overhead light. He sidesteps to the edge of the table, slowly moving toward the open doorway.

"Then I don't know what you want."

"No?" I walk sedately to the other side of the table and pick up one of the papers. "Aiden Steller? Are you shittin' me?" I look at him, dropping my relaxed demeanor and letting the pure hate I feel for the man seep into my eyes. "You're taking your son's first name?"

He swallows again and his face pales. "I-I loved my son. What happened to him—"

I cut him off. "You mean what *you* did to him?"

"I didn't do it," he argues with a shake of his head. A bead of sweat flings from his temple, landing on his hand braced on the table behind him. "The jury found me not guilty."

"It's a wonder they didn't find you guilty, because your ability to lie is exceptionally terrible." I grab the key sitting on top of a stack of papers. "Let me guess, a safety deposit box, right? And I'd bet my left nut it's full of money."

"I don't know what you're talking about," he mutters. "That key is for a trunk in the basement."

I let him think he'll get away as he rounds the corner of the table.

I chuckle. "Sure it does. Tell me, did your son beg for his life before you took it? Did you even feel an ounce of remorse as you raped him?"

His eyes widen further as I stare at him, waiting for him to answer. He opens his mouth then snaps it closed before a word leaves his lips. I know just the moment he decides to make a run for it. His body stiffens and panic flares in his eyes. Not a second later, he's darting for the doorway. Unfortunately for him, he doesn't make it far. He stops abruptly with a muted grunt and begins to move backward. Not by choice, but from the man who has his hand locked around his neck. Emo comes into view, his eyes wild and body shaking with rage. Alec claws at the hand, but it's useless. Even Emo, the smallest of the four of us brothers, has a good foot and at least fifty pounds of muscle on the guy.

Emo slams Alec into the table, bending him backward until his feet lift from the floor. I drop the key back on the table and slowly walk over to the pair. Alec's face is turning purple and his eyes are bugging out. Satisfaction flares inside me at the look of utter terror on his face.

"Did you really think you were going to escape that easy?" I ask, coming to stand at the end of the table beside Emo.

When the only thing that comes out of Alec's mouth is a breathless wheeze, I look to my brother.

"Ease up a bit, Emo. He deserves so much more than to die from simple strangulation."

Grudgingly, Emo loosens his fingers around his throat. As soon as he's free, he tries to scramble back on the table.

Laughing, I grab his ankle and yank him back to the edge. "Nah uh, Mr. Hallson. You won't be going anywhere."

His sits up, his legs dangling over the table's edge, and regards Emo and me with frightened eyes. "Wh-what are you going to do?"

"Kill you, of course," I answer impassively.

His face drains of all color and a glance down shows a wet spot forming on the front of his pants. Why is it that almost everyone pisses themselves when faced with the fear of death? You'd think that they'd want their last moments to be a bit more dignified.

"You can't do that," he argues, his voice sounding on the verge of tears. "The police will catch you."

"Doubtful." I cross my arms over my chest and offer a smile. "We haven't been caught yet."

Tears leak down his cheeks pathetically and his body starts shaking so hard I can feel the trembles through the floor. If it wasn't for the pictures Judge showed me of the condition Alec left his son's body in, I might feel a hint of remorse for the man. But I did see the pictures. The boy was covered from head to foot with bruises. Not only did Alec rape his son with his sick dick, but he used a bat on him as well, after he beat him with it. It was ultimately that bat being forced in the boy violently, causing internal injuries, that killed him.

Alec Hallson doesn't deserve one ounce of remorse or compassion. The only thing he deserves is pain, and the knowledge that his son's rape and death was avenged.

"You want him?" I ask Emo.

The words barely leave my lips before he's growling, "Yes."

Alec's eyes flit to Emo, who up until that point has remained silent. Recognizing the deathly look in Emo's eyes and knowing he'll get nowhere with him, the asshole begins to beg.

"Please, please, don't do this." He throws his hands up and smashes them together, like he's praying to us. "I-I did it. I r-raped and killed Aiden. I'll go to the p-police right now and confess. Just p-please don't kill me."

I contemplate his plea as I pull a chair away from the table and take a seat. "One question. Why?"

His gaze drops and he closes his eyes. His voice is a hoarse whisper when he answers. "I found out my fiancée was trying to seduce him."

"So you decided to punish your son for the sins of your fiancée? Did it work? Did he sleep with her?"

"No." Alec opens his eyes and his mouth forms a straight line. "But he would have eventually. Charlotte can be very persuasive."

"You have some seriously fucked up priorities. I hope the bugs feast on your rotting corpse."

I glance to Emo and tip my chin. He doesn't need to be told twice. Before Alec has a chance to make a sound, Emo has his hand wrapped around his throat. His eyes glaze over in pain as he frantically paws at the fingers restricting his airway. A moment later, there's a sickening crunch as his larynx is crushed, ensuring he can't scream for whatever Emo has planned for him.

His struggles cease as his efforts move to painfully and unsuccessfully pull in much needed air. If given long enough, he'll die from lack of oxygen. That's not the way Emo plans for the man to die though.

He carelessly tosses Alec's weakened body farther on the table and climbs a top to straddle his waist. I get comfortable by throwing my feet up on the edge of the table and cross my ankles.

Emo slides a wicked looking knife from the sheath at his side, the silver glinting off the light. As much as I wanted to slay the bastard myself, I know this is a kill that Emo needs after watching those tapes. Hopefully it'll appease some of his anger.

Holding the blade between his teeth, Emo rips away Alec's shirt. A crazed look darkens his already ominous gaze when he takes the knife and drags it down his torso. The cut isn't deep, but damn sure painful. Alec's eyes widen and the sound that leaves his lips is distorted. What it must feel like to want to scream out in pain and not be able to. It's like stubbing your toe and the pain being so great you expect the appendage to be barely hanging on by a thread, only for it to not even be scratched.

Blood leaks from his wounds, sliding down his body to pool on the table beneath him. Emo likes his kills to be messy. Normally the sight of Emo's work is repulsive, but the images of Aiden's lifeless body has me wishing *I* was the one tearing Alec apart.

It's not long before he's dead. Not from his crushed windpipe, but from Emo slicing and dicing him. I don't stop him when I know Alec is dead. I let him continue to cut away at the demons that are plaguing him.

By the time he's done, he's covered in blood and Alec looks like he's been dissected. Emo's hair falls in his face as he looks down at the mess he's made. Satisfaction mars his face. The only sound in the room is the low hum of the heater and Emo's harsh breathing.

"Are you good?" I ask quietly

"Yes," he grunts. Standing to his feet, he jumps from the table, blood splattering from his hands and onto the floor.

"Let's go and I'll call it in."

With a curl of disgust when he looks at Alec one last time, he turns on his heel and leaves the room without a word. I follow behind him and we leave through the front door. It's dark outside and the closest neighbor is a good hundred yards away, so there's no worry of being spotted. At my truck, parked at a playground a couple blocks away, Emo strips down and uses his t-shirt to wipe away the blood from his hands. Donning clean clothes, he climbs into the cab where I'm already waiting. Before we leave, I call Dax and let him know it's done. After hanging up with him, I grab the secured phone from the glove box and dial the police to leave an anonymous tip about hearing screams coming from Alec Hallson's house.

Starting the truck, I point us in the direction of the hotel we're staying in tonight. Emo's still riding his adrenaline high from slaughtering Alec, so the drive is quiet.

With one bird down and one more to go, the silence gives me time to think about the confrontation with Diego's father tomorrow.

I RAP MY KNUCKLES AGAINST the door and wait. Emo's at my side, tense but alert. After his shower last night, once we made it to the hotel, he let me re-bandage the wounds on his arms, but not his hands. So far, the key has stayed in his pocket, but I have no doubt it'll be in his hand before the day is over.

"We keep this as civil as we can," I tell him in a low voice.

His mouth tightens. He doesn't want to be here anymore than I do, but he has my back, just as I knew he would. Emiliano has a reputation for being a ruthless bastard. My brothers and I have had many discussions about taking him out, but as much as we detest the guy, his role in San Antonio is too important. The city is full of criminals, and of course, Emiliano is one of them, but he's known for despising anyone who hurts women and children. That's probably his only redeeming quality and it works in our favor. He's been connected to several murders of known thugs who have harmed women and children.

"We'll see." Emo answers, his hands fisted at his sides.

The door opens just then, and I turn to face a hulk of a man in a black suit. At least seven-foot tall and weighing over three-hundred pounds—most of it muscle—tree trunk arms, military cut blond hair, and bottomless gray eyes, his expression is blank as he stares at us. "May I help you?"

"We're here to see Mr. Tomas."

"Senior or junior?" he asks tonelessly.

"Well, since junior is currently in my town wreaking havoc, I'd have to say senior."

"And whom may I ask is calling?"

His stoic demeanor remains the same. It makes me want to junk punch him to see if I'll get a different response.

"Sheriff Ward and Emo."

He inclines his head—expression still bland. "If you'll wait here—"

"Let them in, Smalls," a voice says from behind Hulk. He steps to the side, revealing a balding, portly man in an expensive suit.

Emiliano Tomas.

Emo and I walk past Hulk and Emiliano walks our way, holding his hand out to shake. "I've been expecting you."

Gripping his hand, I give a firm squeeze and raise a brow. "Have you?"

When he offers his hand to Emo and Emo looks at it with disgust, he lets it drop to his side. "Come. We'll talk more in my office. Smalls, Maria needs help in the kitchen."

"But, sir—"

Emiliano cuts him off, slicing his hand through the air. "Now, Smalls."

"Yes, sir." He spins on his heel and stalks across the checkered tiled floor. I expect to feel the booms of his steps and see cracks form on the walls, but the huge man is surprisingly graceful as he walks away.

"Smalls? What an unusual name for a man of his size."

He grunts. "His size is the only intimidating thing about him. When God made him, he forgot to add a brain."

He leads us to a set of closed double doors. Pushing them open, we step inside a modern-looking office. Massive desk dominating one wall, bookshelves adorned with hundreds of books, a fireplace —who needs a fucking fireplace in Texas? —a sofa, and two recliners with a small table between them.

Unbuttoning his blazer, Emiliano walks behind his desk and takes a seat. He gestures to the chairs across from him. "Sit."

Declining the offer, Emo and I stand behind the chairs. "We won't be staying."

He laces his fingers and places his hands on the wood surface. "My son tells me you're hiding something of his."

My hands grip the back of the chair, the humor of moments ago gone, and anger taking its place. "Did your son also tell you he beat the shit out of that something and threatened her life?"

Emiliano sighs and reclines back in his chair, frustration marking his face.

"Just tell the girl to give him the microchip. I'll take care of him from there."

"She doesn't have it. Doesn't even know what chip he's asking for," I grit out between clenched teeth.

His eyes turn cold and the cutthroat man I know Emiliano to be, finally makes an appearance.

"She's lying. She was seen on video going into his office and rushing back out the day she took off from his house."

I lean over the chair and hiss, "Tell Diego to back off." I stand back up. "She doesn't have the fucking chip." Or at least I hope like fuck she doesn't. I know hardly anything about Eden Delmont, but I've never gotten the vibe she was hiding anything. Of course, she could just be a damn good actress. I don't think so though.

Emiliano gets up from his chair and walks around to the front of his desk, re-buttoning his blazer, like some kind of uptight rich businessman. He leans back against the desk and crosses his ankle, appearing relaxed, but the rigid set of his jaw tells another story. It's also laughable, really. Emiliano is far from intimidating in stature. He's fat, short, and out of shape. But I'm no fool. He may not be able to handle his own dirty work, so he hires muscle like Hulk to do it for him.

I feel Emo stiffen at my side, and I hope like hell he keeps his cool. He feels the threatening vibes in the room and doesn't like it any more than I do.

"Your man," He juts his chin to Emo, "is bleeding on my carpet."

"Send me the fuckin' cleaning bill," I growl, growing impatient for this to be over with so we can get back to Malus. And Eden.

He opens a box at his hip and pulls out a cigar. Bringing it to his nose, he sniffs it before putting it between his teeth. I've always hated the smell of cigars. After he lights it and releases a plume of smoke, he pinches it between two stubby fingers.

"You know, I've heard about you and your brothers and the infamous town of Sweet Haven. It's truly a shame what the children there went through."

My jaw tightens, and I hold back the need to plant my fist in the guy's throat. Emo, apparently, has no qualms about hurting him as he releases a guttural growl and makes a move to go after him. If there's one thing that pisses my brothers and me off the most, it's pity. Pity is for the weak and we aren't weak. Not anymore. We beat our past, escaped it, and we'll be damned if anyone thinks we're lesser because of it.

"No," I order and grab Emo's arm before he can get too far. "Leave it, Emo."

I can feel the tremors in his body as he forcefully tries to control himself. Thankfully, after several seconds, he steps back beside me. I turn back to Emiliano to find his eyes lit on Emo.

"If Diego insists on continuing his pursuit of Eden, he'll meet a deadly end," I warn him, drawing his attention back to me. "She's under my and the town of Malus's protection."

He takes another draw of his cigar and talks through a billow of smoke. "You're threatening my son's life? To my face?" he asks with a hint of surprise. He may not know the lengths we go through to ensure the safety of Malus's citizens or what my brothers and I do on the side, but he knows our name, and not only because of our pasts. He knows we're not the type to be fucked with.

"Yes."

He considers my answer for a moment. "How well do you know this woman? Is she really worth the risk you're taking coming in my house and telling me you'll kill my son?"

"It doesn't matter how well I know her. I know enough to know she's innocent of whatever Diego claims. And even if she isn't, he's still not laying a hand on her."

Stubbing out his cigar, he leans away from his desk, coming to his short five and a half feet tall height. I glare down at the little bastard.

"I've got too much other shit going on around here to deal with more of Diego's fucked up mess because he was neglectful with one of his women. I've never had any issues with you or your kind, Sheriff Ward. I'll have a talk with him, but he's a stubborn bastard, so I can't promise anything."

I hold his stare. "You better hope he heeds your warning,

because if one hair on Eden's head is harmed, the devil himself won't stop me from putting him down."

His jaw tics and the pulse at his temple throbs, giving away his mounting anger. I have zero fucks to give if he likes it or not.

"I believe it's time you both leave. I've been generous to allow you into my home while offering nothing but threats. That generosity has about run dry."

"We'll see ourselves out." Giving him a tight nod, I spin on my heel, grabbing Emo's arm on the way before he has the chance to permanently mark the older man's face and bring the Tomas family down on our heads. Not that I fear their wrath, but it's something I don't want to deal with. Not to mention, it could cause problems for Malus.

I just hope like fuck Diego listens to his father and leaves Eden the hell alone. Diego will still die by my hands, but at least this way, it'll be on my terms.

chapter fourteen

JW
The Past

I PULL THE COVERS UP CLOSER to my chin when I hear my bedroom door creak open. The light in the hallway is off so it's too dark to see who it is, but I don't need the light to know. This is the fourth night in a row he's come to my room. I don't think Mom and Dad know, and I'm too scared to tell them. They always said what happens on Hell Night is supposed to be special and sacred. That it's the one night a month the adults are allowed to show the kids the true meaning of love. If what happens on Hell Night is love, then I don't want anyone to love me. It hurts too much to be loved.

I hold real still when my covers are lifted, and I feel a warm body climb into bed with me. My eyes sting, but I try to force back my tears. If I cry, my nose will run and I'll be forced to sniff, letting Trey know I'm awake. Maybe if he thinks I'm asleep, he'll leave.

My heart pounds hard in my chest, and I worry he'll hear it. I start counting in my head, trying to make the numbers match my heartbeat to slow it down, but it doesn't work. A hand lands on my hip, and I can't help but stiffen at the touch, giving myself away.

"I know you're awake, Liam," he whispers and moves his body up against my back and butt. I hate the name Liam. My name is JW. It's what my real brothers call me, what Rella calls me, because I love John Wayne movies so much. I wish I was watching a John Wayne movie right now.

Something pokes into my pajama pants. I want to cry out for Mom and Dad, but I worry they won't help me. Why would they when they let Trey do the things he does to me on Hell Night?

"I can feel you trembling. Are you excited I'm here?"

My bottom lip wobbles. "Please, Trey," I whine. "I don't want to do it tonight. I'm tired and want to go to sleep."

His dry lips and the little hairs on his face he's starting to let grow out scrape across the back of my neck. His hand comes around my waist and goes under my shirt, rubbing my stomach.

"It's okay. You don't have to stay awake. I just want to love you for a little while. I can love you while you sleep."

"But it'll hurt, and Mom said we're supposed to wait until The Gathering."

His hand moves down my stomach into the waistband of my bottoms. I squeeze my eyes shut as he touches my privates. His deep groan in my ear almost sounds like he's in pain.

"I can't wait that long. I need to love you now." He squeezes me and it hurts. I let out a small cry. "Shh… little brother, it's okay," he whispers and loosens his hold. "Let me show you how much I love you. I promise I'll be gentle."

He's never gentle. He'll say he'll be gentle, and in the beginning, he is, but he always ends up being rough and hurting me. Sometimes he's so rough that I bleed.

I hate my brother. I hate my parents. I hate every adult in Sweet Haven. The only reason Trey is being nice right now is because he doesn't want me to scream and wake our parents.

"Please, Trey. I don't wanna." Tears leak from my eyes. I clutch my pillow and draw it closer to me.

When he begins pulling down my bottoms, I grab onto the waistband to hold them up. He pinches my side hard. "Let go, Liam. All you have to do it just lay there and let me do what I want."

I let go of the waistband. Not only because he's still pinching me, but *also because the sound of his voice has changed. He sounds like he does on Hell Night. He sounds like the devil.*

My pants are pulled off and his hand runs up my leg and over my butt. I let him push me to my stomach because he's so much bigger and stronger than me. There's no way I could make him stop, and I fear what he'll do if I try. During Hell Nights, Trey is mean. Like really mean.

"Just lay there like a good boy and go to sleep. Let your big brother love you like I'm supposed to," he whispers into the dark.

His weight settles on my back, and I bury my face into my pillow. I push my head so hard into the fluffy surface that I can barely breath. I wish I could just stop breathing. That would mean I wouldn't feel the pain I know is coming.

My pillow case is wet from my tears and snot, but I don't care. I keep my face pressed against it. When the first bite of pain hits, I scream. I scream so hard my throat hurts. No one can hear it though, because it's muffled by my pillow.

I cry and cry and cry some more, wishing the whole time I was big enough, strong enough, brave enough to force my brother to stop. But I'm not. I'm little and weak, so I let him hurt me over and over again, his grunts hitting my ears and his sweat dripping on my back. And when he's done and rolls away to his feet to leave my room, I curl up into a ball as small as I can get and cry even more.

chapter fifteen

EDEN

I POP THE PILL OUT OF THE back of my birth control packet and tip my head back, dropping it in my mouth filled with water. Giving my head a shake, I swallow it down. I grab the packet and stuff it back in my make-up case, making a mental note to find the pharmacy here because I'll need a refill soon.

Once I'm dressed, I go back into my room and grab my phone. I heard it ring while I was in the bathroom. Looking at the two missed calls from Mom, I let out a little sigh. The woman is driving me crazy. I mean, I understand her worry, but no matter how many times I've told her I can't tell her what's going on, she asks me every time I talk to her.

Knowing she'll probably call the police if I don't call her back, I press her name and bring the phone to my ear. She answers halfway through the first ring.

"Eden Marie Delmont, don't you ever scare me like that again!" she screeches over the line. I wince at the high pitch tone. "Why didn't you answer?"

"Jesus Christ, Mom. I was in the bathroom." I huff out a breath, blowing a few strands of hair from my face.

"Don't you take the Lord's name in vain."

"Sorry," I mutter. I'm not really sorry. I love her, but the woman is maddening.

"Tell me what's going on? When are you coming home?" she demands.

Rolling my eyes, I hold back what I really want to say, and try my best to keep my tone light.

"I'm not sure when. I'm still trying to figure things out, but I'll let you know as soon as I do." Before she can grill me further, which I know she wants to do, I ask, "How's Daddy?"

"Your dad's fine. Just worried about you. Still grumbling about his new diet."

I laugh, because I can just imagine Dad fussing over his low-carb diet and trying to sneak in sweets when he thinks she won't see him. Mom sees everything. I swear she has cameras hidden all over the house.

A few weeks ago, Dad found out he was on the verge of diabetic ketoacidosis. Luckily, he wasn't so close that he had to be admitted and was sent home with strict instructions on how to change his diet. Before then, Dad didn't even know he was diabetic. Mom freaked out, of course, and started him on a new diet regimen right away. Any time I was over at the house for dinner, which was a couple times a week, he always bickered about what she made.

"Just keep on him. He'll get used to it eventually," I tell her.

"You know me. He can gripe all he wants, but it'll do him no good." She turns quiet before she says somberly. "We miss you, Eden. I want you to come home. Whatever's going on, we can figure it out together."

A lump forms in my throat and I'm forced to clear it before I can talk. "I can't, Mom. I wish I could, but I just can't. I swear I'm safe where I am."

I close my eyes at the sound of her sniffle. I hate hurting her, but this kind of hurt is much more bearable than the pain she'll go through if I go back home. I have no doubt Diego will go after her and Dad if I'm there.

"Okay," she says after several silent moments. "I trust you. Just promise you're being careful."

"I promise. Give Dad a big hug and kiss for me. And tell him he better continue following his diet or he'll have me to deal with along with you."

Her laugh is strained, but it's a laugh, so I'll take it.

"Talk to you soon."

After I hang up, I flop back on the bed, staring up at the white ceiling and suddenly feeling homesick. I've never been this long without seeing my parents. We've always been close, and I go visit them at least twice a week. Or they come to my house to see me. What I wouldn't give in this moment to have them both wrap me in their protective embrace and tell me everything is going to be okay. I'm not a Momma or Daddy's girl. I'm a parent's girl.

The vibration of my phone against my stomach, followed by Hosier's *Take Me to Church*, has me sitting up in bed. Expecting that it's probably Mom having forgotten to tell me something, I don't even look at the screen.

"Hello?"

There's nothing but static at first, then a muffled sound.

"It's been too long," a dark voice that has shivers racing down my spine answers.

"Diego," I utter through a dry throat.

"You've kept me waiting long enough, Eden. Too long, in fact."

At first, I'm frozen with shock and can only sit there stiffly on my bed. Memories of the pain I endured by Diego's hands, the fear of what he would do next, of realizing there were no lines he wouldn't cross, holds me hostage. The stinging bite of my nails against my palm is the only thing that brings me back to reality. I pull in an encouraging breath.

"What do you want from me?" I ask quietly, trying and failing to keep the fear out of my voice. Diego's the type of person who thrives on fear, and I don't want to give him the satisfaction of knowing he scares me shitless.

His tsk across the line is condescending, like he's reprimanding a child. "You're a smart girl. You know what I'm after. Give me the fucking chip, and I'll leave you be."

"I don't have any chip," I cry then clamp my lips closed, not wanting to alarm Jenny or Judge. "I never did. I don't even know what you're talking about."

"You're a Goddamn liar," he spews furiously. "I have video footage of you running from my office the day you took off from my house."

I frown because he's not making any sense. "What? I only went in to get my purse."

"It's pretty fucking convenient that the day the chip goes missing is the same day you went into my office without me," he growls. "You obviously have a death wish. Now tell me where the Goddamn chip is!"

I shake my head. "Diego, I swear—"

"Hey, Eden, Judge and I are…."

I glance at the doorway just as Jenny pokes her head around the corner. Her voice trails off when she sees the look on my face. Her gaze darts to the phone in my hand then back to my eyes before she spins and hurries away.

"Who is that I hear?" Diego asks. "Is that the pretty blonde you've been staying with? You know who she reminds me of?" he continues. "She reminds me of the girl I had in my room the day you left. The one who was chained so beautifully to my wall. All bruised and bloody, her guts lying at my feet." He hums, like he's savoring the memory like he would a delicious meal. His words make me feel sick. My stomach actually twists and plummets, and I'm forced to cover my mouth. "I bet she'd look just as beautiful, but I think I'd play with her a bit first." His voice changes, deepens into a deathly growl. "Get me that fucking chip or we'll see just how beautiful she'll be with her insides hanging from her body. I have it in my hand, and I'll leave you be."

I gag and it's only sheer force of will that keeps the contents of my stomach down. His words are no idle threat. It's a promise.

He's also lying, because I know damn good and well, he won't leave me alone. He can't chance me staying alive when I witnessed him murder a woman. No, even if I did have the chip and gave it to him, he'd kill me.

I look up just as Judge storms into the room, anger making his scowl look dangerous. Jenny is hot on his trail. He stalks over and grabs the phone from my hand. It's too late though, Diego's already hung up.

"Who in the fuck was that?" he demands once he realizes there's no one on the line.

I hug my stomach and hunch over, feeling drained and helpless. "Diego."

"Goddamn it, Eden," he grates with aggravation. "Why in the hell didn't you get me as soon as you knew it was him."

"Calm down, Judge," Jenny orders, coming to sit beside me on the bed and putting her arm around my shoulders. "She's already upset enough."

"Fuck," he snarls and spins away from us, raking his hand through his hair angrily. He turns back to us. "We could have tried to put a trace on the call."

I lift my eyes. "He's smarter than that. He would have used an untraceable phone."

"What did he say?"

"He wanted to know where the chip was," I answer quietly, dejectedly. Since I don't have the stupid chip, Diego will eventually find me and.... Kill me, I guess. Or at least try. And in trying, he might hurt someone here in Malus. He's already killed my dog, brutally so, hurt that Derek guy, and threatened to kill Jenny. I can't let that happen. I don't know what I'm going to do, but I have to do something.

"Are you sure you don't have the chip?" Judge asks, suspicion evident in his voice.

His question pisses me off, and I jump up from the bed, giving him my best glare.

"I've already said I don't fucking have it," I growl, my balled fists at my side shaking from anger.

"You say that, but we don't know you. You just showed up in town with trouble trailing you, bringing danger to everyone who lives here. Why should we believe you?"

I almost huff out a laugh, because he's right. No one here really knows me, and they've got no reason to take my word. But it still angers me that he would doubt me. I've been through hell by Diego's hands. I witnessed him disembowel a woman, was beaten by him, threatened, then found my dog eviscerated. Why in the hell would I keep the chip after all that? Whatever's on it is something Diego doesn't want people to see, so it has to be bad. If I had it, I would have already handed it over to the police. Or at the very least, given it to JW to handle.

"I'll only say this one more time," I warn, my voice rising. "I don't. Have. The fucking chip. If I did, I would have already handed it over. I don't have a death wish."

"If I find out you're lying—"

"That's enough, Judge," Jenny says, getting up from the bed, angry on my behalf. "If she said she doesn't have the chip, then she doesn't have it."

Judge's eyes narrow on Jenny. "We can't know that for sure."

"I said—" She stalks up to Judge and pokes his chest with her pointer finger, "—that's enough."

A growl rumbles from his throat, but thankfully doesn't question my word further. Instead, he asks a question I don't want to answer, but know I have to.

"Did he say anything else?"

I look to Jenny and see her sweet and innocent face. Even angry, she still appears angelic. The thought of her being hurt, gutted like the woman I saw Diego slice open, sends a violent wave of both anger and fear running through me.

I turn my eyes back to Judge, my voice husky when I answer. "He said if I don't get him the chip, he'll kill Jenny."

Jenny inhales sharply beside me. I don't look at her but keep my eyes locked on Judge, hoping he sees the pain of what Diego's threat did to me. Anger flares in his green eyes. It's so hot it makes his eyes burn brighter. Thankfully, it's not directed at me though.

"I'm calling JW." His voice is tense, resolute. "This shit is being taken care of *now*."

I nod and let out a deep breath. I want JW here too. For some bizarre reason, he makes me feel safe. He left yesterday, said he had some business he had to attend to, and is due back this afternoon. Ever since I watched him pull away from Remi and Trouble's house yesterday, I've felt anxious, edgy. I blamed it on being sexually frustrated; that was the second time something I knew would be amazing sex was dangled in front of my face and it was snatched away. I know now that wasn't it—I mean, yeah, I wanted the amazing sex—but it was JW being away, not near me, not in Malus to protect me if Diego made an appearance.

Judge already has his phone to his ear and walking out of the room. I sit back on the bed and Jenny comes to sit beside me. Her eyes are still wide, and guilt twists my stomach. I grab her hand and squeeze it tightly in mine.

"Don't worry. They won't let anything happen to you."

"I'm not worried about myself," she says, and I look at her. "I'm more worried about you. It's you he really wants. The men will protect us both, but it has to be so scary for you, knowing someone like him is out there."

I try to smile, to act brave, but I'm sure it comes out more a grimace than anything. "I am scared, but I refuse to let him have control over me." I close my eyes for a moment and take a long breath before looking back at Jenny earnestly. "I swear I don't have whatever he thinks I have."

She nods once. "I know you don't. I believe you. And Judge is just worried. He can be an asshole when he's worried. He cares a lot about the people of Malus."

I can understand that. From what I've seen so far, this small community is more like a family than a town. It must be nice to have so many people care about you and care about them in return.

"Thank you," I clear my throat when it comes out hoarse. "Thank you for believing me."

Now it's her turn to squeeze my hand. We both look toward the bedroom door and wait.

chapter sixteen

JW

I DROP EMO OFF AT HIS PLACE, glad to see Grace's car parked in the driveway, knowing she'll take care of him. My tires squeal as I hit the gas hard, pulling away from the curb too fast, but not caring. I'm the damn sheriff of Malus. It's not like someone will pull me over.

I'm impatient to get to Judge and Jenny's house. My jaw clamps shut and my blood simmers, coursing through my veins at a rapid speed.

I got a call from Judge just as we were leaving Emiliano's house, telling me about Eden's phone conversation with Diego. His threat came before Emiliano could issue his own warning to his son, so hopefully his call to Eden was for nothing and he'll forget about his pursuit of her. Something tells me he won't though. Something tells me he won't stop until he either kills Eden or he's stopped by my brothers and me.

I pull up to Judge and Jenny's house a few minutes later. My steps are heavy and quick as I walk up the steps and through the front door without knocking. My eyes immediately lock on Eden's. She's sitting at the bar, a cup of coffee in her hands. It pleases me when her eyes give away her relief when she sees me. Judge and Jenny are on the couch. I ignore them as I stalk over to Eden. She's on her feet before I get to her. I don't stop until I have my arms around her waist and her face is smashed to my chest. I love the way she feels against me. It feels familiar, like we've been doing this for years and not just days. She shudders against me, but when she pulls away a few minutes later, her mouth is set into a firm angry line.

"I need to leave," she says, her chin lifting. "I can't stay here any longer."

"Like fuck you can't," I growl and tug her closer. "You aren't going anywhere, Gypsy."

"Listen to me. All I'm doing is bringing trouble here. If someone else were to get hurt because of me...." Her throat constricts. "I couldn't live with myself."

"You're still not leaving."

"Damnit, JW, just let me leave," she argues foolishly. "I'll find somewhere to hide out until Diego forgets this whole thing."

I narrow my eyes and bend my knees so we're eye-to-eye. "Do you really think he's just going to give up? You know Diego better than me. Does he come across as the quitting type? Especially when you saw what you did and it could come back and bite him in the ass one day."

She huffs out a breath and a small growl of frustration leaves her lips.

"Why are you doing this?" she demands. "I know you said it's your job, but how can you know for sure I don't have the chip he wants? How do you know I'm not lying to you?"

I pause for a moment, because I'm not sure how to answer. How *do* I know she doesn't have the chip? I don't know for sure, but I have a gut feeling, and my gut's never led me astray before.

"I just do," I give her the best answer I can.

The fight leaves her eyes and her forehead thumps against my sternum. I look over her head to Judge and glare at him. I didn't miss the subtle glance in his direction when she asked how I knew she wasn't lying. I also didn't miss the misery in her eyes when she did so. Judge accused her of something, and I'll damn sure find out what later.

I lift her chin with my finger. "Go grab some clothes. You're coming home with me."

Her shoulders slump, but she gives me a nod anyway. Before she walks away, I peck her lips with mine then wait until she leaves the room. I cast Judge another glare as he gets up from the couch.

"What in the hell did you say to her?"

He straightens his spine and glares right back at me. "I asked if she had the chip."

I laugh, but there's nothing humorous in the sound. Nope. It's bitter and filled with loathing. Judge may be my brother and I love him, but he really pisses me off sometimes.

"You," I point my finger at him, "just stay the fuck away from Eden. You don't get to give your opinion anymore."

"The fuck I don't," he grates. "That bastard threatened Jenny's life. Like it or not, I'm smack dab in the middle of the shit now. And fuck you, JW. You're so Goddamn far up that woman's ass that you can't see the possibility that she very well could be lying to us. I'm not one bit sorry for caring for this town enough to think of all avenues. She's a fuckin' stranger, and you're willing to put everyone here in danger, over someone you don't fuckin' know."

I seethe. My chest goes crazy as I breath in and out rapidly. Red clouds my vision, and before I know it, I'm in Judge's face. He doesn't move, not even an inch, as I invade his space. Not that I expected him to.

Jenny squeaks from the couch at my sudden advance, but we both pay her no mind. I've never been tempted to hit one of my brother's before, but right now, as I stare at Judge with contempt, it takes everything in me to not pound his face in.

"You don't think I care about the people of Malus?" I ask with a deceptively calm voice. "You don't think I'd give my life for every single one of them? You, Trouble, Emo, and I came back and rebuilt this town into what it is today. It's not just a town and its people, it's my fuckin' family. I may have been born into a shit one, just as you, Trouble, and Emo, but that doesn't mean I don't know what a real family is supposed to be. It doesn't fuckin' mean I won't do whatever in the hell I have to do to protect them." Reaching in my pocket, I pull out my phone and bring up the picture I got earlier from an unknown number. I shove the phone under his nose. "But it also doesn't mean I'll let an innocent woman end up like the one in that picture. It doesn't fuckin' matter if she has the chip or not, but you want to know why I know she doesn't? Because of that picture. Because anyone with any sort of survival instincts would give it up to avoid becoming that."

I turn away from him, and because I've got so much pent up anger pouring through me, and I'm trying not to release it on Judge, I snatch up a glass from the coffee table and hurl it across the room. It smashes against a wall, pieces of glass raining everywhere. My hands go to my hips, and I drop my head. I suck in deep breaths, willing my body to calm down.

"That's her." I turn at Eden's hesitant voice. Tears swim in her eyes when they meet mine. "That's the girl Diego had chained to his wall."

"How do you know?"

"Because I recognize the tattoo on her arm." She glances back down at the picture, only to lift her eyes again. "But how? Where did you get this?"

"From an unknown number."

Judge snaps his eyes to me. "Was Emo—?"

I'm shaking my head before he can finish. "No. It was sent from a burner phone. The phone was broken and dropped in a trash can; no way Emo could trace it."

"Damnit," Judge mutters, mimicking my same thoughts when Emo and I found the broken phone.

"Do you think Diego sent it?" Eden asks. Her arms are hugging her middle. I hold my hand out to her and she rushes to me. I pull her snuggly to my side. Having her close cools my temper a few degrees.

"When was this sent?"

I look to Judge, still irate at his accusation against Eden, but I answer him. "About five minutes after I got your call."

"Then no, it couldn't have been Diego. I was able to get a general area of where his phone call to Eden came from. It's within a five-mile radius of the center of town. He wouldn't have had time to make it to San Antonio."

"But then who sent it? And why? Was there a message with the picture?" Eden asks, looking up at me.

I tip my chin to Judge and he looks back down at the phone.

"*This is what will happen to her if you don't stop him,*" he recites the message that came with the picture.

Eden trembles against my side, so I pull her closer, trying to absorb her fear into me.

Jenny, who's been quiet this whole time, approaches Judge and tries to look at the phone. He holds it away from her.

"No," he demands. "You don't need to see it."

"Let me see, Judge," she says calmly.

"Jenny," Judge and I both warn. It's already bad enough that Eden saw the picture. Hell, she saw it in person. No one should see something like that.

"Let me see the damn picture, Judge."

With a tight jaw, he holds the phone for her to see, and just as expected, her face pales and she sucks in a gasp. "Oh, God." She throws her hand up to her mouth. Muttering a curse, Judge leads her to the couch to sit down before she passes out.

The woman in the picture is mutilated almost beyond recognition. I'm surprised Eden was able to recognize her. That tattoo her only clue as to who she was. Her face is swollen and bloody, her body covered in bruises and lacerations, and her insides are no longer inside her, but lying next to her body.

"Find that bastard. This shit stops," Judge growls.

I lock eyes with him, both of us silently saying what we can't say out loud.

That woman in the picture, what was done to her... will be nothing compared to the hell we'll bring down on Diego fucking Tomas.

chapter seventeen

EDEN

I'M QUIET AS JW LEADS me into his house, which happens to be just around the block from Jenny and Judge's. My thoughts are scattered and it leaves me feeling numb. I've never considered myself a weak person. I stand my ground, I'm not afraid to give my opinion, I always fight for what I believe in, and I've never let a man treat me like shit.

I feel weak right now though. Diego makes me feel weak and helpless. No matter what I do, I'm going to lose. If I run, I'll be leaving everyone I care about behind, including JW and the others in Malus I've begun to think of as friends, for God knows how long. JW was right earlier. There's no way Diego will give up looking for me. He may go back to San Antonio when he realizes I'm no longer here, but it'll never be safe for me to return, and I'll always be looking over my shoulder.

If I stay, I run the risk of someone else getting hurt. Even if JW and his brothers manage to capture him, there's a chance one of them will get hurt, possibly even killed, in the process. And if they aren't, Diego is part of the Tomas cartel. He's Emiliano's son. He'll no doubt send goons to Malus, and I don't want to imagine the havoc they would cause.

"Hey," JW calls. I blink and look up at him, briefly remembering him walking me to his room and sitting me on his bed before he left the room. I didn't even see him come back. "What's going through your mind?"

I drop my eyes to his shirt where I pick at an invisible string. "Just how stupid I was to ever get involved with Diego. And that no matter what I do, someone is bound to get hurt."

He grabs my chin and forces my head up. His brows are slashed down into a frown. "You need to have more faith in me. Diego's done. He won't be hurting anyone else. That, I can promise you."

I want to believe him. I want so badly to take his word and run with it, but there's no way he can guarantee it. There are no guarantees in life. It's unpredictable, no matter how much we may try to make it otherwise.

"Come on. It's early, but I'm exhausted, and you look dead on your feet."

It's dark, but it's early. Only about nine o'clock or so. He's right, though. I'm exhausted to my bones. Earlier, after the initial shock of seeing the picture of the girl, JW called in Trouble and Emo. Remi and Grace came with them. After Jenny gave the women a short run down of what happened, she quickly changed the subject. I think she knew I was on the verge of a mental break down and needed a distraction. The four men sequestered themselves into Judge's office and talked about... I don't know what, but I know they were planning something and it had to do with Diego. I want to ask JW about it, but a part of me doesn't want to know. I just want to pretend for one night that he doesn't exist.

Pulling in a deep breath, I get to my feet in front of him.

"I want to forget." I run my hands up his chest. "Help me forget, JW."

His eyes flicker back and forth between mine. "Are you sure? You've had a rough day."

I offer him the best smile I have in me. "I'm completely sure. I need this. I need *you*."

His eyes darken when he palms my cheeks, dipping his head

and lightly settling his lips over mine. He's slow and gentle at first, his lips barely touching me. I release a contented sigh and my grip on his shoulders tightens.

His arms lock around my waist, and I'm suddenly smashed against his chest. I curse the long skirt I have on because it's preventing me from wrapping my legs around his hips.

His kiss becomes more demanding, swiping his tongue across my lips and forcing them open. The moment our tongues meet, he lets out a groan so deep I feel the vibrations against my chest.

"Never in my life have I tasted something so good as you. You're addicting, Eden Delmont."

I smile against his lips because I feel the same way about him. I could kiss him all day long and never get tired of it.

His hands leave my cheeks and move down my sides. Once he reaches the bottom of my shirt, he dips his fingers underneath. His touch brings goosebumps to my flesh, and I shiver. I need more of him. So much more. Thankfully, it's only seconds later that he starts lifting my shirt. Our lips part so he can pull the material over my head. His eyes immediately drop to my bra-covered breasts. Using one finger, he traces a line from the hollow of my throat down to my cleavage. I watch his eyes as they follow the movement, desire making the beautiful blue turn to a stormy grey.

"So damn beautiful," he murmurs.

He grabs the lace edge of one of the cups and pulls it down, my boob spilling free of its confinement. His head dips, and I toss mine back when his lips engulf the nipple. He bites down on the hard peak, but not enough to hurt. Just a slight stinging pleasurable pain. My hands go to the back of his head, and I hold him to me.

He yanks the other cup down and palms my sensitive breast, tweaking the tip lightly before releasing my nipple with a pop so he can give the other one the same treatment. My breasts have never been overly sensitive, not like some women, but having JW pay homage to them, already has me on the edge.

Just then, something hairy scurries across my feet, and I really hope it's not a rat. "Umm… JW? You have a cat, right?" I ask, my voice barely a whisper from my brain being so fogged with desire.

"No," he mumbles around the nipple still in his mouth.

My eyes snap open wide, and I immediately scramble up on the bed. JW's still bent over from my sudden movement, his mouth hanging open from where I popped my nipple out of it. I scream when a little furry black head appears over the side of the bead, its beady eyes staring up at me.

JW chuckles as he walks over and scoops up the little critter and cradles it in his arms. I narrow my eyes at him.

"That's not funny," I spit.

"Actually, it was very funny."

I huff and cross my arms over my chest. I almost lose my balance on the mattress when I shift my weight to my other foot.

"You could have answered my question with more than a simple no, you ass. Or given me a heads up or something."

"But this way was so much more fun."

I want to punch the mirth right off his face, but it's really freaking hard to stay mad at him when he allows the cute little ferret on his shoulder to rub its head against his neck. JW pets the animal affectionately as he stares up at me still on the mattress.

"Come meet Piper."

I hedge closer to the edge of the bed. I've never owned a ferret but I've always thought they were cute. JW holds his other hand out to help me from the bed. Once I'm back on the floor, I look at the adorable little creature. Reaching out, I run my fingers over her head and down her long body. She stays idle on JW's shoulders.

"She's so pretty. Her coat is so dark it almost looks blue. How old is she?"

"Three years."

I smile at Piper and continue to pet her.

"I just can't imagine a big tough man like you having such a small and delicate pet."

He grunts, and I lift my eyes to him. He's looking down at his arm, where my bare breasts, still hanging out of my bra, are pressed against him. His eyes flick back up to mine and the heat's back in their blue depths.

"I'll be back."

I watch as he walks out of the room with Piper. My heart begins to pound with anticipation. When he appears back in the doorway, he does that sexy move men do when they reach between their shoulder blades and yanks off their shirt. And holy hell, his chest is a work of art. Tanned skin, hard muscles, and several tattoos. My mouth waters.

"You look like you want to eat me." He stalks slowly across the room toward me.

"Maybe I do."

"Not until I've had you first," he growls, coming to a stop in front of me and dropping to his knees. "Lose the bra."

I reach back and unhook my bra then throw it to the side. He stares up at me, his eyes dark with lust. He grips my hips with firm hands and brings his mouth to my upper stomach. My breath hitches at the first touch of his lips against my skin.

"That feels sooo good," I moan because I want him to know how good he makes me feel.

His mouth moves south down my stomach, leaving a wet trail behind. He stops at my belly ring long enough to flick it with his tongue.

"This is so sexy," he remarks huskily.

He looks up at me when he slowly starts pulling down my skirt. As soon as it's over my hips, he drops his head and kisses each hip bone, across my lower stomach, and over my bare pubic bone.

Feeling his hot breath fanning between my thighs has my legs going weak. I cry out and grip his shoulders to keep from falling when his tongue swipes between my folds. My legs are closed, so he can't get a good reach, but that's all taken care of a moment later when he pries them apart, putting one over his shoulder.

I pant and become dizzy when he licks me again, his tongue snaking between the lips of my pussy. One hand digs into my asscheek to hold me steady when I uncontrollably buck my hips forward. The other he uses to tease my opening. The rumble of his growl and the scrape of his gruff against my thighs has my eyes crossing in pleasure. Nothing in my whole life has ever felt so good.

I come undone and fireworks explode behind my closed eyes when his lips attach themselves around my clit and he sucks on the highly sensitive bundle of nerves. I come hard and fast, faster than I ever have before. My legs start to shake and my toes dig into the carpet. All I can do is hold onto his shoulders as I ride the blissful wave of rapture.

I jerk in his hold when he doesn't release my clit. I'm so sensitive it's almost painful.

"Oh, God," I whimper. "Too much."

"Not enough," he growls in response, repeating the words he said to me that day in Remi and Trouble's bathroom.

He continues to lick, suck, and fuck me with his fingers. I want to beg him to stop and beg him to *never* stop.

When he pulls his head away, I slump down on the bed. My legs feel like jelly and my heart thumps heavily against my ribs. Exhaustion has my eyes drooping, but when I see JW tugging down his pants, fatigue is the last thing on my mind.

I rub my lips together as I stare at his engorged cock. He's long, thick, and looks painfully hard. The head is a deep red and there're thick veins running up the sides. A bead of pre-cum hangs from the tip.

I have the sudden urge to suck that drop away and see if I can get him to produce more.

"Another time, baby," he says, reading my thoughts. "I need your tight pussy wrapped around my cock more than I need your lips around it."

Damn, I seriously love it when he talks dirty.

"Scoot up," he says then walks to the nightstand, pulls the drawer out, and retrieves a condom. Again, he does the sexy man move with the condom; ripping it open with his teeth, before sliding it down his shaft. A hiss of air leaves his throat as he does so.

I scoot back, my legs shamelessly falling open and waiting for him. Anticipation has my heart rate speeding up again as he crawls on the bed and settles himself between my legs.

"I'm sorry," he murmurs against my lips. Gripping his cock, he notches the head at my entrance.

"What for?" I frown in confusion.

"Because this is going to be fast and rough. I've been on edge for days."

Before I can respond, he's sliding in me. His thrust isn't forceful or fast, just a smooth non-stop glide until he's all the way in and his balls are resting against my ass. I let out a soft moan at the welcome intrusion. It's a snug fit, but it's a good snug fit. One that borders on pain but still feels oh so good.

"Sweet Christ Almighty," he rasps.

I weave my legs around his waist and lock my feet at the small of his back. He lifts to one elbow and uses his other hand to lift my ass. When he starts moving, his thrusts are steady and long. Like, he pulls all the way out to the tip and slides back in until he's fully seated. Each time he presses against my pelvis, he hits just the right spot over my clit.

Sweat slides down his temples, and why does that look so damn hot? Why does it make me want to lick away the salty moisture?

He speeds up, his grunts and my moans fill the space around us. My eyes fall closed as an intense wave of pleasure starts in my lower stomach. His fingers dig into the fleshy part of my asscheek, lifting me even higher. When his cock hits something inside me with the new angle, my eyes spring open. A throaty cry flies from my mouth.

"There," I moan. "Oh, God, right there."

Cocking his knee under my ass, he adjusts my angle, and my eyes about roll into the back of my head from the added pleasure that simple move gives me. My legs tense around his hips and my breath gets stuck in my throat, but a moment later, I'm letting out a loud cry as my release slams through me. My nails dig into the muscles of his shoulders, I'm sure painfully so, but it seems to spur him on because he starts hammering his hips forward.

With a grunt, he drops his head into the crook of my neck, and with a final forceful thrust, he stills.

I love the feel of his fevered breath fanning across my sweaty flesh and the erratic beat of his heart against my chest.

After several moments, he moves his hips again. Just lazy slow strokes, but it feels good. His scruff scrapes my skin as he lays tender kisses over my collar bone.

"You undo me," he murmurs quietly. My heart flutters at his admission.

I gently run my fingers through his hair and whisper my own confession. "No more than you do me."

WE'RE IN BED AFTER TWO rounds of bed sex and one round of shower sex. I'm on my stomach, half on his chest and half on the bed. Our legs are tangled together, and I keep rubbing the arch of my foot over the hair on his shin. What can I say? It's oddly sooth-ing. He's playing with my braid, and ever so often goosebumps appear on my arms because the end tickles my back. The only light filters in from the hallway. We've both been quiet for the last several minutes. I hate to break the silence, but there's something I want to ask him. Something I forgot about until his and Judge's argument earlier.

"Will you...." I hesitate, unsure how to ask, but decide to just come right out with it. "Will you tell me about Sweet Haven?"

The muscles in his stomach tense and his hand stops playing with my hair. I hold my breath and wait.

"How do you know about Sweet Haven?" he asks, his voice carrying a hint of.... Anger, maybe?

I opt to keep my head on his chest instead of sitting up and looking at him like I desperately want to do. I get the feeling I wouldn't like his expression if I saw it.

"When I was little, I think I was about eight, I remember hearing the name. It was all over the news for weeks. My parents would always change the channel when it was on the TV and anytime I asked about it, she said it wasn't for my young ears. It kinda stuck with me though, because I know there were some kids hurt, and I felt bad for them. Then years later, when I was an adult, I walked into a coffee shop and caught the end of a news broadcast. They were talking about how the town Sweet Haven had a new name. Malus. What you said about coming back here and rebuilding the town made me think of it again."

I stop talking and hold my breath again. He's quiet for so long that I wonder if he'll say anything at all. I was so young when the news broke out about Sweet Haven that I didn't know what they meant when they mentioned a sex ring. My parents shielded me as much as they could, but I heard whispers from the teachers at school. All I knew about it, was that it was bad. Thinking back now, those teachers were neglectful and should have made sure kids weren't around to overhear them.

When he does begin to speak, JW's voice is flat and devoid of emotion.

"My brothers and I; Judge, Trouble, Emo, and myself, along with many other kids, grew up in Sweet Haven. You were right. The name didn't change until we came back and petitioned the change. The place was a ghost town until we arrived almost eleven years ago, only a few people remaining from when we were kids. A few innocent adults and a handful of kids."

He picks my hair back up and starts twisting it around his fist loosely. I feel the hard thump of his heart under my hand. I hold still, afraid if I move, he'll stop talking.

"When we were little, most days our childhood was normal. Anyone from the outside looking in, they'd see a small town filled with loving families and friendly neighbors." He laughs harshly. "I say that, but we never got outsiders. I fuckin' wish we did." He stops again, and I feel my hair being lifted, then his deep inhale, like he's smelling my hair. "Hell Night is what me and my brothers called the one night a month when the adults changed from loving parents to lecherous monsters. All of the adults called it The Gathering. To us it was a night we were put through hell, while to them, it was a night to show the kids the 'true meaning of love'. Utter fucking bullshit. It gave them the opportunity to rape and molest kids while they justified it as love. The adults didn't just abuse their own children, but others as well. They all shared. Or most of them anyway."

I can't help it. The gasped words leave my lips before I can stop them. "Oh, my God. Those bastards."

"Bastards?" he asks "No, they weren't bastards. They were sick psychos who had a twisted way of spreading love when they didn't know the meaning of the word."

I'm appalled. Like completely, overwhelmingly, horrifyingly appalled. What kind of parents would do that to a child? What kind of parent would allow someone else to touch their child in such a disgusting way? What kind of person *likes* to touch children in that way? They should all be stripped and treated the same way. I've always had the mindset that if you lay your hands on someone in a way they don't want, your punishment should be the same in kind. Inmate rape in prisons against child molesters and rapists…. Yeah, I've never felt sorry for them.

"I am so sorry you went through that," I offer. It's a lame condolence, one I'm sure he's heard many times over the years, but it's the only thing I can offer. I'm still kind of speechless. While I knew what happened all those years ago was horrible, I had no clue just how much.

He moves, rolling to his side, and turning me until I'm facing him. Our legs are still tangled together, but our chests are no longer touching. He gazes at me, and I see the deep pain he's trying to hide but still very much feels.

"Despite what my brothers and I went through, I think we turned out okay. Most of that is due to Mae and Dale."

"The older woman from the diner?"

"Yes. Dale died three years ago. It was with Mae and Dale's help that we were able to get away the night of the raid. Otherwise, we would have been put in the system and separated. They knew how devastating that would have been for us. My brothers and I aren't blood related, but we couldn't be more close if we were.

"What happened to all of the adults?"

His jaw hardens when he answers. "Most were arrested, some died that night, and some got away."

"Were they ever caught?"

His eyes narrow in anger. "A few were, but there are some still out there."

The way his voice deepens at that revelation, the pure malevolence in his tone, sends shivers slithering down my spine. With good reason, he's irate at the fact that some people got away and evaded the punishment they rightly deserved. To know they are out there somewhere, possibly hurting other children, brings on my own anger.

I curl my fingers around his neck and rub my thumb over the heavy pulse, hoping to soothe him. I'd like to think it's that gesture that causes some of the darkness to leave his eyes, but I don't know for sure.

"You were right. You and your brothers have turned out so much better than most people would. You're kind, brave, and compassionate. You've gone beyond your duty to help me. And I've seen the way you, Judge, and Trouble interact with the townspeople. You all seem to genuinely care about them. Emo, I haven't been around him long enough to form an opinion, but he seems to be quiet and guarded. Even so, I bet he still cares, he just doesn't show it well."

His brows pucker as he frowns, and I feel my hair being lifted again. I love that he likes playing with my hair.

"Emo's had it harder than the rest of us. I won't go into detail because it's not my story to tell, but the rest of us at least got breaks in between Hell Nights. He didn't. He lived in hell all the time."

My heart breaks for the silent and withdrawn man. I've seen the fresh cuts and scars on his hands. They're harder to see through the tattoos covering the skin, but his arms carry some too. It's his hands that are mangled terribly though. It makes me wonder if the rest of his body is marked as well. I keep that curiosity to myself. As JW said, that's not my business to know. So instead, I ask him something else.

"Why did you and your brothers choose to come back here?"

"We grew up here. It's a big part of our past. A dark and painful one, but still a big part. We knew some of the good people stayed here. Mae and Dale always kept up with the few people who remained. We wanted to give this town a new history, one that people didn't cringe at. It'll always have a stigma, but eventually it'll fade to where it's barely noticeable. We're helping it along by making Malus a safe place for people who've been abused in some way. Almost everyone here has one thing in common; they all share horrifying experiences. But they also heal, flourish, and become strong here. They don't have to be afraid. We're more than just neighbors and friends, we're a family."

"That's beautiful." Tears prick my eyes at what JW and his brothers have created in Malus. "It's amazing that you want to take the place that caused you so much pain and turn it into something good. Something that will help other people."

His eyes slide away from mine, but I catch something in them before they do. Some emotion I can't name, but it's dark and grim and makes me curious about what just went through his head. When he looks back at me, it's gone, and I wonder if it was just my imagination.

"Enough with the heavy talk," he states and rolls to his back. I'm lifted and placed on top of him, my legs straddling his hips. With my braid wrapped around his fist, he tugs me down. "Now kiss me," he rumbles sexily.

I do just that, because, well.... Who am I to deny him?

chapter eighteen

JW

I WAKE TO THE ANNOYING as fuck sound of my phone ringing. I ignore it, something I usually don't do, because I'm the sheriff and therefore always on call. The soft and warm body in front of me feels way too good to let go of though.

I tighten my arm around Eden's waist and bury my face deeper into her hair, breathing in the sweet floral scent. We're both naked and my quickly rising cock is nestled between her asscheeks. I never want to leave this bed or this position. If I stayed here a year, just like this, I'd be okay with that.

But my Goddamn phone keeps going off. I growl grumpily, ready to slug the person who has shitty timing. Don't they know I'm in bliss right now and should be left alone?

Eden moans sleepily, her ass rubbing against me, causing me to harden further. "You should probably answer that," she says through a yawn.

With a grunt, I roll to my back and snatch the phone up from the nightstand. It stops ringing as soon as my hand touches it. I check the missed calls. Emo. Three of them. I must have not heard the first call.

I'm just about to hit his name to call him back, when it starts ringing again.

"This had better be really fuckin' important," I snarl.

"I need you to come over," Emo states, his voice impassive.

"Why? This couldn't wait until later?"

"No. It's something you'll want to see."

I sit up in bed and swing my feet to the floor. "What is it?"

"Just get here and I'll show you," he answers evasively.

"Fine," I sigh. "Give me thirty."

I feel Eden moving behind me as I toss the phone on the night-stand. A moment later, her naked tits are plastered to my back, her arms go around my torso, and her hands flatten on my pecs. Her sweet lips press against the center of my back.

"Everything okay?"

"Hmm… I don't know. Emo wants to see me."

"Sounds serious," she remarks, pressing a kiss to my shoulder blade.

"Yeah."

I twist, forcing her to lean back, grab her waist, and haul her into my lap. She sits sideways across my thighs and her arms slide loosely around my neck. Her smile is sleepy and entirely way too pretty.

"Hi."

When I lean down for a kiss, she shakes her head, scrunches her nose, and covers her mouth. I cock a brow at her.

"I need to brush my teeth," she mumbles behind her hand.

Chuckling, I grab her wrist and yank it down. "Give me that mouth woman. I don't care about fuckin' morning breath."

Before she can protest further, I swoop down and give her a kiss that makes us both delirious with need. She's panting by the time I pull away, and it's apparent morning breath is no longer on her mind. Even my own breathing is labored.

"Legs around my waist, Gypsy. We're killing two birds since I don't have much time; a shower and sex."

Once she's situated with her legs tightly gripping my waist, I get us both up from the bed and haul her to the bathroom, where I eat her pussy, then fuck her against the shower wall.

FORTY-FIVE MINUTES LATER, because you just can't rush shower sex, Eden and I are walking through Emo's front door. Grace is in the kitchen. With a wave to Grace and a kiss to Eden, I leave the women and go to Emo's office. He's at his desk, reading over something on the monitor in front of him. He looks like shit, but I'm glad to see it's not as bad as the last time I saw him.

"What's going on?"

He gestures to the computer with his chin. "Come take a look."

I walk over and stop behind his chair. At first, I don't know what I'm looking at. It's just a bunch of jumbled medical terms. When I notice the name at the top of the screen though, I take a closer look. It's a medical record. On my father.

I read over the record. Then read over it again. My gaze slides to the doctor's name and address. It's a doctor's office in San Antonio. When I glance at the date, it confuses me.

"Where did you get this?" I ask Emo, reading the record for a third time. "This can't be right."

"There was a floppy disk shoved in between a couple of the tapes. It's all legit." He closes the record and pulls up another one. The name on this one is someone I've never heard of before. "The clinic and the doctor are real. And the signature is spot on." He points to the signature at the bottom on the screen. He's right, it matches perfectly with the one on my father's record.

"But it says my father had a testicular rupture due to an injury. One that couldn't be repaired through surgery. It made him infertile."

"Yes."

I grit my teeth impatiently. "Emo, this has to be a fake. The date on that is eleven months before I was born. I'm here, so apparently, my father could have children."

"Unless your father isn't really your father," he states quietly.

I've already thought of that, but it was so crazy the thought left my mind the moment it entered. I mean, yes, my parents were some twisted individuals because of their roles in Hell Night, but they appeared to genuinely love each other. Always affectionate, always declaring their love. They had stars in their eyes when they looked at each other, for fuck's sake. I can't imagine my mother ever cheating on my father. I also can't imagine my father being okay with her cheating and raising another man's child.

"It was obviously something they didn't want people to know," Emo continues. "That's why he saw a doctor outside of Sweet Haven."

"But why? And more importantly, who in the hell is my father?"

"I don't know, but I figured this was something you needed to know."

I drag my hands through my hair, frustrated with this new development. It doesn't really matter who my father was. Ninety-five percent of Sweet Haven's adult population participated in Hell Night, so the chances of one of the other sick fucks being my father is pretty high. I just want to know who it is so I can make sure he's dead.

"See what you can find out and get back with me." He nods and turns back to the screen. "How're the tapes going?"

His hands freeze on the keyboard, and I see the muscle in his jaw twitch. "I'm almost done." He types something then swivels in his chair to face me. "Do you remember Jenny's parents?"

I think back and vaguely remember the young couple. I don't remember their names, but their faces come to mind.

"I don't remember much about them, but yes, I remember them. Why?"

"So, you don't know what happened to them?"

"No."

He turns his back to me. "I don't remember them much either. But I do remember all of a sudden Jenny living with her aunt and uncle. I don't recall ever seeing them again after that." He pulls a video up on the screen. "Look at this."

He presses play and it takes the video a moment to focus. It's the hall, crowded with adults and children. I ignore the cries and wails and force my attention where Emo is pointing.

"That's Mick and Deanna, Jenny's parents. Watch them."

I lean down, because the quality is shit, and take a closer look, recognizing the two people at the coffee table-sized table. The angle isn't very good with them off to the side, but good enough to tell what's going on. Mick is at the end with his pants around his knees standing between Jenny's thighs. Deanna is at the head of the table, her face to the side of Jenny's, her hand running down Jenny's stomach. The sight makes my stomach twist in disgust, and I force back the urge to hurl.

Looking past the depraved behavior, I look at Deanna's face, which is turned to the camera. I lean closer and notice something. Deanna looks like she's… crying. There's a sheen on her cheeks, and it's not from sweat. Her expression is drawn tight and pained. Glancing at her hands, it looks like they're barely touching Jenny.

"Do you see it?" Emo asks.

Ignoring him, my eyes move to Mick. For all intents and purposes, he looks like he's having sex with his daughter. He has his hands on her thighs and his hips move back and forth, mimicking sex. There's just one small problem.

I look to Emo and he pauses the video. "He doesn't have an erection." It's not very noticeable because of the shadows and the grainy quality of the video, but if you look closely enough when he pulls back, you can tell the man is softer than a marshmallow. "Neither one of them wanted to be there doing what they were doing."

"Exactly," he puts in. "According to the date on this video and Jenny's birthdate, she had just turned the right age to fully take part in Hell Night almost a week prior. This would have been the final stage to complete her initiation. You'd think they would be foaming at the mouth to get to her after waiting so long. They aren't. They look like they're barely holding onto their stomachs."

"You said they disappeared and she moved in with her aunt and uncle. So, what happened to them."

It's more of a statement than a question. Emo and I were both twelve at the time Sweet Haven was raided, and according to the date on the video, this took place about a month before the town was taken down. Unless we were directly involved or overheard something, there's no reason why we would know what happened to Jenny's parents.

"People aren't allowed to leave Malus, so that only leaves one choice."

"They had to have been murdered," I voice our grim thought. "Question is, was it because of their less than enthusiastic participation or did they do something The Council didn't like. Regardless, they must have been murdered not long after this video, because the raid wasn't long after this happened."

"She was only five, but it might be a good idea to ask Jenny if she remembers anything."

I stuff my hands in my pockets. "I've got to drop Eden off at Judge's place for a couple hours so I can take care of a few things, but when I pick her up, I'll have a talk with Jenny. I'll also check the death records my parents kept. See if any of them are Mick and Deanna's."

Emo gives me a stiff nod before turning back to the computer monitor and closing out the paused video. After, we leave his office in search of the women, finding them where I left them in the kitchen. Eden has her hands wrapped around a coffee mug held close to her mouth.

"You ready to go?" I ask, walking up and lightly tugging on the end of her braid.

She moves toward the sink to dump the rest of her coffee, but I grab the cup before she can. "I'll finish it."

"It's hot," she warns, but I've already got it to my lips, tipping it back and swallowing the hot liquid.

She snorts and rolls her eyes, but they sparkle with laughter. "Men," she mutters. "They think they're so tough."

"Ain't that the truth," Grace adds, her own eyes dancing light-heartedly.

"That's because we are," I interject. "Right, Emo?"

His answer is a grunt as he walks to the coffee pot and pours his own cup.

"Besides," I set the cup in the sink and turn to snag Eden around her waist, "You women like us men being tough."

She shrugs. "Eh. Sometimes." She looks at Grace and winks before bringing her eyes back to me. "When it's convenient for us."

I chuckle and playfully smack her fine ass. "Hop to it, woman. I've got shit to do."

She sticks out her tongue, and I lean down to bite it, but she pulls away from before I can. With a giggle, she bids Grace and Emo goodbye.

"See ya later, Grace," I offer. My eyes slide to Emo, and we share a dark look before Eden and I leave.

What Emo showed me today may end up being nothing of importance. Both about my father not being my father and what happened to Jenny's parents. But some internal voice tells me otherwise.

I just need to find out what it is.

chapter nineteen

EDEN

WHEN WE PULL UP TO JENNY and Judge's house after leaving Grace and Emo, I turn in my seat and face JW. I feel incredibly happy right now, so I give him a silly grin. "I miss you already."

His laugh is light as he shakes his head. I'm glad to see the euphoria on his face. It's a big difference from the expression I saw when he first walked in Emo's kitchen after talking to him.

"Pretty corny, huh?"

He lifts his hand and separates his thumb and pointer finger by a fraction of an inch. "Just a bit. But I still like the meaning behind the words."

I jerk my chin down once. "Good, because they were true."

Still smiling, he pulls me to him by my braid until our lips meet. The kiss is heated and leaves me wanting so much more, but we're in a car in someone else's driveway.

"How long will you be?" I ask once we pull away.

"Couple of hours maybe. I've got paperwork I've been putting off."

"Okay." I hesitate for a moment. "Is everything okay with Emo?"

He turns his face away from me to stare out of the windshield. His expression changes from light and flirty to something dim and bitter.

"To be honest, I'm not sure."

I reach over and grab his hand. "Do you want to talk about it?"

He looks back at me and forces a smile. "I'll tell you later."

Picking up the hand I place on his, he brings it to his lips. Goose bumps form on my arm when his scruff rubs against the tender skin on the back of my hand. He hasn't shaved in a couple of days. The prickly hair on his face looks hot as hell on him, and I bet it would feel even better against my thighs.

Down girl, now's not the time.

"Pack your stuff. I want you to stay with me from now on while I'm home," he tells me.

"Are you sure?"

I really fucking badly want to stay with him, but only if he truly wants me there.

"I'm sure. I wouldn't have asked otherwise."

"Alright."

I get tugged to him for another scorching kiss, and this one leaves both of us breathless when we separate.

"You better go now before I put off that paperwork even longer."

Laughing blissfully, because that's exactly the way I feel, I get out of the car. At first, I stand there, wanting to watch him drive away, when I realize he's waiting on me to go inside. Such a gentleman sometimes. With a wave, I spin on my heel, practically bound up the steps, and hear JW pull away as I walk inside.

The TV's on, but Jenny's not in the living room. Judge's office door is closed, so I assume he's locked himself inside again. Dropping my purse and phone on the small table by the door, I go in search of Jenny. The kitchen is empty, so I make my way down the hallway to her and Judge's room, stopping by the door that leads outside and not finding her in the backyard either.

Their bedroom door is closed. I listen closely and don't hear any noise. Even so, I still tap on the door. I certainly don't want to barge in on them having sex. Besides, it's their bedroom, and you just don't waltz right in someone's bedroom without knocking.

When I don't get a response, I try again and get the same thing as the first time. Nothing.

Hmm… maybe she's in the shower or taking a nap. I go to Judge's office door and tap twice, wanting to let one of them know I'm home. When I still get no answer, I begin to worry. They both could be taking a nap, but I really don't see Judge being the take a nap kind of guy. Both his and Jenny's car are in the driveway, but where in the hell are they?

A creepy feeling forms in the pit of my stomach, and I walk back to the bedroom door. I press my ear against the wood and strain to listen. When I hear nothing, I grab the door handle, twist, and cautiously open the door, just in case they *are* having sex.

I know something's wrong the moment the air inside the room hits my nose. A sickenly sweet metallic scent, so strong I throw my hand up and cover my nose. Pushing the door open further, my stomach drops and my heart nearly explodes at the scene before me. Blood, so much it almost covers the entire white bed spread.

"Oh, God," I moan, tears blurring my vision, but not enough to miss the body sprawled out on the bed. "No, no, no."

A sob escapes my tight throat, then another and another, until my cries become hysterical. Her head is turned away from me, but I see the blonde hair and know that it's Jenny. Sweet and innocent Jenny. The pain of seeing my friend, a woman I barely knew, but one I was starting to care for, torn to shreds nearly brings me to my knees. Whoever did this, was ruthless and gruesome. There's blood everywhere. And not just blood, but *parts* of her, parts that are supposed to be *inside* her, are spread out around her decimated body.

My knees become weak, along with my stomach. Bile rises in my throat, and I swallow several times to try and force back the need to throw up.

I spin on my heel and leave the bedroom. JW. I need JW.

This is Diego's work. He warned me. He fucking warned me, but I ignored it, thinking JW would find him before he did anything else. He didn't give me enough time. Even if I did have the stupid chip, which I don't, he still didn't give me enough time. I should have had more time to come up with a plan!

Frantically, I look all over the place for my phone. Not on the kitchen island, not in the living room. Then I remember I put it on the table by the door with my keys. Scrubbing my hands over my eyes to clear my still watery vision, I pull up JW's number. I slide down the wall by the door and listen to the rings. Each one that buzzes in my ear without hearing his voice, I release a sob.

"Hey. I was just getting ready—"

"JW," I croak, completely breaking down. My sobs are loud and my chest rattles with them.

"Eden? Jesus, baby, what's wrong?" he asks, worry making his words come out fast.

"I-I-I," I stutter, unable to form the words, hating that I need to. "J-Jenny. She's, uh…" I cry harder. "Oh, God, JW, th-there's s-so much b-blood."

"Fuck," he curses. "Where are you?"

"I-in the living r-room. By the door." I wipe my nose with the back of my hand. "You n-need to come here."

"I'm on my way, Gypsy," he cajoles softly, but I don't miss the hard edge in his tone. "I want you to get up and go outside. I'm only a couple minutes away."

I sniff, but my nose is so stuffy from crying that it doesn't help. "Okay."

"Get up now and go outside."

I wobble to my feet, my stomach churning with sickness. It takes me a minute to get the door open because my hands are shaking so bad. I step outside, breathing in the fresh air, but I still smell the sick scent of blood. I swear it's seared into my nose hairs. I don't know if I'll ever be able to get rid of that smell.

"Are you outside, Eden?" JW's rushed voice sounds in my ear

"Y-yes."

I sit on the steps and hunch over, resting my forehead on my knees and hugging my legs with one arm. Not even a minute later, I hear JW's truck and look up. He's barely turned the motor off before he's sprinting up the driveway. As soon as he's within reach, I spring up from the steps and launch myself into his arms. I cry so hard and loud, I know I'll have a sore throat later. But I don't care. Jenny is inside with her guts torn from her body. Dead. All because of me.

A moment later, JW's got me by the shoulders and gently pulling me away so I'm forced to look at him.

"What happened? Where's Jenny?"

I swallow and squeeze my eyes closed. "She's in the bedroom," I whisper hoarsely. Fresh tears leak down my cheeks.

"Come on," he urges, turning me back toward the house.

"I can't!" I wail. "I can't go back in there. I can't see that again."

Dark eyes filled with several emotions—sympathy, pain, and rage to name a few—stare back at me in understanding. "Just into the house. I need to go see what happened. You can wait for me in the living room."

Nodding, I let him lead me back into the house. He takes me to the living room and sets me down on the couch before heading down the hall. I pull my feet up on the edge of the cushion, hug my legs, and bury my face in my knees.

"Jesus fucking Christ," I hear JW mutter.

I lift my head when I hear the front door burst open. Judge stalks inside, jaw tense and his eyes darting frantically around the room. When he sees me on the couch, he opens his mouth to say something, when JW walks back in the room.

"Judge—" he begins, but Judge interrupts him.

"Where is she?" he demands.

"Judge," JW tries again, "I don't think—"

"Where. In the fuck. Is Jenny," he booms. I flinch at the loud demand and squeeze my legs tighter, further into myself. More tears burn my cheeks.

JW's eyes narrow, but he gives Judge what he wants. "Bedroom."

He steps to the side just as Judge gets to him and disappears down the dark hallway. JW's eyes meet mine.

"Are you okay?" I nod weakly. "I need to…." His words drift off.

"Go to him," I croak through a dry throat.

He spins away just as a loud crash comes from the bedroom. I drop my head to my knees again and simply let my tears flow, my heart breaking even further at the utter pain I know Judge is going through. He may not love Jenny in the traditional romantic sense, and he may share his affections with other women, but there's no doubt he cared for her deeply. It didn't take long for me to see that.

Judge's roars echo off the walls and there's more thundering crashes. All I can do is sit there and listen. Listen to a man who seems so strong, tear apart his room because of his grief over losing someone important to him. Not only lose someone, but in such a cruel and hideous way.

JW's murmurs drift down the hallway, but I can't tell what he's saying. What can really be said in a situation like this? There's nothing that is comforting enough. There's nothing that can make a person feel better. There are no words that can make this right.

It's been at least ten minutes before JW and Judge come back into the living room. I cautiously cast my eyes at Judge, afraid his wrath will turn my way. If he holds me responsible for what happened, I wouldn't blame him. It is my fault. It's me who Diego wants. Jenny was just an innocent casualty in his sick need to get what he wants.

He stops in the center of the room and faces me, his eyes dark and carry a mountain of pain, but also filled with rage. JW comes to a stop between us. Not blocking Judge from me, but no doubt putting himself close in case he needs to step in. I don't think Judge would hurt me, but words can sometimes be just as painful as a blow to the face, oftentimes more so.

"Where's Benjamin?" Judge demands harshly.

I frown. "Benjamin?" I look to JW then back to Judge. "Who's Benjamin?"

"The guy I left with Jenny while I ran an errand." His answer is a biting growl.

"I was just getting ready to call you when you called me." JW inserts. "My phone was in the truck while we were at Emo's, and I missed Judge's text, telling me Benjamin was here. I wanted to warn you. You didn't see him when you got here?"

I'm shaking my head at the same time I say, "No."

Just at that moment, a loud bang comes from the kitchen, followed quickly by a low moan. I barely have time to blink before JW's rushing toward the kitchen with a gun I hadn't seen until now in his hand with Judge hot on his trail. I get up from the couch, suddenly fearful with the possibility that Diego's still in the house. It didn't even dawn on me that he could still be here. I wrap my arms around my middle and edge toward the wall by the hallway.

A moment later, JW and Judge are leading a guy out of the kitchen, his arms draped over their shoulders as he struggles to stand. He has blood running down the side of his face, dripping from his chin onto the floor. He looks to be in his early-to-mid-thirties. I assume this must be Benjamin.

I hold my place at the wall as the two men set the injured one down on the couch. He groans when his head thumps against the back.

"Eden," JW calls, and I glance at him. "Can you go to the kitchen, find a towel, and wet it for me?"

I nod and rush to do his bidding. Grabbing a dish towel from the drawer by the sink, I stick it under the spigot, and squeeze out the excess water before bringing it back into the living room.

"Trouble should be here any minute," JW is saying when I hand him the wet towel.

"What in the fuck happened, Benjamin?" Judge stands, glaring down at the man, his hands shoved deep into his pockets and his face a thunderous mask.

Benjamin's head is still lying against the back of the couch and his eyes are closed as JW begins to wipe away the blood. There's a huge gash that's left behind.

"I don't fuckin' know," he replies. "I was in the kitchen getting something to drink when the next minute it felt like a bomb was going off in my head."

"Jenny's dead," Judge says grimly. I bite my tongue to hold back the sobs wanting to break free again.

"What?" Benjamin explodes, knocking JW's hand away when he sits up quickly.

"Lay the hell back, you dumb ass," JW growls when Benjamin starts to list to the side from his sudden movement.

"Shit, shit, shit," Benjamin mumbles over and over again, following JW's orders because he has no choice. It's either that or pass out. He already looks like he's on the verge of losing the contents of his stomach.

"Yeah. Shit. She's fuckin' hacked to pieces on our bed." Judge spins away and reaches for the back of his head with both hands, gripping his dark strands and tugging roughly. A guttural growl rumbles from him.

"Son-of-a-bitch, Judge. I'm sorry." Benjamin rubs his hands down his pants, his expression full of remorse. "So fuckin' sorry."

Judge's back stiffens, but he doesn't turn back or say anything to acknowledge the apology.

I'm devastated for him. We may not know each other that well and it's not my place to offer condolences, especially given the reason behind Jenny's morbid death, but I still wish I could go to him and pull him into my arms; give him the soft comfort that normally only females offer. I don't think it would be well received though.

A car door slams outside. Judge stalks across the living room and meets Trouble, a black medical bag in his hand, at the front door. They exchange a few murmured words, Trouble's brows slashing into a frown as he listens to Judge.

"Take care of him," he grunts and jerks his chin in Benjamin's direction.

Trouble steps up to Judge and lays a hand on his shoulder. It shows how close they are when he doesn't knock his hand away.

"I'd like to take a look at Jenny first. See if there's—"

"There's nothing that can be fuckin' done, Trouble. He tore her Goddamn insides out." Judge slams his teeth together and hisses out a breath. "Just fuckin' take care of Benjamin."

After that, he walks out the front door, leaving it open in his wake. I watch him through the open doorway as he marches down the steps and stops in the front yard. His head falls forward and his shoulders droop, like they're holding the weight of the world and he doesn't have the strength to hold it any longer.

Trouble walks by me, his hand squeezing my arm in comfort as he passes by. As soon as he takes a seat on the coffee table in front of Benjamin, JW walks over to me.

"Jesus, you're as white as a damn ghost," he mutters, grabbing my hand and leading me to a chair. He forces me to sit and points a finger at me. "Stay there. I'll right back."

He leaves me and goes into the kitchen, reminding me of my search for Jenny a while ago. I never actually went into the kitchen; I just saw over the bar that it was empty. Or at least I thought it was. Benjamin was only a few feet away, and I didn't even realize it. Had it been Diego, even more destruction would have happened. I shiver at the thought.

JW comes back, holding a glass filled with amber liquid. I take it when he holds it out to me. I'm not a big drinker, but I make an exception this time. Anything to help numb the pain I'm feeling.

I drain the glass, coughing at the burn sliding down my throat.

"More?" JW asks, taking the glass from me.

"No, thank you."

Snagging me around my waist, he lifts me like I weigh nothing, spins to take my seat, and puts me down on his lap. He palms the back of my head and presses my face into his neck, and I'm only too willing to let him. I feel like a child being consoled by a parent.

The kind and comforting gesture brings more tears to my eyes. I don't want to cry anymore, not that Jenny doesn't deserve my tears.

I just want to be strong. Being strong is the only thing that will help me defeat Diego. But strength is the very last thing I feel right now. I feel weak and fragile and regretful. So much regret. Then comes the guilt. Not only for what Jenny went through, but because I'm throwing my own little pity party in my head. It's selfish. My feelings don't count right now.

The soothing feeling of JW's hand running up and down my back comforts me, and after a few minutes, my cries of sorrow become quiet hiccoughing sobs.

He pulls me away from his neck, and I want to protest. I'm not done leaning on him. "Are you okay?" He tucks a piece of loose hair behind my ear.

"I don't know." It's the only answer I feel comfortable giving.

"You aren't to blame for this, Gypsy," he says gently.

"I'm not—" He doesn't let me finish.

"Yes, you are. I see it in your eyes. You didn't do that to Jenny. Diego is the only one at fault here."

"He's right." I look up at Judge and find him only a few feet away, looking down at us. His face is pale and haggard. "That bastard did this, not you."

I'm shocked at first, because I thought for sure he would blame me.

"But if it wasn't for me, she would still be alive," I whisper through a throat thick with emotion.

"Doesn't matter. Don't you dare take this on your shoulders."

"You didn't know who he was when you started seeing Diego," JW says and I look at him. "You didn't ask to be a witness to the murder of that woman. You don't have that chip. And you certainly didn't perpetrate Jenny's murder. This. Is. Not. Your. Fault." He enunciates the last few words slowly.

I don't agree with either of them, but I nod anyway. I'll always feel guilty for what happened to Jenny, no matter what anyone says, but it makes me feel marginally better that neither JW or Judge casts blame my way.

I tuck myself back against JW's chest and let his steady heartbeat calm my raging one. If I knew JW would let me, I'd leave Malus tonight. The thought of someone else being hurt because of me has anxiety clawing its way into my lungs. So I don't think about it. I don't let it pull me under. I don't think about how it would be safer for everyone if I just left. It's pointless anyway, because I know JW *wouldn't* let me leave. And a big part of me is glad.

Although I would sacrifice the happiness I know I could have living here if it meant no one else would come to harm, I don't want to give up Malus or its people. But most importantly, I don't want to give up JW.

chapter twenty

JW

W E'RE ALL STANDING OUTSIDE. Eden is huddled against my side, my arm draped over her shoulder as she quietly cries against my chest. Judge is beside us with Trouble and Emo on his other side. We listen to Pastor Philips preach the graveside sermon, but I don't think any of us really hear him.

It's the typical funeral. A rainy day to match the dark, dismal, and somber mood everyone is in. We're all huddled underneath black umbrellas with our black formal clothes. The women cry softly, while the men comfort them with a gentle embrace. There's no coffin. Jenny wanted to be cremated. I remember her once saying the thought of her decaying body in the ground gave her the heebie jeebies. An open casket before her cremation was out of the question. The reason behind that still makes my blood boil. Jenny wasn't simply murdered. She was fucking slaughtered and gutted like a pig.

What separates Diego from all the other sick psychos out there who like to mutilate their victims is the fact that Jenny was alive when he started cutting into her. I don't know how Emo was able to come to that conclusion, but I don't doubt his findings. He's good at what he does. Another morbid fact about Jenny's death and what she went through the thirty minutes Diego was with her, and it turns even my stomach, is that before he sliced her from pubic bone to sternum is, he shoved that knife inside her privates. The blade, not the handle. When Emo shared that tad bit of information, Judge went ballistic. I've never seen that crazed look in his eyes before. There was damn near nothing left in Emo's living room that wasn't broken. It took me, Emo, and Trouble to calm him down, and even then, Trouble ended up with a black eye and Emo with a split lip. The only consolation was knowing that Jenny probably passed out from the pain of being raped by a knife, and that she more than likely wasn't conscious when he started slicing into her. I kept that bit from Eden, knowing she would only blame herself more if she knew the extent of Jenny's experience.

Pastor Philips finishes the sermon and after a few moments, the cemetery caretaker is lowering the small black box that contains Jenny's ashes into the ground. Judge kept a small urn with some of her ashes for himself. This brings on another round of silent sobs. The women behind us, Judge's other women, all huddled together and cry for the friend they lost.

After the cremation box is in the ground, people start to disperse, most leaving sedately in their cars and some sticking around to talk.

Mae walks over and pulls Judge's stiff body down for a motherly hug. "I'm so sorry, sweetie." He gives her a clipped nod and kisses her cheek. She turns to Eden, giving her a hug too. "How are you holding up?" Mae wasn't given all the details of Jenny's death, we decided to keep the more gruesome parts to ourselves, but she knows Eden was the one who found her.

Eden's eyes are sad as she flicks them to the hole in the ground.

"I'm okay."

She's not okay. She couldn't be further from okay. Using the tissue in her hand, she wipes under her red and swollen eyes. It's a good thing she's not wearing makeup because she'd look like a raccoon by now with all the crying she's done.

Mae's eyes are dull when she nods. "Everyone is gathering at The Hill. Will you two be there?"

Eden looks at me for an answer, but I stay quiet and leave the decision up to her.

"Yeah, we'll be there."

"Alright, honey. I'll see you there then."

She speaks with Emo and Trouble for a moment before turning to Jamie, Gillian, and Layla. Mae's never been a fan of Judge's choice in having multiple mistresses, but she's always been fond of the women.

"You want to go home and change before we go to The Hill?" I ask, because no matter how much you huddle under an umbrella in the rain, you always end up soaked.

Relief flashes across her face, mixing with the look that says she could use a nap, or ten.

"Yes, please. I think my toes have started a mud wrestling match in my shoes."

I grab her hand and pull her behind me. It's probably rude to just leave without saying goodbye, but I want to go before anyone stops us. Besides, we'll see everyone at The Hill later. I want to get Eden out of her damp clothes and into something warm. The temperature isn't too bad, but it'll be dropping once the sun starts going down.

We're both quiet during the short drive to my house. I hold her hand in my lap and her fingers clutch mine tightly, like she's scared to let go, or I'll let go. There's no chance of that. Maybe not ever.

She mumbles something about going to change and walks off toward the bedroom. I watch her go, her black knee-length dress a big contrast to what she normally wears. I don't like her in the drab clothes. She's only worn it for a few hours, but the minute she stepped into the living room earlier, I wanted to demand she go change. I like the soft, colorful, flowy skirts she wears. The bangles and hoop earrings were also absent. I missed the jingle the bangles made. And her hair? Her hair was in a Goddamn bun. A tight one at that. With no loose flyaway pieces.

I pull at my tie, loosening it, then yanking it off and tossing it on the couch. Walking into the kitchen, I snag the whiskey from the cabinet, pour some in a glass and throw it back, repeating it two more times as I lean back against the counter.

My thoughts drift back to Jenny and the death certificates of her parents I found the night she was murdered. She was five when they were killed. I wonder if she knew her parents were against the acts of Hell Night. Maybe it was just their own daughter they were against hurting. Emo couldn't find any more footage that showed the couple, or at least not close enough to tell their demeanor with what they were doing. Like I told Emo the other day, I don't remember them much, but I do remember seeing them a couple of times during Hell Night. I never really paid attention to them though. I was barely twelve when the FBI showed up in Malus. I was too young to pay much attention to other people during those nights. I was busy living my own hell.

It's all pointless now, because Jenny will never know. And that's a fucking shame, which makes me want to carve into Diego just a little bit deeper because of it.

I toss back another shot of whiskey before capping the bottle and putting it back in the cabinet. It's been twenty minutes since Eden went to the bedroom. I had her get her belongings the night Jenny was murdered and she hasn't been back to Judge's since. Seeing what she did, that shit stays with a person anyway, but I don't want her to have any reminders.

I hear the en suite shower going when I approach my bedroom door. Deciding to join her, I start on the buttons of my shirt. The bathroom is cracked open, and not wanting to startle her, I push it the rest of the way open slowly. Dread, anger, and torment take place in my stomach when I don't find her in the shower, but hunched over the sink, naked, her head bowed and her shoulders shaking.

She must sense me, because when I walk up behind her and wrap one arm around the front of her upper chest and the other around her mid stomach, she doesn't even flinch. I pull her back against me and her body sags, physically unable to hold herself up any longer. This is why I'm here. To be her strength when she has none.

Her broken sobs wreck me. The tears flooding down her cheeks make me feel helpless. I hate seeing her like this. I hate even more that I can't take her pain away.

I hold her as she purges out her sorrow through her tears. I don't say anything, because this is what she needs. Grief and sorrow are awful feelings and the only way to move past those emotions is to let them out, to give them an outlet. Only then can you start to move on. Eden will grieve for a long time, we all will, but we'll also eventually begin to heal.

Once her cries have quieted down, I take my arms from around her and pull the pins from her hair. She watches me with bleary eyes, her face red and her breath still stuttering. After I have the long locks loose and flowing down her back, I turn her to face me. Using my thumbs, I wipe away the dampness from her cheeks.

"Thank you." Her voice is hoarse and it breaks my heart even more.

"I haven't had a chance to tell you yet, but I spoke with Diego's father the day Emo and I got back to town. We had actually just left his house when I got the call from Judge telling me about Diego's call to you."

"What?" she squeaks. "What did he say?"

I clench my jaw and leash my temper. "He said he'd talk to Diego. Emiliano isn't stupid. He knows it's in his best interest to rein in his son, but apparently, Diego didn't heed the warning."

"I hate him. I hate him so much that I wish he would just die."

Guilt makes its way into her eyes at her confession. I'm glad she feels that way, because Diego will most certainly die a very painful death. Whether she wishes it or not. I keep that to myself. Wanting someone dead and them actually dying are two different things. It's easy to wish for someone's death. It's not so easy knowing they *will* die.

"Don't feel guilt for thinking that way, Gypsy. It's a normal reaction after everything he's done."

She bites her lip and tilts her head to the side. "Why do you call me that?"

"Because you remind me of one with the clothes, bangles, and the scarf you wear over your hair sometimes." She smiles a little, and I'm so damn proud of myself because of it. "And speaking of clothes, that shit you have on the bed is a no. I want you back in your skirts, light tops, and bangles."

"What about the scarf?" She quirks a brow.

I shake my head. "You may as well toss all your scarfs. If I see another one on your head, it'll be too soon."

She points her eyes to the center of my chest, morose once more. "I wear those clothes because they make me happy. I'm not really in the mood—"

I tip up her chin with my knuckles. "You can't let this change you, Eden. Jenny wouldn't want that. Grieve for her, miss her, but don't let what happened make you a different person."

She nods after a moment.

I bend down for a kiss and she rolls to her toes to meet me halfway.

"Get in the shower. I'm right behind you. Then we need to get to The Hill."

She gives me a half-hearted smile before walking into the shower. I make quick work of my clothes and follow behind her.

THE PARKING LOT IS SO FULL when we pull up to The Hill that we're forced to park along the road. Jenny was well loved by everyone in Malus. She was one of the few original children who stayed here after the raid, so everyone knew her. She was also one of the first people we told about how my brothers and I were going to handle assholes who like to hurt women and children. She was on board immediately.

I grab the umbrella from the back floorboard, get out, and walk around to Eden's side. It's cute how she huddles against me on our way to the entrance of The Hill so I won't get wet either. Not that I give two shits about getting wet, but the fact she worries I will, is sweet.

Leaving the umbrella on the stoop of the steps, we walk inside. The atmosphere is different than it was at the funeral. Light and less bleak. People are obviously still morose, but there're easy chuckles from the men and soft giggles from the women.

Spotting Trouble holding Elijah, and Remi over by Benjamin, I lead Eden in that direction. It almost makes me laugh at the look on Trouble's face and the tight grip he has around Remi's waist with his free hand. He doesn't care for Benjamin too much. Before he and Remi got together Benjamin showed interest in her. Ever since then, Trouble can't stand the guy.

When we walk up to the trio, I notice the haggard look on Benjamin's face. He's pale and looks like he's lost some weight. He also has dark circles under his eyes and his clothes are wrinkled to shit.

I feel sorry for the guy. No man wants to feel like a failure. Diego got the jump on him, and because of that, Jenny died. Not that anyone blames him. There wasn't anything he could have done to save her. He was passed out and bleeding from a gash bad enough to need stitches, for fuck's sake.

When we stop in the small circle they formed, Benjamin's eyes dart away from Eden and me.

"Hey, Eden. How are you holding up?" Remi asks, her eyes almost as red and swollen as Eden's still are.

She shrugs against my side. "Could be better."

Remi nods in understanding. "I still can't believe she's gone."

Eden sniffs, indicating she's on the verge of crying again, so I change the subject.

"You never officially met Eden," I tell Benjamin. "Eden, this is Benjamin. Benjamin, meet Eden."

They shake hands, and I notice Benjamin still doesn't look at Eden. He quickly withdraws his hand.

"It's nice to meet you, Benjamin. I just wish it was under different circumstances." She offers a sad smile.

"Yeah," he responds.

"How's your head?" she inquires.

He reaches up and fingers the bandage on his forehead. "Still hurts a little. It should have been worse," he finished on a mutter.

I look around the room. "Where's Leddy?"

Benjamin swallows thickly, his throat bobbing, and he shoves his hands into his pockets.

"With her mother. They're in San Antonio for several days visiting her family. I didn't want her to come to the funeral."

"Is that your daughter?" Eden asks.

"Yes."

Grace appears by my side holding two glasses in each hand by their bottoms.

"I figured you all could use a drink," she states and passes them around. We all take one, except Benjamin, who declines the offer and excuses himself.

"Where's Emo?"

Using the hand that's holding a glass, she points with her finger behind me. "Talking to Mae and Judge."

I glance back and see the three deep in conversation. Emo has his arms crossed over his chest, looking like his usual emotionless self. Judge has a couple days' growth of beard, something that you normally don't see on him. He's always impeccably dressed and groomed.

"He's done, by the way."

I turn back to look at Grace. "He told you that?"

She nods. "Yes. He watched the last one last night." She takes a sip of her beer, her eyes turning sad. "Because of what this Wednesday is, I'll be staying a few more days, but after that, I need a break."

I dip my chin in understanding. The woman's been through

Hell the last week, and it's only about to get worse. She never complains and is always there when he needs her. It's just another testament to how deep her feelings for him run. It's a shame, because Grace is a good woman. She'd be good for Emo. But that part of him was broken by his father when he was still a child. The only girl who could ever tame the darkness in him died by her own hands as a child.

"What's Wednesday?" Eden asks.

I look to Trouble and see his eyes darken in pain. Remi has her hand underneath Elijah, gently rubbing soothing circles on Trouble's stomach.

"The anniversary of my sister's death," he answers Eden's question.

She jerks her head around to look at Trouble, her eyes widening. "I'm so sorry."

"Don't be," he grunts. "It was a long time ago." He pauses for a moment. "Emo and Rella were close," he explains. "He never does well on the anniversary."

Her hand in mine tightens.

Elijah begins to fuss, and Remi turns and holds out her hands. "It's time for my little man to eat. Eden and Grace, you want to get a seat somewhere?"

"Sure." Grace drains her glass then holds the glass up. "I'm stopping by the bar for another. You want a refill?" she offers only to Eden since Remi still breastfeeds Elijah.

"I'm good."

The ladies walk off and Trouble and I head toward Judge and Emo. Mae's back behind the bar helping Doris and Meryl serve customers. When we make it to our brothers, Judge gestures for us to follow him down the hallway. Once we're inside the office that Mae, Doris, and Meryl share, he closes the door. Curious what this is about, I turn to face him, just as my brothers do the same. His eyes focus on me.

"I got a phone call from an old friend in Pennsylvania before the funeral. He's pretty sure he's found your mom and brother."

My back stiffens and the muscles in my neck cramp. "What?" I ask, because I want to make sure I heard him right.

He nods. "He won't be able to confirm for several days, maybe a week, but he's pretty confident."

All the air in my lungs whooshes out on a hiss. When I draw in my next breath, it's not only air that rushes through me, but pure, raw rage. It fills me up so fucking fast that I become dizzy with it.

It's been almost twenty-four years since I've set my eyes on my mother, father, and brother. My father died in the raid, but my mother and brother managed to escape. I've hunted them for years and have never come up with even a smidgeon of a clue as to where they might be. Every year that went by without any word of their whereabouts, made my anger grow.

The bones in my fingers creak and pop from clenching my fists so hard. Blood rushes to my head furiously. I want them now. I want them in front of me. I want to see the blood drain from their faces as the man they hurt as a boy stands before them, knowing he's about to take their lives. With not once ounce of mercy.

"Where are they?" I demand, my voice sounding demonic even to my own ears.

"You'll get that information when it's been confirmed."

"Judge," I growl, "So help me God, give me what I fuckin' want."

He straightens his spine and it only pisses me off more. "Not until it's confirmed."

I take a step toward him, ready to rip his head off, when Trouble steps in front of me. He places a firm hand against my chest. I glare down at it before shooting my eyes to his.

"A few more days won't make a difference, JW," he says. "It's better to know for sure before you take off. Besides, Eden needs you here right now."

It's Eden's name that cools me down enough to think properly. She needs me to protect her. I can't leave right now even if I did have the address of where my bitch of a mother and bastard brother have been hiding out, in my hand.

It's in that moment that I realize that Eden is more important than my vengeance. The pain of something happening to her, of Diego getting his hands on her and gutting her like he did that girl and Jenny, far outweighs my anger toward my mother and brother.

"As soon as I have the confirmed address, I'll give it to you," Judge says, stepping forward. "If you don't want to wait and Diego hasn't been dealt with yet, I'll personally watch over Eden twenty-four seven. I'll even sleep in the same bed as her."

He's joking, which is strange coming from Judge, because the man doesn't have a humorous bone in his body. He would never touch her inappropriately, and Eden wouldn't allow it either, but even joking around about it still pisses me off.

"Fuck you," I grit out.

His lips twitch and the tension leaves the room; or it does Judge anyway. I'm still tense as fuck. Knowing Diego is still out there and then finding out I'm real damn close to finding my mother and brother sends my anxiety through the roof.

I'm close. So damn close to finding all three of them that I can practically feel it slithering down my spine.

chapter twenty-one

JW
The Past

I PRESS MY EAR TO DAD'S *office door and listen carefully as Mom, Dad, and Trey talk. I'm supposed to be in bed when I came downstairs for something to drink and heard their voices. I'd get yelled at for being up, so I keep as quiet as I can.*

"I think it's time too, Robert. He's six. Trey's waited long enough," Mom says. She's using her soft voice. The one I like. The one that makes me want to believe she's a good Mom. She's not though. She lets people touch me in places they aren't supposed to, so she can't be a good Mom, right?

"The others aren't going to like it," Dad warns.

"Doesn't fucking matter. He's mine, and I want him," Trey growls.

A shiver races down my spine at the anger in his voice, and I swallow hard. They haven't said my name, but I know they're talking about me. My brother scares me. The way he looks at me sometimes makes me feel the same way I did the one time I ran across a rattle snake in our back yard. My stomach drops, I begin to sweat, and all I want to do is run away. I told Mom about it one day, and she just laughed at me and said my imagination was too active. I don't think it is. I think Trey wants to hurt me.

I told Judge, Emo, and Trouble about it too, and they said they'd protect me, but Trey's a lot older and a lot bigger than them, so I don't think they'll be able to stop him if they tried.

"You need to let the other adults know they can't touch him anymore. I won't allow it. He's mine from now on, starting at the next Gathering."

"Trey—" Dad begins, but my brother's hard voice cuts him off.

"No, Dad. I'm not sharing. I waited like you asked. I'm done waiting. Tell everyone else whatever you have to. I don't care."

My mouth starts watering like it does when I'm getting ready to throw up and my teeth begin to chatter. I know what he's talking about. Hell Night. The night my parents let some of the other adults touch me and do things to me and make me do things to them. Things I hate doing and things that make me feel sick to my stomach. No matter how much I begged my mom and dad or cried for the adults to stop, they wouldn't. They'd just say that it was okay. That they were supposed to do those things.

Trey says he doesn't want others to touch me anymore, but does that mean he wants to? He's never touched me during Hell Night, but I've seen him watch others while they do so. I hate it. And I think he hates it too, because he always looks like he wants to hurt them. I'm scared when Trey does touch me, it'll be worse than all the others.

While I'm thinking all this, they must have stopped talking, because I can't hear their voices anymore. Footsteps thump across the floor, coming toward the door. Fear has me backing up, and I almost trip. I stayed too long. I won't be able to make it upstairs before someone sees me. I turn around to run anyway, when a hand reaches out and grabs my arm.

I try to yank my arm back, but he won't let me go.

"What are you doing up, little brother?" he asks. When his finger starts rubbing over my wrists, I get that tight feeling in my throat again like I'm going to puke.

"I was thirsty."

"Bet you heard me, Mom, and Dad talking, didn't you?"

I shake my head hard, not wanting him to know I did hear them.

He lets go of my wrist but comes closer to me. He's so much taller than me that I have to tilt my head way back to look at him. Using the same hand, he runs his fingers through the hair on top of my head, his head tilted to the side giving me a strange look.

"You know you can't lie to me," he says. "I know you heard."

I try my best to be a big boy and blink my tears away, but I'm really scared and one falls down my cheek. He uses his thumb to wipe it away and then put his finger in his mouth. He gets down on his knees in front of me. Even like that, he's still taller than me.

"You know I love you, Liam, don't you?" he asks.

My lip begins to wobble, but I nod anyway. Trey loves me, Mom and Dad love me, the other adults love me, but if they truly did, would they really hurt me like they do?

He pulls me to him until we're hugging. I put my arms around him because I worry he'll get angry if I don't. Something pokes me in the stomach and I try to wiggle away from it, but Trey's arms are too tight around me. He groans in my ear, and I wonder if he's hurt.

He puts his hands on my butt over my pajama bottoms. I squeeze my eyes shut, wishing he'd move them away. Instead he begins to rub my butt. Something wet touches my neck, and I realize it's his tongue. He groans again and this time I know it's not because he's hurt.

"Next week, at The Gathering, I'll be able to show you just how much I love you, little brother. I've waited a long time to show you." His voice is deep and sends goosebumps over my skin.

"Release him, Trey," Dad barks. I look up and find him and Mom standing behind Trey. "You're getting what you wanted, but you'll wait until next week. You know how it works. We reserve these things for The Gathering. That's the only night that it's not a sin."

Trey kisses my neck before letting me go. He gets up and turns to face Dad, his eyes barely open as he looks at him angrily. Trey's not a kid anymore. He's nineteen, so he's an adult and can do whatever he wants, but he still keeps quiet.

I'm grateful my dad stopped him, but it makes me sad. He only did because it wasn't Hell Night and not because he cares.

Mom's eyes keep flickering between all of us. She opens her mouth like she wants to say something, but she doesn't.

"Go on up to bed, Liam," Dad instructs, his eyes never leaving Trey.

"Yes, sir," I mumble and run up the stairs.

As I crawl into bed, two feelings have my body shaking.

The first is relief that I'm no longer downstairs where Trey is.

The second is fear, because I know when Hell Night gets here, I'll be hurting more than I ever have before.

chapter twenty-two

EDEN

"SO, TELL ME THREE THINGS about yourself that most people wouldn't know," JW says as we drive through town. He decided to take me with him today, and I couldn't have been more pleased. It gives me the chance to get to know him more. See him while he works. Of course, in a town this size, there's not much that goes on. But that's okay. I'd rather him have a boring day with no crime than have him out fighting dangerous criminals on the regular.

Apparently, by his question, he's taking advantage of our time together as well, which brings a secret smile to my face. I love that he wants to know more about me.

"Hmm... let's see." I tap my finger against my lips as I think. "I always eat the chocolate chips first in mint chocolate chip ice cream. And it has to be the Breyer's brand, because they make the best." I roll my eyes upward and try to come up with something else. "I have an addiction to coffee cups. Three of my cabinets back home are full of them, and I have four more boxes in the attic."

"Jesus," he chuckles and shakes his head. "Why in the hell would you need that many coffee cups? There's no way you can use them all."

I shrug. "I don't know. I just like them, and I rotate them out, so they do all get used eventually."

He grunts, but his lips twitch. "And number three?"

"I don't have a favorite color."

He lifts a brow and moves his eyes from the road long enough to send me disbelieving look. "A woman without a favorite color? Aren't all girls supposed to have a favorite color?"

"Well, I guess I technically do. Right now, it's baby blue, but next week it'll be something different. My favorite color changes all the time."

"Why?" he asks, laughing lightly.

"It changes when I see something I really like. Whatever color that is, is my new favorite color."

He pulls up to a stop sign and looks over at me. "And what did you see that's baby blue that made it your new favorite color for the week?"

I look away from him, my cheeks heating with embarrassment. I really don't want to answer that question. It'll sound silly and childish. He reaches over and laces our fingers together, putting our conjoined hands on the center console.

"Gypsy?" he calls, and I can't help but slide my eyes his way. He already knows. I can tell by the softness in his gaze, but he wants me to say it anyway.

Clearing my throat, I confess, "It's the color of your eyes."

His grin starts on one side and slowly creeps across the rest of his face. He has on a pair of sunglasses, which is a shame in this moment, because I can't see his eyes.

"Yeah, I know. Corny, right?" I ask, my already red cheeks turning a shade darker.

"Not at all." He lifts my hand and kisses the back of it. "*This* actually may be corny, but that's one of the nicest things a woman has said to me. And I have to say, I really fuckin' like that your favorite color is the same color as my eyes."

My embarrassment slides right off my face, and I smile big at him.

"Now, give me those lips."

He snatches off the sunglasses, tosses them on the dash, he tugs me across the console, and he meets me halfway. It's not a hard kiss, but one that's soft and sweet and sends flutters to my stomach. I let out a sigh against his lips and we lazily stroke our tongues together.

All too soon, there's a catcall from outside the truck. We pull away but don't lean back in our seats. We stay only centimeters apart and look at each other. The color that I just mentioned in his eyes, changes. It's no longer the pretty baby blue, but a darker hue. More like steel, which is just as pretty, and probably my second favorite color.

There's another jeer and JW's eyes narrow as he turns in his seat, rolls down the window, and yells, "Fuck off, Aaron, and mind your own damn business."

The man, who's barely a man and has to be in his early twenties, just snickers with a couple of other guys standing with him. "Shouldn't the sheriff know he's not allowed to make out in public? Didn't you just bust me and Lisa last week for doing the same thing?"

"I'll be busting you in another way if you don't get going the hell on your way," JW throws back. The words are growled, but his eyes give off amusement.

"We're goin', we're goin'. I just had to give you shit," Aaron yells back.

"Time and place, and now ain't the time nor place."

With a chuckle, Aaron gives JW a two-finger salute as he and his crew walk off.

"Dipshits," JW mutters, and I can't help but giggle. He gives me a look that suggests I may be losing my mind, which only turns my giggles into laughter.

He grabs my hand again, pulls it to his lap, and eases his truck forward.

"So, what about you?" I ask.

"What about me?"

"Tell me three things about you that most people might not know."

He's quiet as he thinks over my question.

"I've never told anyone that I love them," he says quietly, thoughtfully.

His statement shocks me for several reasons. First, he has to be in his early-to-mid-thirties. How could he have lived for so long and not said those words to anyone? It makes me incredibly sad for him. Second, why would he tell me that? It's scary to even contemplate, but is that how he feels about me? Is he trying to say something without actually saying it? Third, I'm surprised at the violent urge I have to wrap my hands around someone's throat and squeeze as hard as I can. There's no doubt in my mind that it stems from his childhood. Those dirty bastards fucked with JW in more ways than one.

"Really?" I can't keep the disbelief from my tone.

"Nope," he answers casually, like it's no big deal when it's a huge one. I mean, I don't expect him to have just thrown the words to just anyone, but surely there has been someone he loves.

"Not even to your brothers?"

He side-eyes me as one corner of his mouth quirks up. "I love them, but we're brothers, Gypsy. Men don't tell each other they love them."

"Eh, I guess they don't. Not that there would be anything wrong if they did," I tack on. I'm not the type who thinks men are weak for talking about their feelings. "What about Mae?"

"Mae knows I love her. She doesn't need me to say it."

I almost say that sometimes people just need to hear those three little words, but decide to keep that to myself.

"Why? If you feel it, why don't you say it?"

The hand that's gripping the steering wheel turns white as he grips it harder. "Growing up, love was used as an excuse to hurt children. I'm not real fond of using the word now."

My throat constricts. What I wouldn't give to have the opportunity to give his parents a piece of my mind.

His phone rings through the speakers and he lets my hand go to press the *Answer* icon on the screen on his dash.

"Sheriff Ward."

"Cliff and Dorothy are at it again," an older woman says through the speakers. "She whacked him with a broom and he fell. He busted the back of his head open. Trouble's on his way, but I figured you'd want to be there too."

"Fuckin' hell," JW grumbles. "I'm on my way. Thanks, Rita."

He hangs up, and I grab the oh shit handle above my head as he does a U-turn in the center of town.

"What was that about?" I relax back in my seat once he straightens the truck.

"Cliff is an old grouchy bastard who keeps doing stupid shit to his neighbor. The both of them are stubborn as hell and can't get their shit together."

As we drive, he tells me about Cliff losing his wife six years ago and about him turning to alcohol to help with his grief. My heart aches for the old man. He said when Cliff's drunk, he becomes unreasonable and blames his neighbor Dorothy for the leaves that fall into his yard from her tree. I barely hold back my laugh when I imagine an old man raking those leaves up in a trash can lid, only to dump them in her yard. It's not a laughing matter, but then again, it's so ridiculous, it kind of is. JW also explained his belief that the reason Cliff is the way he is when he's drunk is out of guilt for caring for another woman who isn't his wife. Minus the leaf dumping part, the whole thing is incredibly sad. I can't imagine loving someone for so many years and then all of a sudden not be there anymore.

When we pull up to a brick house a few minutes later, Trouble's truck is already in the driveway.

"I can wait here?" I suggest.

He doesn't answer. Just gets out, walks around to my side to open the door, and grabs my hand.

"Cliff won't care."

He taps his knuckles against the door once before going inside. A strong scent of pine hits my nose.

Trouble's at the couch with an older man lying down on his side with the back of his head facing him. Trouble's dabbing something on Cliff's head. An older woman is hovering over them both. She's frowning and there's no mistaking the worry on her face.

"How is he?"

"Bleeding like a bitch." He casts a glance to who I assume is Dorothy. "Sorry," he mutters. "It's not bad. It's a head wound and they always bleed profusely. Not to mention the alcohol in his system has thinned his blood."

JW shoots Dorothy a wink before turning to Cliff as Trouble helps him sit up. "You done with this foolish behavior?"

"You hush it, boy," he grumbles.

JW rocks back on his heels, his lips twitching. "You wanna press charges against Dorothy?"

"Are you fuckin' stupid? I ain't pressin' no charges, you dummy," Cliff growls angrily.

JW laughs. "I'm not the dumb one."

Dorothy comes to sit beside him. She grabs his frail hand in her equally frail one. "I'm sorry, Cliff," she says with sincerity. "This is all my fault. I shouldn't have hit you with a broom.

JW snorts and Cliff shoots him a dirty look before looking at Dorothy.

"Nah. I shouldn't have been throwing those leaves in your yard. You were only protecting your property."

From the deepening frown, Cliff's words don't appease Dorothy.

"Apparently, the alcohol has worn off because he'd never admit that he was wrong."

He casts JW another contemptuous look at his quiet words. "If you're here to cart me off to my cell, get it over with."

JW's right. The man isn't acting drunk at all. His speech is too good and his eyes are as clear as glass.

"Nope. Just came by to make sure your stubborn ass doesn't do anything else moronic."

I'm surprised when Cliff, a man who has to be in his seventies, pulls off an immature stunt by using his middle finger to scratch his cheek. I laugh. There's no way I can't *not* laugh at the silly behavior.

My laughter pulls his eyes to me. "Who's the lady?"

JW tosses his arm over my shoulder. "This is Eden. She's visiting for a while. Eden, meet Cliff and Dorothy."

I wave. "It's nice to meet you both."

Cliff grunts his greeting while Dorothy smiles and offers her hand. "It's good to meet you too."

"Am I going to get called out here again in a few days?"

Cliff rubs the back of his head, like he's embarrassed. I can't be sure, but I think he mutters "asshole" before he looks back at JW.

"I'm done. I'm pouring my alcohol stash down the drain. If my yard fills with her leaves, then so be it."

"'Bout Goddamn time," he mumbles. I elbow him in the ribs and he just shrugs.

"Alright, fun's over," Cliff announces. "Get the hell out of my house. It's about time I feed my woman some lunch."

"Excuse me?" Dorothy asks, her eyes darting to Cliff in surprise. She's very pretty, and I'd bet she was a knock out back in her day.

"You heard me woman." He stands up and grabs her by the elbow to help her up beside him. "You've been mine since that cheating bastard of a husband you had kicked the bucket two years ago. Before that even. I've just been too stupid to say it. I ain't stupid no more. Those leaves I hate so much won't matter any longer, because I've decided you're moving into my house. You sell your house, but I'm cutting that tree down before you do."

My brows jump up at his demand.

"Well, I never," Dorothy sputters, her hand flying to her necklace and fingering it. "You have lost your mind Cliff Levins. You can't demand I move in with you."

His eyes narrow and it takes iron will to not laugh at the two old people bickering back and forth.

"The hell I can't. I'm old and you ain't much younger than me."

I wince at his implication that Dorothy is old. Doesn't he know you're never supposed to say that about a woman? Especially to her face?

"You're an asshole," Dorothy throws at him in a high-pitched voice.

"Yep, sure am. But I'm an asshole who's claiming what's his. I ain't wasting anymore years, because I don't got much left. That fall made me realize somethin'." He steps closer to Dorothy, his gaze softening. "Betty would do more than just hit me upside the head with a broom with the way I been treatin' you. She would also want me to grab whatever happiness I had left. That's exactly what I plan to do. Having you will make me happy. You bein' in my house would make me happier. And don't even try denyin' it won't make you happy too. We need to make the best of the time we got left."

Okay, so the man isn't as stupid as I thought he was. I damn near melt at his words and they weren't even directed at me. I hold my breath and wait for Dorothy's response, secretly hoping she'll give in. What Cliff said sounds barbaric, but at the same time sweet. How can you fault an old man for wanting to spend the rest of his days with someone he cares for? If you have a heart, you simply can't.

"I'm not cutting down my tree," she persists stubbornly.

Cliff's serious expression morphs into a playful one. "Fine, but I ain't raking the yard. We can hire someone."

After a moment of silence, she slowly nods. Without warning, Cliff drops his head and kisses her. It's not a simple peck on the lips either. It's a full-on, lips, tongue, and soft moaning kiss.

"And that's our cue to leave folks," JW says, already turning me toward the door. "That's something I sure as shit don't need to see."

Trouble and I both laugh as we walk down the steps toward the trucks.

"I think it's sweet," I interject.

"What he *said* was sweet. What he's *doing* to Dorothy is disturbing."

"They're flesh and blood, just like the rest of us."

"Yes, but they're old. Old people don't do shit like that."

With a chuckle, Trouble waves goodbye as he gets in his truck. JW opens the passenger for me to climb inside. When he gets in behind the wheel, I ask, "So, you won't be doing that with your wife when you're that old?"

He starts the truck but doesn't pull away from the curb. His eyes jump merrily when he looks at me. "Oh, I'll be fucking my wife until the day I die or until I can't get it up anymore. And even when I can't, I'll still be fucking her in ways other than with my dick."

I snort and shake my head. "You're so crass."

He wiggles his eyebrows. "Crass maybe, but no less true."

I roll my eyes. "Just drive, you deviant."

With a chuckle, he pulls away from the curb.

chapter twenty-three

JW

"HOLY FUUUCK," I GROAN, my eyes closing in pure bliss. "It's like my mouth just had an orgasm or some shit."

Eden chokes on a laugh, her eyes bugging out and her mouth falling open. She slaps my arm with the back of her hand. "JW, really?"

"I'm not kidding." I stuff my mouth with more of the gooey orgasmic goodness, giving not one fuck that my teeth are covered in chocolate when I flash her a grin.

"That is so disgusting," she says, wrinkling her nose.

"What in the hell are these things?" I shove another brownie looking thing in my mouth. Fuck it, I'm going to be fat because of these things, and I don't even care.

She looks damn proud of herself when she answers. "They're called crinkles. It's my mom's recipe."

"Oh no you don't," I reprimand as I scoop up Piper before she can climb on the table and investigate. "I'm stingy. You can't have any."

Eden giggles as I set Piper back down on the floor and throw the squishy ball with a bell inside across the room. She scampers off after it.

I take a big gulp of milk, and damn if it doesn't make the crinkles taste even better. "What else you got?"

She pushes another plate toward me, and I snatch up what looks like a hunk of chocolate. "It's chocolate peanut butter fudge. Another of my mom's recipes."

I take a bite and fall even further into sugary heaven. I'm normally not a sweet eater, but this stuff is too damn good to resist.

"Damn you, woman." I look at the chunk of half-eaten fudge in my hand. "I'm going to end up with diabetes because of you."

She giggles again, looking pretty pleased with herself.

"What's up with all the sweets?" I ask, nodding my head toward the rest of the dishes on the counter filled with all kinds of sweet shit.

Her smile loses its luster and she shrugs. "I bake when I get nervous or upset. It keeps my mind occupied."

I drop the rest of the fudge on the plate, lick my fingers clean, and snag her chair with my foot. When she's close enough, I grab her up from the chair by her waist and plant her ass across my lap. One arm goes around my neck and she presses her other hand on my chest.

"Look at me," I say firmly. Once I have her eyes, I tuck some loose hair behind her ear. "Don't let that asshole do this to you, Eden. He's not worth one second of your worry. We'll catch him and he'll be dealt with accordingly."

"What does that mean exactly? He'll be dealt with? What are you going to do?"

I hold her stare and fight with myself on what to tell her. In the end, I leave it up to her.

"Don't ask questions you don't want the answers to, Gypsy. You might find they aren't something you can handle."

Her eyes slide away from mine and she chews on her bottom lip, her brows dropping into a frown. After a moment, she straightens her spine and looks back at me, conviction written on her face. "I want to know," she says determinedly.

Her bravery would make me smile if the situation wasn't so

dire. The answer to her question isn't simple, and it's not one I should give. It's dangerous and has the potential to be hazardous to my brothers and myself. It's an answer that could be our downfall, but for some inexplicable reason I trust her with it.

I tighten my arms around her waist and give her the truth. "He'll die. By mine and my brother's hands."

It's not shock I see on her face. It's not disbelief or contempt or even fear. No, her eyes light up with interest, like the idea isn't one she's against, but one she actually agrees with. For some reason, I expected this response from her. Eden doesn't have a vindictive bone in her body, but with *this*, I knew she would be on board.

"How will you do it?"

I clench my jaw and blow out a harsh breath between my teeth. "That's something you don't need to know." She opens her mouth to ask again, but I cut her off. "No, Gypsy."

Her lips clamps shut and her shoulders fall an inch. "Okay," she says quietly. "But can you answer one question?" I keep quiet. "Will it be painful?"

"Extremely," I answer gravely.

She nods, her expression fierce. "Good."

"It doesn't bother you that I plan to kill Diego?" I ask, looking at her curiously.

A wrinkle appears between her eyes, giving away her uncertainty. Her gaze moves to her hand resting on my shoulder.

"I know it should." She looks back to me. "But with Diego…. What he's done, the pain he's caused; to me, to the people who live here, and Lord only knows who else, the damage I have no doubt he'll continue to inflict…. He needs to be stopped. He needs to atone for what he's done. And he and his father have got too many people in their pockets. He'll never see the inside of a cell."

She's right. The chances of Diego spending time behind bars is slim to none. But it wouldn't matter. The man doesn't need to sit in a cell and reap what he's sewn. He'll never regret his actions, only that he was caught. He'll never rehabilitate. He'll serve his sentence, be released, and do the same shit over and over again.

Fuck. That.

Diego will pay for what he's done in a way that's fitting. In a way he *will* regret his crimes. He'll be given just as much mercy as he gave his victims. Not one fucking ounce.

My phone chimes an incoming text and Eden startles in my lap from the sudden sound. I snatch it off the table and pull up the message from Judge.

Judge: It's been confirmed. We have an address.

I damn near crush the phone in my grip when I read his text. As it is, it creaks in my palm. He doesn't need to elaborate. I know exactly what he's talking about; my bastard brother and bitch mother. He has the address where they are. After years of searching for them, they're right there at my fingertips. *Right fucking there.*

Eden shifts in my lap. "What's he talking about?" she asks, and I lift my eyes from the phone.

And I can't do a Goddamn thing about it. Not right now anyway. Not until I know Eden is safe. I glance down at my phone and grit my teeth as I type out my reply, because this shit is hard. I want to jump up right now and hunt the bastards down, but Eden is too important. I can't leave her.

Me: Don't give it to me yet. I'll let you know.

I toss my phone on the table and circle my arms around Eden's waist again.

"JW?"

My hand shakes when I pick up the end of her braid and twirl it around my finger. My body radiates with the knowledge that my past is almost resolved. That I'm so close to closing the door on that part of my life.

"It's my mother and brother," I tell Eden. I twirl her hair tighter around my finger. I watch as the tip turns red as it fills with blood. "Back when Malus was Sweet Haven, my brother was the one who took me most of the time during Hell Night." She sucks in a sharp breath and my eyes move to her. "I don't know what I did to make him hate me, but he was always mean and unforgiving during those times. He was older than me by thirteen years, so my parents had no control over him by then, but they always let him have me. I was his fuck toy, and they just watched. Didn't matter what he did or how rough he was, he had full rein over me. It was different every other day. He wasn't particularly nice, but he wasn't cruel either. On the occasions when he did show his darker side, my parents acted like real parents and protected me from him."

Her fingers dig into the muscle in my shoulder. The bite of pain distracts me from some of the anger building inside me.

"What about your father? You said it was your mother and brother."

"He died during the raid. The stupid bastard pulled a gun on one of the agents while my brother and mother were escaping out the back door. They shot him. Or that's what the reports say." I tip my chin over her shoulder. "He died right over there."

Her eyes widen as she turns and looks into the living room. "This is your childhood home?"

"Yes. When my brothers and I came back we took back our childhood homes, but we had them gutted and remodeled. None of them resemble what they were."

My phone chimes again, but I don't pick it up this time.

"They got away that night. I've been searching for them for twelve years."

Her voice is quiet when she guesses correctly, "And Judge just found out where they are?"

I give her a clipped nod and loosen her hair from around my finger.

She tilts her head to the side, assessing me with fierce green eyes. "You plan to kill them, don't you?"

There's no point in denying it. She already knows I plan to kill Diego. What's adding two more to my list of crimes?

"Yes."

Her lips purse and she gives me a short nod.

"You know," I start and rub the end of her braid down her arm. She shivers in response. "You're kind of ruthless. I wouldn't have expected that from someone like you."

She arches a brow. "Someone like me?"

"You're tough, Gypsy. I have no doubt about that, given what you've been through with Diego. But you have this sweetness about you that portrays innocence. Almost like a purity that shouldn't be tarnished with the harsh realities of life."

She shifts in my lap so she's facing me better.

"I may appear that way, but I'm far from innocent. I grew up in San Antonio and not on the best side of town. My parents didn't have a lot, so they didn't have a lot to give me. I had what I needed, and I had their love, which was enough for me. No matter how much they tried to shield me, I still saw the cruelties in life. I just refused to let it be a part of mine. Life can be ugly and it can be downright nasty at times. It's left to the good people to fix those parts that the assholes of the world have destroyed. Murder is wrong, no matter why it's doled out or who it's against, but I recognize in dire circumstances, it may be a necessary evil."

She squeaks when I pick her up, put her to her feet, and spin her to face me, her hands landing on my shoulders. Starting with the material at her knees, I grip it and start pulling it up. Once the end of her skirt reaches the bottom of her thighs, I pull her forward until she's straddling my lap.

"You're pretty fuckin' spectacular," I admit. When her ass meets my thighs, I push her skirt further up her legs until her pussy is just barely hidden from my hungry eyes. The soft blue material of her skirt pools down around our legs.

She tilts one side of her mouth up and her eyes sparkle in delight. "You're not so bad yourself."

That makes me grunt. "Not so sure you'd be sayin' that if you knew the things I've done."

She rakes her fingers through the hair on the top of my head and leans closer. "We'll have to agree to disagree, because something tells me what you may think of yourself would be completely different from what I think of you."

Fuck, but this woman does me in. I tell her I'm going to kill a man, then tell her I'm going to kill my mother and brother, and on top of that, all but admit to committing whatever other crimes her mind could conjure up, and she thinks I'm good. What kind of person does that? Only someone with a pure soul and wholesome heart.

I pull her down to me by the back of her neck. Taking her lips, I kiss her like a starved man. Because that's what I am. I'm starving for the taste of her. Hungry for the touch of her. Ravenous to possess her and devour her and make her mine until she wants nothing else except me.

She tastes like chocolate and paradise and Eden. An aphrodisiac combination that I wish I could bottle up and carry around in my pocket so I could have it anytime I wanted. This woman drives me crazy but makes me more sane than I've ever been.

Her hand is still in my hair and she digs her fingers against my scalp when I bite down on her lip. I growl and yank her toward me by her hips. Her warm center, covered only in a pair of silky panties, meets my stiff cock. I flex my hips upward at the same time I grind her down against me.

She rips her lips away from mine and throws her head back on a low moan. My eyes zero in on the slender column of her throat, and that's where my lips go next. I suck, nibble, and lick up her neck, leaving behind little red marks from the bristly hair on my cheeks and chin. I fucking love knowing she'll be marked up by me.

I lean her backward until her spine meets the edge of the table. Her eyes open slowly, the beautiful greens much darker than normal. Her shirt is flimsy, so it doesn't take much to yank it down until her breasts pop out. I thank my lucky stars, because she's not wearing a bra.

Her breasts are exquisite. Perfect in size—not too big, just the right plumpness to fit into my hand— and creamy-white with little blue and purple veins just under the surface of her skin.

I cup them both, undecided which one to love on first. I choose the right and pinch the tip on the left so it doesn't feel neglected. I'm all for equality and shit. I'm sure it's my imagination, but I swear to Christ, she tastes sweet. Like a peach, which makes sense because the little buds are a peachy color.

I pop her nipple free from my mouth and lave the second one. Both are hard little points by the time I get done with them. Leaning back, I grab the rope of her long thick hair and feather the end over the stiff nubs. When she sucks in a breath, I lift my eyes to her and wink.

"Told you there were benefits to not cutting your hair."

Her giggle turns into a moan when I lazily trail her hair between the valley of her breasts. I eye her shirt for a moment, deciding if I like it too much to rip the thing from her body, and determine that I want her naked more than I want to see her wearing the slinky material again. Her head jerks up at the sound of her shirt ripping and her mouth falls open in shock.

"Hey!"

Her attempt at yelling the word falls flat when I tweak her nipple.

"It was in the way," I grunt. "I'll buy you another one. Hell, I'll buy you one in every color if you want."

My dick throbs painfully in my jeans, so I open them to give myself some room.

"I hope you don't like your panties too much."

Before she can form a reply, my hand's under her skirt, and I'm ripping them off her too. Her body is bent backward and my dick's too hard to force it down to touch her, so using my thumb, I wipe the moisture from the tip and smear it over her clit. She twitches. Not her body, but her clit, and fuck if that doesn't make my cock jerk in return.

"Mmm... more please," she whimpers, moving her hips up to meet my finger.

I flip up her skirt so I can see her pussy, and I'm not surprised to see her thighs glistening with her desire. Using my other hand, I place two fingers at her entrance and swirl them inside her opening. I wait until she's panting before slowly sliding them inside. My thumb continues to work her clit as I steadily pump two fingers in and out of her. When her walls begin to swell, I pull my fingers free.

"Wh-what are you doing?" she whines. "Why did you stop?"

Instead of answering, I hoist her up from my lap and get up from the chair. I lay a hard kiss on her lips that has her moaning against my mouth before spinning her in place.

"Grab the table, Gypsy. I've always wanted to fuck you wearing one of your skirts."

She peeks at me over her shoulder but bends forward and grabs the table. I almost come right fucking there at seeing her like this. Her skirt has fallen back down, but I know she's bare underneath. Her tits sway as she stands there ready and willing, waiting on me.

I hike the skirt up over her hips. Her breaths come in labored pants and her hair is draped down her back. It's so long that the end lays between the globes of her ass, no doubt getting wet from her arousal.

Grabbing the end, I wrap it a couple of times around my fist. Have I said I loved her hair yet? It's one of my favorite parts of her.

Her asscheeks are pale and round and what they hide is something I can't ignore. With her hair still in my fist, I separate the two mounds of flesh and reveal her tempting asshole. Starting at her clit, I gather some moisture and rub all the way up to the puckered hole.

She stiffens but doesn't try to pull away.

"You gonna let me fuck you here one day, baby?" I ask huskily.

She wiggles her ass when I apply a little pressure, and I swear she's pushing back against my finger.

"I've never done it before."

"I'll make it feel damn good for you," I promise.

Her breath hitches when I add a bit more pressure. I don't push past the sensitive bundle of nerves. I want to take my time with her when it comes to anal play, and I'm too impatient to get my dick inside her pussy to pay it the attention she deserves.

I quickly pull my pants off, kicking them to the side to land beside her torn shirt and panties. Gripping the base of my cock, I slap her drenched pussy with it a few times. She whimpers and shoves her hips back.

"Please, JW."

"What do you want, Eden?" I swirl the head over her engorged clit. "Say the words, and I'll give it to you."

"Fuck me. Fuck me hard," she answers without hesitation.

I put us both out of our misery by notching the head at her opening and slamming home.

Home.

She feels like fucking home. Not just her body and what she does to mine, but in every way possible.

I use her hair as a means to pull her back into me with each forward thrust. I've only been inside this woman for a few seconds, but I'm already precariously close to the edge. She does this to me every single time.

Our bodies slap together and our grunts and moans of pleasure intermingle, creating a sound so beautifully hot it has my control close to snapping. Bending down, I rain kisses along her spine, slowing my thrusts. I'm not ready for this to be over. She tries to get me to move faster, but I keep my steady rhythm.

She's bent over the table, her face forward, and I have the sudden need to see her face. She's stunning when she comes. It's not only her body that reacts but her whole face lights with pure ecstasy.

"I'm close," she moans. Her walls clamp down on me, strangling my cock in the most delicious way.

I'm past the point of holding back. Standing back up to my full height, I release her hair, grab her waist and pound into her like it's the last time I'll have her. I feel crazed with my need for her. Downright insane with my lust.

"Damn it to hell," I groan and pick up speed. My balls draw up and a spark of electricity travels down my spine when I feel her pussy convulse. She falls over the edge, and I've got no choice but to go with her.

"Son-of-a-bitch," I pant. "No condom, baby. I didn't wear a condom."

She's breathing heavily as she leans more of her weight against the table. "I'm clean and on birth control."

I nod, then say verbally. "I'm clean too."

Once I can breathe properly again, I pull out of her delicious pussy and turn her to face me. Her arms drape languidly around my shoulders as I sit us both down in the same chair I was in before. She looks at me with droopy eyes and a contented smile.

"You wear me out, lady."

I drape her skirt back down her legs and tuck her close to me. Her breath tickles my neck when she draws in a deep inhale and releases it.

"Yeah, but it's worth it right?"

"Fuck, yes, it is."

Her giggle sounds sleepy. Leaning forward, I kiss her temple and snag one of the crinkle things she made. I hold it to her lips and she takes half of it into her mouth.

"Just so you know," I stuff the rest in my mouth and talk around it, "you're not making these for anyone else. I don't share well with others and these are too good to share."

She laughs against my neck and the vibrations I feel from it against my chest send a charge to my heart. In that moment, I realize something.

This woman has captured my heart and claimed it as her own.

chapter twenty-four

JW

E DEN – WOULD YOU MIND grabbing my prescription from the drug store on your way back here?

Me: You got it.

I pocket my phone and let myself inside Emo's house. I come to a stop when nothing but an eerie silence greets me. He's here, and so is Grace. I saw her car parked outside beside Emo's black Impala.

Today is the one day a year that Emo's at his darkest. Normally it would be Trouble who came to check on him, but he had a couple of patients call in at the last minute with emergencies. We all loved Rella, and we all felt the pain of losing her, but she was Trouble's sister. Emo feels immense guilt over what he was forced to do to her when we were kids. Because of that, they share a bond. He has better luck calming the raging fire that burns through Emo.

I know right away where Emo and Grace are. My stomach drops as I make my way to the door that leads to the basement. It's normally locked up tight, but right now it's cracked open a few inches. Before I take the first step, I hear it. A whoosh and a sickening slap. I take another couple of steps and hear it again. Another couple of steps down the sound becomes louder. What makes this so much more painful is the lack of cries or grunts of pain.

When I reach the bottom of the stairs and look to my left, my fucking heart constricts. Emo has always enjoyed a twisted sex life. I don't think he particularly likes sex. It's more of an outlet for him when he feels extreme emotions. It's not pleasurable for him. He doesn't hurt his partners, or rather, he doesn't hurt them more than they want to be hurt. He never goes overboard and the person he's with at the time knows exactly what they are getting when it comes to sex with him. He likes to feel the pain more than he likes giving it.

Even though Grace is clad in only a men's black long sleeve dress shirt and Emo is butt ass naked, what I'm witnessing right now has nothing to do with sex and everything to do with a sick sense of punishment. Punishment Emo feels like he deserves.

He's bent over a table with his hands braced against the surface, his ass facing my way. His head hangs, his black hair falling in his face. Grace is behind him holding a belt. I flinch when she rears back and brings it down against Emo's back. His back, already full of old scars, is red and raised with new marks. A few of the new marks have split open, leaving trails of blood to run down his back. It looks like they've been at this awhile already.

She lifts the belt again, and I take a step closer, ready to put an end to what's happening. The floor squeaks beneath my feet and Grace's head swivels my way. Her cheeks are soaked with her tears. She looks tortured by what she's doing. Grace likes a little pain mixed in with her sex as well. That's why she's here. She's one of the very few who can keep up with Emo and his sinister cravings. I know what she's doing now is something she doesn't enjoy. She hates hurting Emo to this extent, but she stays because she knows this is what he needs.

"Enough," I bark and stalk over to them. I hold out my hand and she immediately places the belt in my palm. Fresh tears fill her eyes, but relief flashes across her face. Emo doesn't move. He just stays in the same position.

"More," Emo grunts hoarsely.

"No," I answer firmly.

His hands fist on the table they lay against.

"Goddamn it, I need more!" he roars.

I look at Grace and gesture to the stairs with my chin. "Go upstairs and call Trouble. Tell him he needs to get here. And to bring Eden with him."

She nods and looks back at Emo, her eyes full of sadness.

"I tried, JW. I tried to talk him out of it, but he wouldn't listen." Her voice cracks.

"I know."

After a moment of silence, she leaves us alone. I pick up Emo's discarded jeans and throw them at him. "Get dressed."

I understand his pain. Had I been put in his situation when we were little, I have no doubt I'd be just as messed up as him. But I can't sit around and let him torture himself like this. He was a fucking kid. He had no control over what happened.

He chucks the jeans back down to the floor.

"You need to finish it, JW," he says.

"It's already finished. You've had enough."

Hitting the table with his palms, he springs up to his full height and turns to face me. His eyes are black, not only in color, but in rage and pain as well.

"Finish it, or I'll find someone to do it for me," he growls.

I take his threat seriously. As much as I hate what he's asking of me, I hate even more the thought of someone else hurting him. He knows I won't let anyone else do it. It should be one of my brothers or myself. Grace did it because she was the only one here and he demanded it of her.

"Fuck, Emo." I smash my teeth together and scrape my fingers through my hair. "You don't have to do this anymore. You're back is already torn to shreds."

"Doesn't fuckin' matter. It's not enough."

"It wasn't your fault," I grit out between clenched teeth.

"I touched her. I'm the reason she's dead. Now fuckin' finish it."

"Because you had no other choice." I bellow.

The muscles in his neck bulge as he glares at me.

"I'm still the reason she's dead, whether or not I hurt her willingly."

The belt bites into my palm. There's nothing that my brothers and I can say to ever change his mind. He's hell bent on destroying himself.

"How many?" He's leaving me no fucking choice but to give him what he wants.

"Five more."

"Jesus Christ," I mutter.

We stare at each other for several long moments before I give him a reluctant nod. I hate this shit so damn much. I hate that he's making me do this. I hate knowing the pain he's going to be in by my hands. I hate the pain he's already feeling.

He turns and leans back over the table. The blood that's dripping down his back reaches his butt and travels down his legs.

When I swing the belt back, it feels ten times heavier than what it is. I grip the leather strap so tight, my joints protest. Swinging it forward, it hits Emo square on the center of his back. I wince at the sound it makes, and I swear I feel the hit myself. Emo doesn't move an inch. Not a twitch or even a sharp inhale of breath.

"Harder," he demands harshly.

I grit my teeth as I hit him again with more force. Air whooshes out of my lungs, and I feel like I've just run ten miles.

He looks at me over his shoulder with a pissed expression, his black hair falling in his face giving him an evil appearance. "Stop fuckin' around, JW, and hit me harder."

I scowl at him as I rear back and slam the belt forward again, making sure to hit him in a new spot. This time, he hisses out a breath, and I spot the slight tightening of his back muscles. His head drops forward.

"Two more." He grits out, his shoulders stiff. "Make them fuckin' count."

"Goddamn you, Emo," I snarl, baring my teeth, and land a

fourth blow against his lower back. Blood beads at the new laceration, trickling down his spine.

I'm sweating and breathing heavily. My head feels like it's going to explode. And my heart, my damn heart is hammering so hard I hear it in my ears.

I crack the belt down one last time, then immediately drop it to the floor. My hands go to my hair, and I grip it tight, pulling at the strands.

"Fuck!" I roar out in rage to the ceiling. If I didn't love the bastard so much, I'd beat the shit out of him for making me hit him like that.

Emo sags against the table, the adrenaline coursing through his body finally running out. When his legs collapse and his knees hit the hard concrete floor, I rush over to him. Blood continues to seep from his wounds and there's a fine sheen of sweat coating his body. I hoist him up by his arm and toss it over my shoulder.

"You've gotta stop doing this to yourself, Emo. It's slowly killing you," I tell him as we slowly walk to the stairs.

"You know I can't, so stop wasting your breath." He sounds weak and drained. Of not only energy, but life.

"You wanna die?" I force the words out between a tight jaw. "Is that it?"

He stops when we get to the bottom of the stairs and lifts his head. His face is pale, except for the dark circles around his sunken eyes. He's also lost a bit of weight.

"Maybe I do," he answers in a low voice devoid of emotion. "Maybe I'm just tired of fighting the black nothingness that's always there, waiting for the right time to suck me under. Maybe I don't want to fight it anymore."

I tighten my arm that's around his waist and don't give a flying fuck when he winces. My eyes turn hard, and I've got no doubt they're flashing fire when I glare at him. I bend down until my nose almost touches his. He needs to hear this and he needs to hear it well.

"And maybe you should think about someone else besides

yourself. How in the hell do you think I, Trouble, and Judge would feel if you weren't around anymore? Have you thought of that? Have you thought of what it would do to us? Do you have any fuckin' clue how much that would hurt us? We're brothers, Emo, the four of us. If one of us dies, it wouldn't be like losing an arm or leg, we'd lose a part of our Goddamn hearts."

He doesn't say anything, just looks at me with emotionless eyes and gives me a silent nod. Emo's talked about letting the blackness take him a few times before—usually when he's going through a particularly rough time—and each time it does, it pisses my brothers and me off. I don't know if he would actually go through with it, but even the thought sends my heart rate into overdrive.

We walk slowly up the steps and into the living room. Grace jumps up from the couch, a pair of jogging pants in one hand and a wet rag in the other. She doesn't look much better than she did when I found her in the basement. I take the pants from her and give them to Emo. After he puts them on, I help him lay down on his stomach.

"Trouble should be here any minute," Grace says quietly, kneeling down beside the couch. Carefully, she starts to clean his back. She doesn't touch the abrasions, only cleaning the trails of blood they've caused.

A few minutes later, Trouble walks through the front door with Eden behind him. His eyes meet mine and I give him a clipped nod, silently letting him know he's okay. For now, at least.

He walks straight over to the couch and drops his medical bag on the floor. Grace moves out of his way. The pulse in his temple throbs and pain flashes across his face when he sees the damage on Emo's back. Wordlessly, he begins pulling items from his bag. He knows I've already laid into Emo and him adding to it won't do a damn bit of good.

Eden's voice trembles when she asks, "What happened to him?"

I wrap an arm around her waist and pull her to my side. "He's going through some shit. Today hasn't been a good day for him."

"It looks like… he was beaten."

I close my eyes and pull in a deep breath before replying. I keep my voice low. "When we were kids, he was forced to…." I try to find the right words. "touch Rella. He blames himself, even though he had no choice but to do what his father made him do. He punishes himself for it."

She sucks in a ragged breath, and I drag her closer to me.

"Poor, Emo," she whispers.

We both watch as Trouble cleans Emo's wounds then lathers an ointment on them. Grace sits on the love seat, an unopened bottle of whiskey in her hand. As soon as Trouble is done, he helps Emo sit up and Grace walks over with the whiskey. Before she can hand it off to Emo, Trouble snatches it up, pops the lid off and guzzles several swallows. He wipes his mouth with the back of his hand and passes it to Emo, who tips it to his mouth.

Trouble grabs Emo by the back of the neck and pulls him toward him until their foreheads are touching. Emo closes his eyes as Trouble whispers something to him too low for us to hear. His eyes squeeze shut tightly and he nods at whatever Trouble says. I take a good look at Trouble. He looks like shit. Not as bad as Emo, because he manages to hide his grief better, but I know he's in incredible pain as well.

The two break apart and Trouble gets to his feet.

"I'm gonna stay here for a while. There's no reason for you two to stay."

I nod. "Where's Remi and Elijah? You need me to pick them up?"

"They're with Judge at Mae's house. They knew I'd be here a while, so he's going to stay with them until I get back."

Reaching out, I grip his shoulder. "You okay?"

Pain etches his face, but he answers with a drop of his chin.

"Call me if you need anything." I turn to Emo. "You good?"

"Yes," he grunts with the bottle at his lips. I'm just turning away to lead Eden to the door when Emo's words stop me. "Thank you."

There's no fucking way I'm going to say you're welcome for

what he forced me to do to him, but I still acknowledge his thanks with a nod. I don't blame Emo for what he puts himself through. Hell, I'd feel just as guilty had I been in his childhood shoes, but it still hurts knowing he feels he deserves to inflict pain upon himself.

I tip my head to Grace and she returns it with her own solemn nod. Eden and I are silent as we make our way to my truck. Today has been emotionally draining, and all I want to do is go home, crawl into bed, and get lost in Eden's arms. After a quick stop, that's exactly what I plan to do.

"Where are we going?" she asks when I point the truck in the opposite directions to my house.

"Prescription, remember?"

"Oh, yeah."

I run into the pharmacy, grab her pills, and a few minutes later, we're walking into the house. I go straight to the kitchen and grab out two bottles of beer from the fridge. Eden is fiddling with her birth control pack, slipping the old one out of the small plastic case to put in the refill. I set her beer on the counter in front of her when she sucks in a startled breath and her hands freeze.

"What's wrong," I inquire

I look down at what she's looking at and my blood runs cold. There's a tiny micro-chip lying on the counter. I reach for it and her eyes shoot up to me.

"Do you think...." She pauses for a moment and clears her throat. "Could this really be the chip Diego's been talking about? It was behind my birth control pack."

I scowl down at the small piece of plastic in my hand like it's ticking time bomb I can't defuse. "I don't know."

"I swear I don't know how it got there."

I snap my head up at her wobbly voice. "I know you don't, Eden. Someone must have slipped it in there somehow."

Relief has her shoulders sagging. "I don't see when they could have. I always—" She stops abruptly, a frown appearing between her eyebrows. Her shocked gaze jumps to mine. "I left my purse downstairs that last night I was with Diego. That has to be when they put it in my birth control pack. But why?"

"It's obvious whatever's on here is damning. Maybe they wanted you to use it against him." I grab Eden's hand and pull her behind me into the living room where my laptop is. "There's only one way to find out."

chapter twenty-five

EDEN

JW AND I WALK INTO THE HILL, the dim light momentarily blinding us. Instead of stopping and looking around for who we're meeting, JW keeps going and turns to the left. Apparently, it's a usual meeting spot because he leads us straight to a big table that's already full with people. There's Trouble holding Elijah with Remi beside him, her brother, Kian, Judge, Jamie, Gillian, and a lady named Susan I met yesterday while I was with Trouble and Remi when JW went to go check on Emo. I'm surprised to see Emo sitting at the end of the table with Grace to his left. From what I saw of his mangled back yesterday, he has to be in a lot of pain. After what JW told me, something tells me he likes the pain. The sight of the damage done to his back broke my heart. I can't imagine living with such heartache all the time.

We're all here because Remi wanted us together on her brother's last night in Malus.

I take a seat beside Jamie and JW sits next to me, putting him at the end of the table. Judge is to his left.

I reach over and grab Jamie's hand. "How are you holding up?" I ask quietly.

It's been a week since Jenny died, but the pain is as fresh as if it happened just moments ago.

She gives me a sad smile and squeezes my hand in return. "I'm getting there. It'll just take a while. I loved Jenny like she was a sister."

My heart pinches. "I'm so so sorry."

She's shaking her head before I get the words out. "There's nothing for you to be sorry for, Eden."

No matter how many people have told me that over the past week, I still feel responsible.

I look around the table. "Where's Layla? Isn't she supposed to be here too?"

"She wanted to come, but Trouble ordered her on bedrest. She has the flu."

"Oh, no. That's horrible."

"She'll be better in a few days. He gave her some medicine to help with her symptoms."

We talk for a few more minutes. Danaka, our waitress, comes to take JW's and my order since we were the last ones to arrive and everyone else has already given theirs. After she walks away, JW's quiet words capture my attention.

"I've made a copy of it, and I'm sure Diego isn't stupid enough to not think I did, but I plan to call his father tonight to pass along a message." He stops and flicks his eyes to Kian down at the other end of the table to make sure he can't hear him. Kian doesn't know about Diego or what JW and his brothers have planned for him. As he's in the military and essentially government property, it's best it stays that way. "If he doesn't back the fuck off, he'll not only have me after his ass, but the state police as well."

A shiver races down my spine, and I fight the bile rising in my throat. The chip that fell out of my birth control pack yesterday? Yeah, there was some pretty gruesome footage on it. Diego is a lot more acquainted with eviscerating people than I thought. I don't know how many girls there were, because I only made it halfway through the third one before I couldn't watch anymore and had to run to the bathroom to empty my stomach. What makes it so much more horrendous is he would be raping them as he sliced into their stomachs. They actually died while he was still inside them; him coated in their blood and guts.

What kind of sick person does that? And how in the hell did I not know what he was? Was I so enamored by his good looks and his gentlemanly treatment toward me that I overlooked the signs? How did he keep that hidden from me so well? We weren't together that long, and I didn't know him that well, but there had to have been signs that he wasn't right in the head.

When I think about him touching me, using his hands that've gutted God only knows how many girls, sickens me. It makes me want to soak in a bathtub full of bleach and scrub every inch of my body with a steel wool brush.

"That bastard is mine when we find him." I can barely hear Judge's words, but it's enough to bring me back to the present.

JW offers a nod, but tacks on, "You can finish him off, but I get him first."

Listening to the two talk about murdering another human being should frighten me, but it does the opposite. Diego deserves every bit of what's coming to him. Thoughts of the pain Jenny went through the last few minutes of her life, mingled with what the other girls went through, has me hoping he suffers greatly. It may make me a bad person, but I can live with that as long as Diego in punished.

Our food is dropped off and the rest of the time there's idle chitchat around the table. I don't eat much of my dinner, my stomach still in knots over what I saw last night. It's going to take a long time before I'm able to wipe those images away.

Unable to stomach anymore, I toss my napkin on the table.

"I'm going to the lady's room," I inform JW.

"I'll go with you. It's not time to feed him yet, but I want to before he gets cranky," Remi says, getting to her feet and taking Elijah from Trouble.

JW pulls me down by my shirt for a brief kiss before letting me go. I'm only going to the bathroom and will be gone for few minutes, but it melts my heart that he wants a kiss before I go.

The bathroom is in the opposite corner of where our table is located. There's a couple of empty pool tables and high-top tables.

"It's been years since I've played pool," I tell Remi and run my fingers over the felt as we pass by one. "Wonder if I can tempt JW into a game before we leave."

"Just don't play Jamie. I thought I was good, until I played her. She won before I even got a chance at a shot," she laughs. "Although, it was fun to watch her beat Kian. He's cocky when it comes to pool. Thinks he's the master."

I hold the bathroom door open for her. "I'm sure anyone could beat me. I suck, but it's still fun to play."

Remi sits and lifts her shirt to feed Elijah as I walk into one of the stalls.

"I think it's great that you still breastfeed him. I've heard that a lot of women don't make it past the first month or two."

She snorts. "It's been a struggle for sure. Those first couple of weeks I felt like my nipples were falling off, but I love knowing that I'm giving him the best nutrients I can."

After doing my business and flushing the toilet, I go to the sink to wash my hands. I look at her through the mirror. She's staring down at Elijah with a look of love on her face.

"I'm scared of failing at it when I have kids. I've heard it can be extremely painful."

She lifts her head and meets my eyes. "I'm sure you'll be just fine. Get past those first couple of weeks and it's a breeze. My main issue now is if people are secretly criticizing me if I do it out in public. That's why I try to do it in private if there's an option."

I can't imagine anyone at the table would have an issue with her breastfeeding Elijah. I don't say that though, because really, how well do I know them? I could be wrong.

She guesses where my thoughts went and smiles. "Nobody out there would care. I don't really think many people in Malus would have an issue with it either. That's why I love Malus. It's the outside world that concerns me. Sometimes I just simply want to do it in private. It's a sacred bond between Elijah and I, and sometimes I don't want others to witness it."

"I can understand that and think it's incredibly sweet that you want to keep it between you and him at times."

A few minutes later, Elijah finishes feeding and Remi recovers herself.

"The downside to breastfeeding is the leakage. There's been many times I've been out grocery shopping to realize my shirt has soaked through."

I wrinkle my nose at that. "Yeah, that would suck."

Once she's finished straightening her clothes, we make our way to the bathroom door. Before I can grab the handle, it's shoved open. I stumble back a step, almost tripping over my feet. Confusion has me frowning when Benjamin steps inside. He looks terrible, like he hasn't slept in a week and his eyes carry a crazed look.

"Benjamin, what are you doing in here?" Remi asks, stepping up beside me.

"I'm sorry," he says, his voice deep and scratchy. "I have no choice."

"Sorry for what? What's going on?"

His answer is to lift a gun and point it directly at my head.

I COME TO WITH A KILLER headache and my arms feel like they're being pulled from their sockets. It only takes me seconds to understand why and panic sets in. My head is hanging from my shoulders, so when I pry my eyelids apart, that panic turns to terror.

I'm naked. And hanging by my arms.

Diego.

The name whispers in my head. Despite Benjamin being the one who held the gun on me, it's Diego who has me. I know this with one-hundred percent certainty. The question is, why would Benjamin help him?

A more pressing question is, what happened to Remi and Elijah?

Oh, God, please let them be okay.

The last I saw of them, Remi was trying to talk to Benjamin right before he hit her with the butt of his gun. Thankfully, he was prepared to catch Elijah before the baby hit the floor when she passed out. Anger and fear mingled together as he held that baby in his arms to calm him down and kiss his forehead, like he cared for him. He then pointed the gun at me and told me to tie her up with the rope he threw at me. I did as he commanded, but did a shit job at it, hoping she would get loose as soon as she woke up. After I was done, he set Elijah down beside his mother, whispered an apology, and then turned to me. The hit to the side of my head was fast, and it only took seconds for my vision to blur and darkness to consume me.

My shoulders and neck scream in protest, but I manage to lift my head. It takes me a moment for my eyes to focus. I'm in a house. A nice-looking house with pictures on the walls, decorative pillows on the couch, DVDs and CDs on a shelf beside a flat screen TV. Everything looks so normal, warm and inviting. It's all very deceptive.

"Lookie who's finally decided to join us."

The familiar voice sends chills down my spine. I glance over to where it came from and see Diego sitting in a chair, one leg crossed over the other, a glass filled with amber liquid in one hand and the other stroking a woman's head. She stares at me with wide scared eyes as she clutches a little girl to her chest. The woman only has on a pair of panties and bra and her face sports several bruises. The little girl has on a long sleep shirt with matching sleep pants. She has a scratch beside her eye and one on her chin, but otherwise she's got no other visible wounds that I can see. I just pray there're not any that are hidden.

Pain slams into my chest at the fear on the girl's face. Her chest heaves and she hiccoughs as she cries.

From the pictures on the wall of Benjamin, this girl, and woman, they have to be Benjamin's daughter and her mother. Is that why he helped Diego? To protect them?

"Where's Remi and Elijah?" I croak.

He flashes his teeth. "The bitch and brat are still at the restaurant as far as I know."

My eyes flicker back at the woman and child. "Let them go, Diego. You have me now. There's no reason to keep them."

With his eyes still locked on me, he fists the woman's hair and yanks her head back. She winces but doesn't cry out.

"I'm still undecided if I want to let them go. I guess it really depends on how cooperative you are."

I lick my dry lips. "I have the chip. Let them go, and I'll give it to you."

His laugh is evil and filled with menace. "After weeks of denying you had it, why would I believe you have it now? How do I know this isn't just a ploy to get me to let them go?"

"Because I've had it this whole time, I just didn't *know* I had it. Someone hid it in my birth control pack."

He lifts his glass to his lips, takes a sip, and sets it down before getting up from his chair. The little girl whimpers and the woman shoves her face against her chest, shielding her eyes from whatever Diego has planned.

"Now who would be stupid enough to do that?"

"I don't know." It has to be one of his staff. They were the only ones who had access to my purse that night.

"Hmm…. You know, that's pretty fucking funny," Diego remarks, coming my way. "All this time you had the chip." He puts a finger on the center of my stomach and trails it down to my public bone. My arms jerk in their bindings when I try to lean away from his touch. My feet are barely on the floor, so I don't get far. "All this time you could have stopped your dog from being slaugh tered. You could have stopped your friend from being sliced up by my knife. This poor woman and her child would be safely nestled in their cozy house painting each other's nails or some shit. And Benjamin…." He trails off and laughs. "The unlucky bastard on the floor behind you would still be alive."

"I hate you," I choke out on a sob. "I hate you so much. I hope whatever JW does to you is drawn out painfully slow."

He tsks. "Now, now. Your little sheriff boyfriend won't be doing any such thing."

He produces a knife. One that I've seen before. It's the same one that used to sit on Diego's dresser. It's long and looks just as deadly as it actually is. I asked him about it once and he said he likes to hunt sometimes and he uses it to gut his kills. My stomach swirls with nausea when I realize his prey wasn't animals like I assumed, but people. Women in particular.

"He'll come after you and he won't stop until he finds you."

I try to put on a brave face, to not let him see the fear coursing through me. But when he places the tip of the blade at one of my nipples, I can't help the terror-filled whimper that leaves my throat.

Hurry, JW, my mind screams.

"Oh, I'm counting on him finding me." He trails the flat part of the blade down my stomach, pressing harder each inch he goes. The pain is bearable at first, but the lower he goes, the sharper it gets. I know soon the blade will sink into my flesh. "I want him to see the beauty I make with your entrails. And once I'm done, since you seem to like him so much, I'll make a matching canvas with his."

"You're sick."

His eyes flash up to me. "I prefer to call it creative." He grabs my braid and yanks my head back. "It's just a shame I can't be inside your tight pussy when my blade sinks inside you. Nothing's better than a body's muscles tightening up when there's intense pain involved. It grips my dick so tight."

He closes his eyes and moans, while my mouth waters from the bile working its way up from my stomach.

His eyes snap open and his head drops down. His lips slam

against mine. I'm shocked at first but recover quickly. Unfortunately, before I get a chance to bite his tongue off, he pulls his head back.

A moment later, a sharp pain slices through me. I suck in a painful breath and glance down to see half of the blade stuck in my left side below my ribs. Black spots dance in my vision and my legs become weak. In the distance, I hear a child scream and the cries of a woman. They're only a few feet away from me, but they sound a mile away.

My body sags and more weight is added to my arms. With my slumped form, the knife moves inside me, sending another white-hot pain shooting through my side. Diego bends his knees so his face fills my rapidly dimming vision.

"I think you're going to be my best work yet," he whispers and shoves the knife in deeper.

The pain becomes unbearable and all I can think is that I never got the chance to tell JW that I love him. That he'll never know how grateful I am for everything he's done for me.

The next time I blink, my eyes stay closed and blackness takes me under.

chapter twenty-six

JW

I GLANCE DOWN AT MY WATCH and frown when I realize Eden and Remi have been gone for almost twenty minutes. I'm not sure if I should worry or not, because I have no clue how long it takes to breastfeed a baby. Eden wouldn't have left Remi by herself, so I know she stayed behind with her.

When I look over to Trouble and see his own frown, I have my answer.

Yes, I should be worried. He looks up just then and we lock eyes. Neither says a word as we get up at the same time. The table turns quiet, but we ignore the questioning glances at our abrupt departure. Our steps are long and determined as we make our way across the room.

"Should they have been back by now?" I ask.

"Normally no, but it wasn't time to feed Elijah, so he shouldn't have been that hungry."

My hands ball into fists as fear spikes through my system. At the mouth of the hallway that leads to the bathroom we hear it. It would be hard to recognize over the low music coming over the speakers, but once we reach the hallway, there's no mistaking the wailing of a baby. We both sprint the rest of the way to the bathroom. Trouble makes it first and shoves the door open. When I step in behind him, he's already skidding across the floor on his knees to a screaming Elijah.

The sound is heart wrenching. It's not a scream of pain, but one of fright. No child should ever emit that sound.

He's on the floor beside his mother, crying so loud his entire body shakes. Remi, who's tied to the plumbing underneath the sink is just now coming to.

I frantically look around the room. All of the stall doors are open and empty. Eden isn't in here.

Fuck! Eden isn't here!

"What happened? Where is she?" I demand, my voice raspy.

I wait, my skin tightening over my bones and my scalp prickling, as Trouble helps Remi sit up. She has tears leaking down her cheeks as she desperately reaches for Elijah. Trouble's on the floor, still on his knees, with Remi and Elijah between his legs. I bite my tongue to keep back my impatience.

It's not until she has Elijah tucked against her chest that she looks up at me. Worry and fear line her face.

"It was Benjamin," she wheezes. "He came in just as we were going out and held a gun to us. He had to have taken her."

What in the fucking hell? Benjamin? Why?

Her eyes glisten with more tears. "He looked scared and half-crazed, like he was forced to do what he was doing." Her eyes move to Trouble's. "I don't think he wanted to hurt us, but I don't think he had any choice."

I glance at Trouble. "You good here?"

He gives me a clipped nod. Before I spin on my heel and stalk out the door, he stops me. "I want to see Benjamin." His deadly voice matches the dark look in his eyes. I tip my chin in affirmative.

Judge and Emo are halfway down the hall when I step outside the bathroom. I don't stop as I give them a rundown of what's going on. They follow me as I stalk over to the table we were seated at.

"Your sister needs you in the bathroom," I tell Kian.

Not waiting to see if he replies, I turn and head toward the door. An eerie calmness washes over me as we leave The Hill.

This is Diego's doing. Benjamin was just a pawn. I don't know why he helped him, but I know it wasn't by choice. Even so, Benjamin will be punished for playing his part. How severe that punishment will be depends on what condition I find Eden in.

By God, if she's dead, Benjamin will feel the full wrath of my anger.

And Diego. What he did to Jenny and those other women will pale in comparison to what I'll do to him.

AS JUDGE AND I QUIETLY WALK up the steps to Benjamin's house, I realize I could be wasting time coming here, but something tells me this is where they'll be. Diego doesn't want to keep Eden, he just wants the chip and to kill her. There's no reason for him to take her out of Malus. She doesn't mean shit to him, so he wouldn't waste the time.

Which in itself doesn't bode well because he could have already killed her. Thankfully, he couldn't have had her more than thirty minutes. Men like Diego like to play with their victims before putting them down.

We keep our steps light as we both head to a window on either side of the door. Sweat pops out on my forehead when I realize I can't see shit because thick curtains cover the windows. A look to Judge says he has the same problem.

My phone vibrates in my pants, and I pull it out to see a message from Emo.

Emo: He has her in the living room. Naked and strung up from the ceiling.

I've never in my life felt so much rage consume me. It fills my veins like tiny sparks of electricity. I close my eyes and count to ten in my head, trying like hell to calm the furious need to bust down the door and slay Diego in the most brutal way.

My phone vibrates again, and I force my fingers to loosen their hold enough for me to see the screen.

Emo: Knife, no gun. Charlotte and Leddy are on the floor by the chair.

Motherfuckin' hell.

It's no less than what I expected. Benjamin wouldn't have taken Eden on his own. He had to have had an incentive. Holding someone's child hostage is a damn big incentive to get a person to do your bidding.

The question is, how long has Diego had them? A week ago at The Hill, after Jenny's funeral, Benjamin said Leddy and Charlotte were visiting her parents. I have no doubt that was a cover up. Which also means he probably had them the day Jenny died. Diego fucking used him to get inside Judge's house. Benjamin was distraught about what happened. Guilt plastered all over his face both right after we found him in the kitchen and at the funeral. Guilt that we mistook for self-blame for being knocked out and not saving Jenny. While a lot of men would feel responsible for that, he wore his guilt because he let the bastard in the house.

No fucking wonder we couldn't find Diego. He was hiding in plain sight.

I walk across the porch to Judge and keep my voice low. "He has Charlotte and Leddy inside. Eden is strung up from the ceiling. No sign of a gun, but he has a knife."

His jaw clenches as he listens, his thoughts no doubt running along the same lines as mine.

I turn back to the door. I've been in Benjamin's house a few times, so I know just beyond the door is a small foyer. From there is the living room. If Diego has them in that room, there's no damn way I can pick the lock and open the door without him knowing. I either take the chance and kick the door in and hope for the element of surprise, or wait until Emo, who walked around to the back door, gives me a signal. Neither choice sits well in my stomach. The only thing keeping me sane right now is knowing that in order for Emo to know where Eden is, he has to be in the house.

The decision is made for me when a child's scream comes from inside. Without thinking, my shoulder slams against the door and the wood splinters. It only takes me a second to absorb the scene before me, but every second feels like agonizing hours.

Right in the middle of the living room, tied to the ceiling by her wrists, her body sagging, her head hanging, her beautiful fucking hair lying limp down her back, and blood dripping to the floor at her feet, is Eden.

In front of her is Diego, his hand at her side, holding the hilt of the knife he has buried in her. His head turns my way and a demented smile curves up his lips.

The smile doesn't last long though. My blasting through the door distracted him enough for Emo to move into place. One second, he's pressed up against Eden, and the next he has a knife shoved against his throat.

"Pull the knife out, nice and slow," Emo says in a lethally calm voice. "My knife isn't sharp for a reason. Makes it more interesting to have to saw back and forth through flesh, tendon, and bone. You so much as even think about twitching that hand a centimeter in the wrong direction, I'll make sure to take my time hacking through your neck."

I tense, ready to charge the bastard if he decides to go against Emo's orders. My eyes stay locked on the knife sticking out of Eden. More torturously slow seconds pass before he slowly withdraws the knife. I don't know if it's the sight of all the blood or the fact that Eden doesn't so much as spasm as the knife is being extracted from her that fills me with fear.

As soon as the knife leaves her body, Emo pulls Diego backward and I'm rushing forward. I almost slip in the blood surrounding her on the floor. Her legs are fucking covered in it.

"Eden," I say her name through a raw throat. "Jesus, Christ. Eden, can you hear me?" She doesn't answer.

I pick her up below her butt and take some of the weight off her arms. Judge appears by my side, holding the same knife Diego used on her. He easily slices through the rope, attesting to how easy it was for Diego to stab her with it.

With her loose, I gently lay her down on the floor. I briefly register another body on the floor only a few feet away, but I don't take the time to see who it is. All I can see is Eden; deathly pale face and the bottom half her body covered in blood. Her head lists to the side away from me, and I grip her chin to bring it back. Placing my fingers under her chin, I feel for a pulse.

It's there, but sluggish. Feeling the slow beat only relieves a little of my fear and anxiety. She could still easily bleed out.

Judge drops down beside me holding a towel. I take it from him and press down on her wound. She doesn't flinch at the pressure.

"Fuck, *fuck*! Judge, call Trouble and tell him to meet me at his office. Tell him what happened and that Eden might need a blood transfusion. And let him know we may need the 'copter."

I look up when I hear a sickenly sweet crunch sound and find Emo with Diego still in front of him. His blade is still at his neck, except it's no longer a threat, but a promise, as half of Diego's neck is split open with blood rushing down his chest. A look of dark satisfaction glosses over Emo's face as he watches the life drain from Diego.

I can't even be pissed at Emo for taking Diego's life when I craved to do it myself. I'm just glad the fucker is dead. Right now, I need to focus on Eden and saving *her* life, because there's one thing I know of for sure. If she dies, she'll be taking a vital part of me with her.

My heart.

chapter twenty-seven

EDEN

I TRY TO OPEN MY EYES, but I can't. Either they're too heavy or I'm too weak. Or maybe someone superglued my eyelids shut. Crazy thought. Why would someone superglue a person's eyes shut?

It's not just my eyes that won't work, but my mouth as well. My lips won't even so much as twitch, let alone open so I can ask what's going on. And the rest of my body, it just lies there. My mind is fuzzy too.

Am I broken? Why can't I open my eyes, talk, or move? What's going on?

Voices start drifting in and out, but I can't understand what they're saying. One particular voice sounds really nice. It's deep and smooth, but I sense worry in the baritone. What is he worried about?

I try my best to focus on that voice.

"Why hasn't she woken up?" it says.

There's warmth at my side, and I want to reach out and grab whatever it is.

"She lost a lot of blood. Her body is healing," another voice answers.

"How long will it take?" says the voice I like.

"It's up to her."

My throat tightens as I attempt to scream that I'm awake. Why can't they see that?

The voices drift off, but I still sense a presence. The one I like. I wrack my brain, trying to remember who he is. It's small glimpses that come to me at first.

Shaggy blond hair and baby blue eyes. Sometimes his eyes are darker, like a storm cloud. Tall with a strong body. Someone who makes me feel safe.

More images come, clearer ones. And a name.

JW.

Everything comes back at once and my heart begins to pound erratically in my chest. My side hurts, and I remember Diego stabbing me with a big knife. Memories of hanging from the ceiling, of Benjamin's daughter and ex-wife huddled on the floor, of Remi lying unconscious on the bathroom floor at The Hill with Elijah sitting beside her.

It's all too much. My head feels like it's going to implode.

It's not until a warm hand grips mine that I realized I'm moaning.

"Eden?" the voice comes again. "Gypsy, can you hear me?"

The voice is calming and the pain recedes some. My eyelids begin to work enough for me to slit them open. The light is dim in the room and a shadow falls over my face. It takes me a moment to focus. A smile pulls up my now working lips at the face hovering over mine.

"JW," I whisper through a dry throat.

"Jesus," he mutters, closing his eyes for a moment before opening them again. "You scared the shit out of me."

I attempt to lift my hand to touch his face, but my arm's too heavy.

"I'm sorry."

He shakes his head and drops down to place a kiss on my forehead. "Don't apologize. I'm just glad you're awake. You've been out of it for a couple of days."

I frown. It's been two days?

"Really?"

"Yeah." He clears his hoarse voice. "You lost a lot of blood and needed a transfusion, but thankfully, the knife didn't hit anything vital. Trouble says you were lucky."

"Remi and Elijah?" I croak, worry for my friend and her child making my already low voice even lower.

"They're both fine. Remi just has a bump on her head."

I close my eyes in relief but pop them back open. "Diego?"

"Dead," he answers, his tone hard. Before I can ask who killed him, he says, "Emo did it."

I never would have thought I would be happy another human being was murdered, but Emo did the world a favor by killing Diego.

"And Benjamin, his daughter, and her mother?"

Something flashes in his eyes. Both remorse and bitterness. "Benjamin is dead. Diego stabbed him and hit his spleen. It was too late by the time we got there. And physically, Leddy and Charlotte are okay. Diego had them ever since Derek found him in his shed. The fucker was hiding in plain sight and forced Benjamin to take you from The Hill. He didn't touch Leddy, thank goodness, but he raped Charlotte multiple times. In front of Leddy."

My throat grows tight, and I swallow several times when my eyes water. That poor child. Diego may not have touched her, but he still hurt her in the most vile of ways. She'll carry the vision of her mom being violated forever. That's not something you ever get over. And she's lost her father on top of it. The rest of her childhood will be a struggle. Hell, even adulthood will be hard.

A tear slides down my cheek and JW wipes it away with his thumb. The gesture is sweet and comforting. He reaches over to the table beside my bed, grabs a Styrofoam cup and brings the straw to my lips. I didn't realize how thirsty I was until the cool liquid hits my throat.

He leans his weight on the bed, careful not to jostle me, and puts his face back to mine. It's not until then that I notice how tired he looks. His face has more scruff than normal, his eyes are blood shot, and the shirt he's wearing is wrinkled.

"How are you doing?"

I should ask him the same thing, because it looks like he hasn't slept in a week.

"My side hurts a little. And I'm tired."

He grabs my hand and brushes his lips back and forth across the back of it. Closing his eyes, his brow pinched, he pulls in a deep breath before kissing my hand and putting my palm against his cheek. He's in pain, and I hate it.

"Hey," I call. When his beautiful blue eyes open, I reassure him. "I'm okay."

His frown deepens. "But you almost weren't. I came too close to losing you."

A stinging pain hits my side when I force him to let go of my hand so I can cup it around the back of his head. I push past the pain and pull him down closer.

"But you didn't. I'm here. Okay?"

His throat bobs as he swallows and his eyes flicker back and forth between mine, like he's making sure I really am here. He drops his head until his forehead touches mine. "Yeah."

We stay that way for several moments, just sucking in the breath of the other, relishing the closeness we almost lost.

"I love you, Eden," he whispers. His words both shock me and sends a crazy amount of happiness through me. He pulls back to see me better. "I haven't said it until now, but I've felt it for a while. Hell, maybe even that first day. But finding you hanging from that ceiling, that knife sticking out of you and all the blood, knowing you could have easily been taken from me…." He stops, closes his eyes, and twists his neck to the side, as if pained by the very idea. His eyes are stormy when he opens them again and clears his throat. "I've never been so scared in my fuckin' life, Gypsy. I've never felt pain like that before. I would probably survive if you lived but chose not to be a part of my life. But you dying being the cause?" He shakes his head, his eyes turning more serious than I've ever seen them. "I wouldn't be able to survive that. I wouldn't *want* to survive that. I'm a strong man and can handle damn near anything, but I'm not that strong."

My lip wobbles as I try my best to stop the new tears. That's one of the most beautifully tragic things I've ever been told. Of course, I would want JW to move on if something ever happened to me, but knowing he loves me, that the pain of losing me is overwhelming for him, makes me feel more special than I ever have before.

I twist my hand around so I can grab his wrist and put his palm over my thumping heart.

"Do you feel how crazy my heart's beating in my chest right now?" He nods. "It's beating that way for you. It does that every time I'm with you. It *only* beats that way when I'm with you. You make me happy, you make me feel cherished, and you make me feel loved. I'm the luckiest woman in the world to have met you, and I hope to stay the luckiest woman in the world because I get to keep you." I take a deep breath and let it out slowly. "I love you too, JW. Probably an insane amount, but I don't care. I love you," I repeat. Those words feel incredibly good rolling from my lips after thinking I wouldn't be able to say them.

I know he just told me he loves me, but I still hold my breath as I wait for his reaction. It comes not a second later. His eyes light up, showing more life than I've seen since I woke in this bed, and he smiles. His smile is beautiful.

He drops his head and his lips settle over mine. It's a soft kiss, a gentle kiss. I want more, so much more, but me lying in bed with a hole in my stomach makes it pretty much impossible for us to do more.

When he pulls back, I notice his hand lightly holding onto the end of my braid. Is it strange of me to think his obsession with my hair is sexy? I don't care if it does. I'll gladly be strange as long as I get JW.

"I love you," he whispers again, and I smile, suddenly feeling giddy. "I'm going to go get Trouble so he can look you over."

I relax against the pillow and nod. "Okay."

"I'll be right back." His voice is still low. "I love you."

I giggle because I'm happy. I giggle because I'll never get tired of hearing him say it. Doesn't matter if he said it a hundred times over and over again right after the other. Maybe I'll record him saying it on my phone so I can hear it any time I want.

I grab the bottom of his shirt when he turns to leave. He spins back.

"I love you," I tell him.

Instead of leaving, he comes back to me. His hands go to the pillow on either side of my head and he lowers himself. His nose rubs alongside mine and then he's kissing me again.

This time I let him leave, but my eyes track him until he's out the door. Once I lose sight of him, I close my eyes and smile. My side is starting to hurt more, but there's nothing that can take away my happiness.

JW loves me. That's all I need.

chapter twenty-eight

JW

I DROP DOWN INTO MY DESK chair at the station and pick up my phone. Scrolling through my contacts, I find the name I need.

"Yes?" a man's voice comes across the line after the third ring.

"Your son is dead." I get right to the point.

There's a pause before Emiliano blows out a breath. "Why?"

It doesn't surprise me that I don't note any remorse in his tone. Just disappointment.

"Because he killed my woman's dog. Because he killed another woman who was a good friend. Because he held a child and her mother hostage, repeatedly raping the mom in front of the child. Because he killed that child's father. But *especially* because he kidnapped my woman, stabbed her, and almost made her bleed out."

"Shit. Stupid fucking idiot." he mutters.

I clench my jaw. "I'm letting you know as a warning, just in case you have a mind for backlash toward me or anyone in this town, including Eden, that it would be a very grave mistake."

He laughs. He actually laughs, and it makes my back molars protest as I grind them together.

"You're threatening me? After killing my only son?" he asks, incredulously.

"It's no threat, Emiliano. You come after me or anyone I care about, and your days attempting to rule San Antonio are over. You know I can make that happen."

I lock eyes with Judge as he appears in the doorway to my office. Noticing me on the phone, he quietly makes his way to the chair across from my desk, takes a seat, and gets comfortable.

"I don't take well to threats, son," Emiliano says, no longer amused.

"And I don't take well to people threatening what's mine. Your son's half-severed head can attest to that."

It doesn't matter that it was actually Emo who killed Diego. He would have still ended up just as dead.

He sighs, his breath crackling over the phone. "That boy has always been bad news. I knew it when he was a child and would slaughter the neighborhood cats. He knew I forbade any harm coming to women and children, especially after the brutal way his mother died, but he thought, as my son, I would protect him. People like him disgust me, and it's been a long time since I've been able to look at him with anything other than revulsion."

I remember a few years back hearing about Maria Tomas being raped and murdered by the Santiago cartel. It was all over the news because she was found beaten to a bloody pulp in one of the local school's playground. One of the children found her.

"He was my son, and a part of me loved him, but he's caused enough problems. He was going to be put down eventually anyway. Either by another cartel or myself." He turns pensive. "It's over. You have no need to fear retaliation."

"How do I know you're not spewing shit to bide your time?"

"If I gave you my word, would you take it?"

I stay silent. Fuck no, I won't take his word. He may have integrity when it comes to women and children, but as far as he knows, I killed his son. Grieving an offspring can change a person's principles. I trust his word about as far as I can throw a semi-truck.

"It's all I have to offer," he says in my silence. "No harm will come to you or yours. Take it or leave it."

"See that it stays that way. I'll have his body sent to you." I grunt. Hanging up, I toss my phone on my desk and scrub a rough hand down my face.

"Think he'll retaliate?" Judge asks, throwing an ankle over his knee.

"If he's smart, he won't, and Emiliano has never come across as stupid. I'll still keep an eye on things for the time being."

He nods. "How's Eden?"

"Better. Trouble said the wound isn't infected, so that's a scare we don't have to worry about."

The knife Diego used on Eden was the same one he used on all of his victims in the video footage we found on the chip. Once Eden came to and I could think properly again, Emo showed me the knife and I recognized the handle. It appears that Diego at least kept the knife clean. Thank fuck for some miracles.

Judge pulls something from his coat pocket and tosses it on my desk. I reach up and grab the envelope, looking down and seeing Jenny's name and address, but no return address.

"What's this?"

His voice is gruff when he answers. "A letter that was delivered a couple of days before shit went down with Diego. It's from Jenny's parents."

My eyes shoot to his, my brows lifting in disbelief.

"That's not possible. Her parents are dead. They died just a few weeks before Sweet Haven was taken down."

"Emo told me." He jerks his chin to the envelope in my hand. "Read it."

I flip the envelope over, pull out the two folded pieces of notebook paper and smooth it out.

Dear Jenny,

I'm sure you'll find this as a big shock, and I wouldn't blame you if you throw this letter straight into the trash without opening it, but it is my hope that you'll read it.

Mick and I have fought with ourselves for years if we should write this letter or leave well enough alone. In the end, I knew in my heart I couldn't pass onto another world without telling you the truth. I don't expect it to change your view of your father and me, but you deserve to know everything.

When you were born, Mick and I were so very happy. You were the most precious little baby with your blonde hair and innocent beautiful blue eyes. The minute we saw you, we fell in love. You were simply perfect. We were also terrified because of where we lived and what would happen to you once you were old enough.

I'm extremely ashamed to admit, and no punishment will ever be enough for what we did, but up until you were born, Mick and I willingly participated in the monthly Gatherings. We were both young when you came along and all we had ever known was that it was okay for an adult to touch children during those nights, because it was their special way of showing love.

We don't ask for, nor expect, forgiveness or understanding. There is no excuse for what happened those nights.

It wasn't until you came along that we realized the wrongness of what we were all doing. The thought of us or someone else touching you in such a way made me violently ill. Mick felt the same way. You were our precious daughter. You were sent to us to protect and cherish. To love in the right way, with caring and compassion and protectiveness. Unfortunately, Mick and I both knew we couldn't leave Sweet Haven. We had already witnessed other people being murdered because they tried. The children who were left behind were given to another couple in the community. We also couldn't stop The Gathering from happening. We did the only thing we could do. We pretended. We pretended so we could keep you safe. We pretended because if we didn't, they would take you away from us and the person they would give you to wouldn't love you like we did. Really love you. Not the sick and twisted love like most adults did in Sweet Haven.

Jenny, I want you to know that Mick and I never ever wanted to hurt you. During every single Gathering, when we were forced to touch you, a part of us died. There are no words to express the pain or shame and guilt and complete disgust we felt for ourselves for doing what we did. I swear we tried so very hard to make it as painless as possible, but there was no way we could get around it. The Council, although they were there to participate as well, were always watching.

Once you reached five years old, the age a child is to finish their initiation, we knew we couldn't continue. We knew there was no way we could convincingly go on with our deception. We knew you would more than likely go to your aunt and uncle, who were very much into The Gatherings, if something were to happen to us. We knew what they would do to you, but it was the only choice we had left. It was either spend the rest of your childhood being sexually abused or spend one night with the full effects of The Gathering. It was one of the hardest decisions we've ever had to make.

A week after your fifth birthday, Mick and I died. Or that's what The Council believes. To them, we were attacked by a wild animal, but in reality, it was Mr. and Mrs. Swanson's bodies, who had died a couple of weeks before from smoke inhalation when their house caught fire. We dug up their graves, put our clothes on them, and left them out in the woods. We made sure several people in town knew we were going for a walk in the woods, so it wasn't a surprise when the bodies were found. We waited two days out there for a wild animal to find Mr. and Mrs. Swanson. Once they did, and The Council believed it was our bodies, we left Sweet Haven. I cried every mile that separated me from you.

As soon as we hit San Antonio, we made an anonymous phone call to the police. We gave them as much information as we could about what was happening in Sweet Haven. We kept in contact with them by using different payphones and found out they would be moving into Sweet Haven soon. A couple of weeks later, Mick went back to Sweet Haven and left a note under Shane and Delia's door, knowing they were against The Gatherings, and warned them of the imminent raid on the town.

Months later, after everything was over, we went back to Sweet Haven to find you. To make sure you were okay. We found you with Shane and Delia. We missed you so much and wanted to take you with us, but we knew you were better off with them. After everything you went through, after all the times we were forced to take you to The Gatherings, we didn't deserve you. Our punishment was to let you go. We knew Shane and Delia would care for you the way you deserved. We knew they would make you happy. They didn't have any children, and because of that, weren't forced or volunteered to participate during those horrible nights. We left you because it was the safest place for you.

Every day since we left, we mourned your loss. Every minute of every day, we wished we could be with you. We watched over you from afar and were so proud to see the young woman you became. You always looked happy, and that's all we ever wanted for you. You were our greatest and most treasured gift.

You're getting this letter because your father and I are no longer of this world. I left instructions with someone that if anything ever happened to us, to deliver this letter. This is not me asking you to forgive us. There is nothing we could ever say or do to redeem ourselves for what we have done. I simply wanted to let you know the truth. And to say that we have always loved you, in the proper way. In the most beautiful way a parent can love a child.

It is my greatest wish that this letter finds you well. I hope with all my heart you have found true happiness, Jenny, and it continues to follow you for the rest of your life. You deserve it and so much more.

Love Always,

Deanna and Mick

Holy fucking hell. I drop the letter on my desk, shocked as shit at what it revealed. Leaning both elbows on my desk, I drop my head and rub the tense muscles on the back of my neck.

"Her parents died in a car accident three months ago," Judge says. I lift my head and glance at him. "Head on collision with a drunk driver. They lived just outside of Odessa."

"There's no return address. How did you find out where they lived?"

"Had a private investigator look into it. That's why I waited to tell you about it. I wanted to find out what happened to them."

I nod and scrub a hand over my jaw, still astonished about this new revelation. I pull open my drawer and grab out the whiskey I keep tucked inside.

Uncapping the top, I take a pull straight from the bottle. With the bottle still in hand, I wipe my mouth with my forearm, then pass it to Judge. He takes it and tips it to his lips.

"Guess that answers one of the mysteries of that night," I muse out loud.

"Shane and Delia must have slipped the note under Mae and Dale's door. They were close friends with them."

There are several things that happened that night almost twenty-four years ago that we never had the answers to. One being the mysterious note that alerted Mae and Dale of the raid.

"Mae needs to know."

"I'm heading there next," he replies.

I look back down at the note. Although their excuse for what they did to Jenny matches the video clip Emo showed me—that they hated what they were doing—I'm not sure I could forgive them if I were in Jenny's shoes. Especially since they willingly participated in Hell Night before she came along.

"It's a shame she'll never know," I murmur.

His lips stiffen to form a straight tight line. "I think it's better this way. She didn't really remember her parents. There would be no point in bringing something up that would only hurt her."

I dip my chin in agreement. He's right. Jenny was young enough that she didn't really remember much about Hell Night. In a sense, she was lucky.

I refold the letter and slip it inside the envelop before handing it to Judge.

"I'm headed over to Trouble's office. Eden gets to come home today."

We both get to our feet. "Is she staying in Malus?"

I pocket my phone and grab my keys from my desk. "I haven't asked her yet." I cut him off when he looks like he's going to say something. "She knows everything, except for the Finishing. I plan to tell her today before I ask her to stay here." I hold up my hand to warp him off. "She's okay with everything else we do. She'll be okay with that too."

He looks doubtful, but wisely keeps quiet. He knows I would never put anyone in Malus in danger. Informing Eden of how we deal with abusive predators is a hurdle for sure, but one I know we'll safely get to the other side. I trust Eden with my life, and that's essentially what I'll be giving her.

We both say goodbye to Rita as we pass by her. Once we're outside standing beside our vehicles, Judge pulls another envelope from his pocket.

Reaching out, I grab it with my brows raised in question.

"It's information and the address. Figured you'd want it now."

I clutch the envelope in my hand with a tight fist. Anger begins to bubble up as I stare down at it.

"If you want someone with you, give me a call," he says.

I give him a grim nod without looking away from the envelope. Without another word, Judge gets in his car and leaves.

Of course, I'm not leaving yet; I want to make sure Eden is fully recovered before I do. Not to mention, I don't want to leave until I'm certain Emiliano doesn't come after her. But as soon as she's completely healed and I'm sure there's no retaliation in store for her, I'll be on the road.

Mother and brother dearest have no idea what's coming for them.

WHEN I WALK INTO THE ROOM Eden has been using while she recovers, I find her sitting on one of the comfortable chairs, looking out of the window. She's so deep in thought that she hasn't noticed me yet. I lean against the doorframe and give myself a moment to take her in.

She's in one of her usual gypsy skirts and tops. When she lifts her arm to push back some hair from her face the bangles on her wrists clink together. I've come to love that sound. She's lost some weight since she was hurt. Not much, and it won't take much for her to gain it back, but it's still enough to notice. Eden is already slim, so she can't afford to lose much weight. She's done her long red hair in some type of quadruple style braid. She's sectioned her hair off into three long braids then braided those three to make one thick rope.

I only have a profile view of her, but from what I can see, her naturally pale face is devoid of any make-up.

Beautiful is too simple a word to describe Eden, but that's exactly what she is. Beautiful.

I push away from the doorframe and walk into the room. "What has you so deep in thought?"

She spins to face me and my chest tightens when she smiles.

"Just anxious to get out of here."

She gingerly gets to her feet, but I'm already in front of her before she can take a step. I wind my arms around her waist and gently pull her to me, making sure to be careful of her wound. Her hands lay flat against my pecs.

"How are you feeling?" I ask after kissing her sweet lips.

"Better."

"Are you all packed?"

She nods. "Yes."

"Should I get a wheelchair for you?" I give her a mischievous smile. I'm joking, but I want to gauge her reaction to see if she really needs one. I'd carry her to my truck, but that might be more painful than her walking.

She scrunches her face in an adorable expression. "Uh, please don't."

I laugh and kiss the tip of her nose before pulling back.

"I was able to identify the woman you saw Diego murder the day you fled from his house."

Her eyes widen in surprise. "You did?"

"Yeah. Her name was Miranda Simone and she was twenty-two. She was a known prostitute who ran away from home when she was sixteen. Her family has been looking for her for years. Judge sent an anonymous letter to them, explaining what happened to her."

Tears gather in her eyes, but she sniffs and blinks them away. "I can't imagine what her family must be going through," she says, her voice cracking.

I run my hand down her back soothingly. "At least they don't have to wonder anymore."

"Yeah."

I let her go and grab her bag from the bed. Trouble, Remi, and Susan meet us in the hallway when we leave the room. Trouble hands her a small white prescription bag.

"Pain meds. Every four hours as needed. I have you down to come back in a couple of weeks to remove the stitches. Call me if you need me before then."

"I will," she says, taking the paper bag.

Susan steps forward and carefully hugs Eden. The two women have become close over the last few days as Susan's helped care for her while she's been staying in the office. Each night that Eden's been here, I've stayed as well, reluctant to leave her side. After seeing her bleeding out on the floor of Benjamin's house, I've been terrified to leave her. I swear I've aged twenty years since then. And those two days she was unconscious will forever be some of the worst days of my life.

Remi steps forward and gives her own hug to Eden. "Let me know if you need anything. I'll be by tomorrow, regardless, to check on you."

"Thank you, Remi. You're a good friend."

She smiles and steps back. The worry that's been lining her face the last few days is no longer present. Between being knocked out and having her son in danger, her concern over Eden, and her worry on how to handle her brother over the Diego issue, she's been under a lot of stress. Thankfully, Eden is on the mend, Elijah doesn't seem to have any lasting effects from his frightening ordeal, and Kian believed the story we gave him about Diego's death being self-defense. He left a couple days after the incident, believing Diego's body would be delivered to San Antonio and an official report would be made. Of course, none of that happened.

We talk for a couple more minutes before we leave through the rear entrance. I parked in the back because I wanted to avoid running into anyone who would ask Eden how she was. I want to get her home and settled as soon as possible.

A few minutes later, I'm helping Eden get comfortable on the couch with a pillow behind her and a blanket over her lap.

"I'm not an invalid, you know?" she complains good-naturedly.

"You're right, you're not." I finish tucking the blanket around her waist and look up at her from my kneeled position beside her. "But you very easily could have died. Give me this, Gypsy. I need to take care of you."

Her amusement drops from her face. She takes my hand and twines our fingers together.

"You're a good man, JW, and I'm so lucky to have you."

I hope she feels the same way after she hears what I need to say.

I ask if she's hungry and she says no. I ask if she's in pain and needs a pill, and she informs me she's fine and took one a couple of hours ago. I ask if she'd rather take a nap in bed, and again, she declines. With nothing else to do, I grab us both a bottled water and bring them back with me to the living room. I take a seat on the couch, lift her feet to my lap, and work my fingers in the arch of her foot.

She closes her eyes and moans. "That feels really good."

And of course, the sound has my dick picking the most inappropriate time to stand at attention. What a prick.

I know she feels the growing hardness behind my zipper because her other foot is positioned directly on top of it. She confirms this when her eyes slit open and she gives me a wicked smile. Her foot gently nudges my cock.

"Someone's missed me," she says with a giggle and then a wince.

"No giggling if it causes you pain," I reprimand. She rolls her eyes, her lips twitching, and then nudges me again with her foot. "And none of that either." I grab her foot. "At least not for a month.

Maybe two." It's my turn to wince, because a month, let alone two, without sex with Eden is going to kill me.

"I think you might be exaggerating my healing time a bit."

"I may be damn near crazy by the time I can have you again," I grumble. "But I'm not fucking around with your injury."

"But we can do other things, right? Like maybe getting to my knees, and I suck you off?"

Fuck me, this woman just does it for me. And from the look she's giving me, she knows it.

"We'll see," I answer huskily. I foresee many long showers in my near future.

"There's something I need to talk to you about," I tell her once I'm done massaging her feet.

Her brows jump up. "Sounds serious."

"It is. There's a question I want to ask you, but there's something you need to know before I do."

"Okay." She settles back against the pillow and folds her hands over her stomach.

I rub my jaw, suddenly feeling anxious. What if I'm wrong? What if she can't get past the way we handle things here in Malus? I have no doubt in my mind that she wouldn't report what we do, but I need more than that. I need her to be okay with it. I need her to want to stay, because if she doesn't, if she can't look past what we do, I have no fucking clue how I'm going to live without her.

"You're starting to worry me, JW," she says, pursing her lips into a frown.

I turn to face her, cocking one of my legs up on the couch. I need to see her face when I tell her.

"SO, YOU ONLY SENTENCE people to the… Expiration Penalty —" I nod my head when she looks at me in question, "—who have hurt women and children?"

"Yes," I answer. I'm still not quite sure how she's feeling about what I just unloaded on her, but she's not scrambling to get away from me, so I call that a definite plus. "It's case by case and depends on the severity of the crime."

"What about people who hurt men? And what happens if it's a woman who hurts another woman or child?"

"It doesn't happen often, but they're given the same sentence."

Her finger is at her mouth and she's chewing on her nail as she thinks. "How many have you had to do?"

"Seven." I keep my voice calm when inside my nerves are still shot.

She drops her hand to her lap, her thumb nail bitten to the quick.

"What happens if you later find out they weren't guilty?"

I shake my head. "That's never happened and won't ever happen. We don't dole out the punishment lightly. We make sure all evidence points to them committing the crime. We only use the penalty if we're one-hundred percent sure. We don't kill for the fun of it, it's not something we enjoy, but it's something we feel is deserved if the crime warrants it. It's what makes Malus so safe, because everyone knows crimes such as those will not be tolerated."

Her eyes slide away from mine and she looks off toward the kitchen. I watch as the expressions on her face change several times. Some make me even more nervous and some make me believe this might end in my favor. All of them have my heart pounding in my chest.

Finally, after what feels like a thousand minutes, she looks back at me. Her expression has settled on acceptance.

"Okay."

I lift a brow. "Okay?"

She nods. "Yes, okay."

The simple word makes me want to laugh. Just okay. No, I need time to think or this is too much to take in. Just okay. I can work with that. Even so, I want to clarify.

"You're okay with what my brothers and I do here? You're okay with us taking the law into our own hands?" I pause and level her with a look. "You're okay with us killing people we feel deserve it?"

She attempts to sit up, and I try to get up to help her. She stops me with a raised hand. "Stay."

I sit back and clench my jaw when she struggles. She moves slowly, but she eventually moves down to my end of the couch and settles her ass right over my thighs, sitting sideways. One arm goes around my neck and her other hand cups the side of my neck.

"I trust you, JW. I trust that you'll do the right thing. I trust that you wouldn't harm anyone who doesn't deserve it. I think it's amazing and kinda heroic that you protect the people of Malus, even if it's not always in the traditional way."

My heart settles. It's now that I truly believe that this woman was always meant to be mine.

"You're really somethin' special, you know that?" I rumble.

A big grin forms over her face. "I know."

I chuckle and steal the grin right off her face with my lips. We're both breathless by the time I pull back.

"Stay," I whisper. "Move to Malus. Live here with me, Gypsy."

I'm not beyond begging if it comes to it. Luckily, I don't have to.

"It's about damn time you ask that."

"That's not an answer."

She leans down until her mouth is only a whisper away from mine and says softly, "Yes, I'll move in with you."

I want so badly to crush her in my arms. To take her to my bedroom and worship her body like it's the holy grail.

For now, I settle for a feather soft kiss.

chapter twenty-nine

EDEN

JW AND I WALK UP THE STEPS to my parent's place. When I agreed to move to Malus and live with him, he wanted it done as soon as I was well enough. Had I not been recovering from a stab wound, I don't doubt he would have hauled my butt to San Antonio that same day to get my stuff. I have to admit, I was anxious myself. I'm going to miss my parents, Millie, Clayton, and Hannah, but I'm close enough that I can visit them often.

Before I get the chance to open the door, it's flung open and Mom's pulling me into her arms. I close my eyes and release a long breath, basking in the warmth of her tight embrace. The last month has been hard not having Mom and Dad around.

"Sweet Jesus, Eden," she murmurs against my hair. "I'd take a switch to your hide for scaring me so much if I wasn't so happy to see you."

I wince at the pinch of pain in my side from her hug, but I mask it when she pulls back. I never lie to my parents, but this one time, I won't be revealing the full truth. There's no point in telling her about Diego stabbing me when the problem's been taken care of.

I laugh and wipe away the moisture forming in my eyes. "Hey, Mom. I've missed you too."

She palms both of my cheeks, her eyes flying all over my face critically. Lines appear by her eyes as she frowns.

"You've lost weight," she accuses.

I quirk my lips up. "It's nothing I won't gain back in a couple of weeks."

As if she just noticed him standing there, her eyes leave my and settle on JW, who's a couple of feet behind me."

"Who's this?" she asks just as Dad walks up behind her.

Instead of answering, I move around her and walk into Dad's arms. His familiar masculine scent comforts me. I reluctantly pull back.

"Don't pull any shit like that again, you hear me?"

I nod, remorse over their worry for me making my chest tight. "I promise."

I step beside JW and he laces our fingers together.

"Mom, Dad, I want you to meet JW. These are my parents, Melanie and Charles."

JW holds out his hand for them to shake. "It's nice to meet you both."

They assess him as they shake his hand.

"You the reason my girl couldn't come home?" Dad asks bluntly.

I cringe.

"No, Sir."

Dad's eyes move to me. "You finally going to tell us what's going on?"

My gaze slides to JW's before I look back at my parents. "Yeah."

"SO, YOU'RE TELLING ME THIS DIEGO, a man you never told us you were seeing, murdered a woman and you saw it? Then proceeded to threaten you if you didn't give him back a microchip you didn't know you had?" Dad asks, pacing the floor in front of us. Mom's on the couch, her hands clasped together in worry.

"Yes," I answer.

He stops, propping his knuckles on his hips and glares at me. "You could have come to your Mother and me. We would have helped you."

"I couldn't, Daddy. You don't know the things Diego was capable of. I wasn't going to put you and Mom in danger."

He opens his mouth to speak, but JW does so first.

"With all due respect, Sir. I have to agree with your daughter," he states calmly. "Diego Tomas wasn't the type of man to get involved with."

Dad's eyes narrow. "I know all about the Tomas family and what they're capable of. But I'll be damned if I sit around and let someone threaten my daughter."

"That's exactly why I couldn't tell you. I knew you would try to help, which would have only put you and Mom on his radar. I couldn't take that chance."

Mom comes to her feet and takes one of Dad's fisted hands from his waist. "Let it go. It's over and done with. She's home and safe. That's all that matters."

I can tell Dad wants to say more, but he turns his gaze to JW and asks something else instead. "You said Diego *wasn't* the type of man to get involved with. What does that mean?"

I shift on the couch, uncomfortable with telling him he was blatantly murdered. Apparently, JW has no qualms with it though.

"He's been taken care of. He's no longer a threat to Eden."

Dad gives a stiff nod.

"You the one who kept her safe?"

"Yes, Sir. My brothers and me."

He gives another nod. "Then I'm in your debt," he says gruffly.

"That's not necessary." JW puts his arm around my shoulders and tugs me closer. "I did it for purely selfish reasons. I love, Eden."

Dad crosses his arms over his chest and regards JW. I almost laugh at the stern look on his face. It's fake. I can see the mirth in his eyes he's trying to hide. "Do you now?"

"I do."

"Stop it, Daddy." I roll my eyes, get up off the couch, and go to him and Mom. "JW's asked me to move in with him, and I said yes."

"But, sweetie, you've only known him a few weeks," Mom says, grabbing my hand.

"I love him, Mom."

She searches my eyes, and finding the truth, gives a single nod. "Okay."

When we were explaining what happened with Diego, JW told them he lives in Malus and that was where I was the last few weeks. They immediately recognized the name from when it was changed from Sweet Haven and what happened all those years ago.

"I expect you to come visit often," Dad states.

"I will."

I feel JW's hand settle against my lower back. "And you're more than welcome to visit Malus. Just give us a couple of days' notice so we'll have a room ready for you."

"I'm sure we'll take you up on that."

"Who's hungry?" Mom asks suddenly. "I was just getting ready to put together a pot of goulash. I insist you both stay for lunch."

Seeing the hopeful look on Mom's face and having not seen them in so long, I turn to JW. "You don't mind, do you?"

His lips tilt up into a smile. "Of course not. I'd like to get to know the two people who raised such a wonderful young woman better anyway."

I hear Mom's sigh as I lean up and press my lips against his in an easy peck. "Thank you."

"Come on, dear. I'll help you in the kitchen."

Mom and Dad leave, giving us a few minutes alone.

"You're something special, you know that?" I ask as I wind my arms around his neck and finger the small hairs there.

His smile is still in place. "Only because you make me so."

"Thank you for pulling me over that day."

His chuckle is deep and raspy. "I never thought I would say this but thank you for speeding."

I toss my head back and laugh, happy knowing that something that started out ugly and disturbing turned out to be something beautiful and forever lasting.

chapter thirty

JW

I WALK UP THE STEPS TO the older brick house and ring the doorbell. The sun has already set and with the warm temperature, there're bugs flying around the porch light.

As I wait for someone to answer the door, I think back to the note Eden received a week ago. It was from a female housekeeper who used to work for Diego. Apparently, one of the girls on the microchip we found in Eden's birth control pack was her daughter. She had suspected Diego had done something to her. One day, when she was cleaning his office, Diego left his computer on. Frozen on the screen was a video of Diego with his knife jammed in her daughter's gut. She found other videos of him murdering women and took the microchip. She planted the chip in Eden's birth control pack, knowing she would eventually find it. She didn't go to the police herself because she was living in the states illegally and was worried she would be deported back to Mexico, where her husband, who had been abusing her for years, was looking for her.

I understand her fear, but it still pisses me off that she put Eden's life on the line. She apologized in her letter and Eden forgave her. Me, not so much. I'd never want what happened to her daughter to happen to anyone else, but I'll always chose Eden's safety over anyone else's.

She went on to explain she sent the picture I got the day I visited Emiliano, gathering more evidence against Diego. When he went to take a shower, she snuck in the room and took the picture of the girl, then sent it to me, hoping that it would motivate us even more to turn over the evidence to the police.

I'm brought back to the present when I hear footsteps on the other side of the door, and I brace myself. I recognize the man who answers right away, and it takes every bit of will power I possess to not plant my fist against his face. He's older, twenty-four years older to be exact, but he's smaller than I remember. Smaller than I am by several inches and at least forty pounds.

"Can I help you?" he asks, his brows lifted in expectation.

Instead of answering, my hand darts out and my fingers wrap around his neck before he knows what's happening. His hand flies up to mine and he tries to pry it away as I shove him inside, slamming the door closed with my boot. Spotting a couch in the living room, I push him backwards until he falls onto it. He coughs and sputters as he tries to catch his breath.

"Who... in the fuck... are you?" he wheezes.

I cross my arms over my chest. "I'm shocked, Trey. You don't recognize your little brother?"

His hands are braced on his knees while he leans over to pull in much-needed air. At my words, he sits up straight and stops breathing again. His eyes narrow as he looks me over.

"Liam?" he croaks, his eyes growing big in disbelief.

I spread my arms wide. "In the flesh."

I have to give it to my brother. He's not stupid. He knows just what this little visit means for him. He proves this when he jumps from the couch and tries to dart to the hallway. He only gets three feet before my fist is in his stomach and he's once again wheezing for breath. I throw him in the closest chair and he slumps over.

A shocked gasp has me turning. An older version of the woman

I remember my mother being walks out of the dark hallway. Judge is at her back, not letting her too far out of his grasp.

"Liam?" she whispers in a broken voice through the hand she has covering her mouth.

Like Trey, she looks a lot older. Her hair is mostly grey and her face has wrinkles now. I fucking hate that I have her eyes and nose.

"Hello, Mother."

When she stops walking, Judge nudges her forward. She stops about five feet away.

"Oh, my, God. I thought you were dead," she breaths.

"As you can see, I'm very much alive, but I can guarantee you'll wish I were dead by the time I'm through with you and Trey."

Tears appear in her eyes before they run freely down her face.

"I can't believe it." Her voice is still low and she still appears surprised. "I can't believe you're really alive. Your father died that night. I thought you did too, or we would have looked for you before we left."

"Thank fuck for small miracles," I mutter. I jerk my chin to the couch beside Trey. "Take a seat."

Seeming to come out of her stupor, she glances back and sees the hunched over form of Trey. Her head swings back to me. "What did you do to him?"

"Not nearly enough. Now sit down," I order in a hard tone.

Her chin quivers, but she does what she's told. Judge stands off to the side with his hands shoved into his pockets.

"I've been looking for you both for a long time. Imagine my surprise when I find you've been running a daycare here in Arizona. And to name it Sweet Haven Tykes, no less."

That tidbit of information that was in the envelope that Judge gave me that day almost a month ago damn near made me lose it. The only thing that kept me from going after them the moment I read the report was knowing Eden needed me. She knew of the information Judge gave me because I told her. She tried a couple of times to force me to go take care of things—she saw how much it bothered me—but I refused until I knew she would be okay.

"And to make it worse, you're playing husband and wife?" I spit that last part out in disgust. That piece of information almost made me vomit. "I thought you both were sick back then, but that's just fucking repulsive. Are you two actually sleeping together?"

"We love each other," Trey states simply, sitting up more in his seat.

I bark out an incredulous laugh. "Like you loved me?"

"We did you love, Liam," Mom inserts.

"You didn't love me. You loved the sickness that resided in you. If you loved me you wouldn't have let those twisted fucks touch me. You wouldn't have let my own brother rape me."

My mother opens her mouth to response, but Trey cuts her off.

"You don't have a brother," he says, his voice gaining strength. I cast my eyes his way. A slow smile creeps across his face.

"What in the fuck are you talking about?" I demand.

His teeth shine from the light in the room as his grin grows. "I'm not your brother." Before I can order him to explain, he does so on his own, revealing my family is more fucked-up than I thought. "I'm your father."

I can't hide the shock from my face, and from the expression on his, that was his intention. I cast a glance at my mother and see dismay mixed with a hint of resignation. I look back to Trey.

"You're fuckin' lying," I snarl.

He sits back against the cushions and throws an arm over the back, pulling my mother to his side. It turns my stomach when she actually lays her hand on his lower stomach and leans into him.

"Actually, I'm not," he states, looking smug as fuck. He kisses the top of my mother's head before continuing. "Due to an accident, dear old Dad couldn't have any more kids and Mom was desperate for one more. Being the stand-up son that I was, I volunteered."

"You people disgust me."

As disturbing as this revelation is, some small part in the back of my mind suspected this. From the records Emo found, I knew Robert wasn't my father. I also remembered a few times when I was little walking in on my mother and brother in a position that a mother and son should never be in. At that young age, I assumed it was them showing each other their "love", like the adults did to the kids during Hell Night.

Even so, the thought is sickening to say the least. What in the fuck is wrong with these people?

Trey shrugs, like it's every bit normal for a mother and son to have sex, have a child, and pretend to be husband and wife.

I look at my mother. "Why in the fuck wasn't I ever told?"

She sniffs, her chin jutting up stubbornly. "Because The Council didn't allow incest babies."

Members of the same family are not permitted to create a child together.

Rule number six in the laws of The Gathering. No doubt, if anyone knew of their deception, the Council would find out and they would be punished. It wouldn't matter that Robert and Annette were part of the Council.

"How many kids have you touched at the day care?" I ask, changing the subject.

My mother shifts uncomfortably and adverts her eyes away from mine. Trey just sits there, his expression still amused.

"The better question is, how many have we not touched. The older ones you have to be careful with because they may go blabbing. It's the wee little ones who give the most satisfaction."

One minute he's sitting on the couch, and the next he's dangling with my hand wrapped around his throat. My fist plows into his gut and he tries to double over, but I don't let him go.

"Liam," my mother screams, jumping up from the couch and grabbing my arm.

I look down at her hand with contempt then lift my eyes to hers. "Get your filthy fucking hands off me." The growled words are deep and filled with hate.

Her eyes widen and she quickly releases me to take a step back. Judge steps forward to make sure she doesn't go anywhere. Her eyes fill with tears as she clutches her chest.

"We loved you," she whispers.

Trey begins to struggle in earnest in my grip, his air supply running low. I tighten my grip and bare my teeth at her. "I don't want to hear that word come out of your fuckin' mouth. You don't know the meaning of love. When you love someone, you protect them with your life. You put their safety before your own. When they hurt, you hurt with them. You do whatever it takes to make them happy."

She stays quiet after that. There's not a damn thing she can say. When Trey goes lax in my grip, I release him. He falls to his hands and knees before me, gasping for breath.

"Judge, take my mother and tie her hands together. We're leaving."

"What?" she squeaks. "Where are we going? We can't—"

"Mom? Dad?" A small feminine voice calls from the hallway.

I whip around and see a little girl about ten-years-old standing just inside the living room. She's wearing a blue nightgown that falls to her mid-thighs, her long blonde hair is pleated so the braids hang over her shoulders, and she has her hands clasped tightly in front of her. Her frightened eyes move to my mom, then down to Trey still on the floor, then up to me.

My throat tightens as I look the girl over. She looks like a female version of me when I was younger. I close my eyes and blow out a harsh breath. I silently gather every shred of control I have left and turn to the girl.

"Hey there, sweetie. What's your name?" I keep my tone light and make sure my expression appears calm.

She keeps darting her eyes to my mom and Trey. Her bottom lip begins to wobble and her eyes turn glassy. The look breaks my fucking heart. I step in front of her, not too close to frighten her, but blocking her view of her parents, hoping with them out of sight, she'll relax enough to talk.

"We won't hurt you." I gesture to Judge and me. Her eyes flash to Judge and they widen fractionally, like she just realized he was there. He offers her a kind smile. "My name's JW, and my friend there is Judge."

She tilts her head to the side and frowns. "Those are weird names."

I smile and nod. "They are, but they're not our real names. They're just nicknames."

"Oh." She takes a step toward me. "What're your real names?" she asks innocently.

I never give my real name to anyone; well, anyone except Eden that is, but I want this girl to trust me. I glance at Judge and he gives me a nod.

"I'm Liam and he's Kayn."

She licks her little pink lips and takes another step closer. "My name is Thea."

I keep the smile on my face. "That's a very pretty name. It's nice to meet you, Thea."

Feeling movement at my back, I subtly cast my eyes to Judge. He casually walks over to the couple behind me to make sure they don't do anything stupid. I take a step closer to Thea, blocking more of her view of them in case Judge has to do something drastic.

"I know this is going to come as a shock to you, but I'm—"

"You're my brother," she finishes for me, her innocent eyes wide. Now it's my turn to cock my head to the side.

"Yes, but how did you know?"

She twists her gown in her tight grip. "Because Mama said I had a brother named Liam and you sorta look like me."

"You're right. We do sorta look like each other."

She gives me a tentative smile.

"Have you ever been to Texas, Thea?" She shakes her head. "How would you like to visit there?"

I move a step closer when I hear a gasp and a thump behind me.

"Will Mama and Daddy be there?" she asks in a trembling voice.

I turn her around gently by her shoulders so her back is to our mother and Trey and get to a knee.

"Do you want them there?"

She drops her eyes, but there's no mistaking the fear and troubling look that comes across her face.

I lift her chin with my finger. "Have they hurt you, Thea?"

Seeing the tears sliding down her chubby cheeks crushes my heart. I blink away the red haze clouding my vision. She doesn't need to answer for me to know they have. It's written all over her face.

Tears drip from her chin when she nods, confirming what I already know. "I don't want them to go. I don't want them to hurt me anymore."

Throwing caution to the wind, and hope like fuck I don't scare her, I pull her into my arms. I close my eyes and suck in a labored breath when her tiny arms move around my neck and squeeze me tight, as if she's afraid I'll let her go.

"I promise they'll never hurt you again. I swear, Thea, no one will ever hurt you again."

"You won't hurt me, will you?" Her whispered words send a pain so sharp to my chest it nearly steals my breath.

I pull back and look deeply into her eyes. "I swear on my life, I'll never hurt you." I vow.

She looks at me for a minute, and I don't know if it's because she truly does believe me or she just desperately wants to, but she nods.

As soon as I pull her back into my arms, I open my eyes and lock them on the two people I hate most in the world. My mom is sitting on the couch, her hand at her mouth, alarm making her eyes appear bigger than they are. Trey's still on the floor, but he's up on his knees with Judge standing behind him. His eyes are defiant.

I kneel there with my baby sister in my arms, a sister I didn't know I had, but already love, and glare every bit of hate I feel for the two people.

Thea won't know it, but our mother and father will be coming to Texas with us.

TWO DAYS LATER, I stop at the back of Judge's car, pull the keys from my pocket, and pop the trunk. Two people stare back at me, the light they haven't seen for days making their eyes squint from the sudden brightness. One set of eyes are filled with terror and the other set filled with hatred. I don't give a shit what either of them feel.

We made it back to Malus yesterday afternoon. While I was helping Thea pack some clothes for our trip, Judge was loading a gagged, bound, and an unconscious Trey and my mother into the trunk of his car. Trouble sent me with a concoction that would knock the two out for the trip to avoid any trouble along the way. Except for a few pit stops, we drove straight through.

When we first arrived, I took Thea straight home. She was still scared and timid because of the sudden change in her life, but being around Eden for only thirty minutes had loosened my sister up a bit. I have no doubt what she went through by Trey and my mother's hands was terrifying, and it'll stay with her forever, but I hope living in Malus, surrounded by family and friends who will protect and care for her, will help her heal. She has a long road ahead of her. I'm just glad I found her and was able to take her away from the nightmare she had been living.

During one of our gas stops, I called Eden to warn her. She met us outside as soon as I pulled into the driveway, as if she were anxiously waiting for our arrival. As soon as she laid eyes on Thea, I saw the same thing I felt when I first saw her. Instant love and profound pain. Eden let the love shine through and worked her best to hide the pain.

Trouble appears beside me, and I feel the rage radiate off him as he glares down at the two huddled in the trunk.

"How is this going down?" he bites out.

"I figured The Finishing would be appropriate for them."

The Finishing is normally reserved for citizens of Malus, but since Trey and my mother used to be part of what Malus used to be,

I think it's poetic justice. It's not what I originally had planned for them—I wanted them to suffer more—but I have more important things to do than to spend any more time on these two. Like get to know my sister. And ask Eden to marry me.

My mom whimpers behind her gag when I reach inside for Trey. Their hands and feet are bound, so I'm forced to carry him over my shoulder. Trouble follows with my mother over his. Emo and Judge are already out in the field waiting for us by two freshly dug graves.

I dump Trey on the ground, satisfaction hitting me when I hear his grunt of pain. Trouble drops my mother beside him, only slightly less haphazardly. We both prop them up on their knees.

I stare down at the woman who gave birth to me and feel nothing but loathing, disgust, and hatred. Remembering the many times she watched as Trey raped my small body—not just raped, but viciously abused—while her and the man who I thought was my father did the same to another child filters through my mind. There were times she would stop with her own actions and touched herself as she watched Trey with me. Hatred isn't a strong enough word for what I feel for the woman.

"Last words?" Judge asks, bringing me back to the moment.

"They don't deserve them. There's not a damn thing either can say that I want to hear." A thought comes to mind, and I hold up my hand when Judge pulls out his gun. "Actually—" I walk over to Trey and rip off the tape over his mouth, "—there is something I want to know." I glare down at him. "Why? If I was your son, why did you hate me so much? Why volunteer to get our mother pregnant if you were only going to detest your offspring?"

A lecherous look crosses his face.

"Because I wanted another hole to fuck. I wanted something tighter to force my dick into. To put it simply, *son,*" he sneers the word, "you were my new toy and fuck if I had a lot of fun playing with you."

Emo emits a low growl and I glance up to see Judge holding him back. I ignore the distressed moans coming from my mother and look back at Trey. As disturbing as his words are, they're nothing less than I suspected.

"And Thea? Was she the same?"

His eyes close and a lewd smile curves up his lips. "Thea is our little princess. We took care with her, because we didn't want her to break too soon."

An animalistic roar comes from behind Trey and the next moment he's down on the ground with an enraged Emo on top of him. I hold my hand up to Trouble and Judge, warding them off, and let him get a few good punches in. My eyes flicker to my mother. She's fallen on her side, sobbing as she watches her son-slash-husband get beaten.

Trey's barely conscious by the time I pull Emo off him. Emo's hands are covered in blood, some of which is from Trey's face and some from the key he kept in his hand as he was pummeling him.

Trouble takes over holding Emo back until he's calmed down. I pick Trey up so he's on his knees again. Grabbing the front of his shirt, I rear back and put every single bit of fucking strength I have behind the punch I deliver to his face. It's not nearly as satisfying as slowly killing the bastard, but it'll do. After propping him back on his knees again, I take a step back and nod to the others.

Judge walks around until he's to my left, about ten feet away from the couple. Trouble does the same on my right, making sure he's not in a direct line across from Judge. Emo, who's practically foaming at the mouth, mirrors my position behind them, but slightly to the side.

I pull out my gun from the holster on my side as my brothers do the same. Raising my arm, I aim at Trey first, the others following suite.

"May Lucifer welcome you with open arms," Judge begins the dictum reserved for all Finishings.

"And deliver you to the darkest pits of Hell," comes Emo's growled words.

"To live out an eternity for the evil deeds you've bestowed," I deliver my part, my voice filled with menace.

"Shall you *not* rest in peace."

As the last word leaves Trouble's mouth, four shots are fired. Before Trey's body hits the ground, the same shots are delivered in the same locations to my mother. Between the eyes, the heart, base of the neck, and the groin.

My mother's lifeless eyes are wide as her body falls on top of Trey's. I holster my gun and walk over to them. I don't spare them a glance as I kick their bodies into the two graves. Silently, we all shovel dirt over them.

Once we're done, I toss my shovel to the side and wipe sweat from my brow with my arm. Something that feels like peace settles over me. The door to my past is finally closed.

"You good, brother?" Judge asks.

I look over at him. "More than good."

My hands move to the small lump in my pants pocket. It may seem kind of twisted for me to kill two people the same day I plan to ask the woman I love to marry me, but to me it's the perfect time.

What better way is there to shut the door on a past that was dark and painful by celebrating a future that'll be bright and beautiful?

Eden and Thea are my future. One I plan to cherish, protect, and love for the rest of my days.

epilogue

JW
Several Months Later...

I STAND AT THE FRONT OF THE church with my hands clasped together in front of me. Sweat beads my forehead and anxious nerves have me constantly shifting my weight from one foot to the other. Every person in Malus is crowded inside the church. Soft whispers and rustling of clothes can be heard throughout the room. I keep my eyes pinned on the back, waiting impatiently.

"Will you stand the fuck still? You're starting to make *me* nervous."

I shoot daggers at Judge. "I'm not nervous," I bit out.

"Then why in the hell do you look like you're getting ready to haul ass out of here?"

Ignoring his question, I grumble, "What in the hell is taking so long?"

"They're women," Trouble answers. "They always take a long time to get ready for shit like this."

I look down at my watch and frown when I notice the time. Eden, Remi, and Millie should have been here ten minutes ago. What in the hell is going on? Has something happened to them?

Did she change her mind? Did they get into a wreck on their way to the church? Are they lying in a mangled car on the side of the road? There's no one in town who could come across them because they're all fucking here.

"Check your phone, Trouble, to see if Remi's messaged you."

Before he has a chance to pull out his phone, music starts through the speakers and Thea appears at the end of the aisle. I let out a relieved sigh.

Thea is beautiful in a light blue dress with white bows around her waist. Her hair is done up in some fancy do and she looks happy. She still has a long way to go to mentally heal from her life with our parents, but she's different from the quiet frightened girl when I first brought her here months ago. Despite the first eleven years of her life being anything but easy, she's smart, caring, and very much loved by everyone in Malus.

My eyes move past her to Remi. I hear Trouble blow out a breath beside me. She has on the same dress as Thea's, except hers show off her womanly curves. Trouble's a lucky bastard to have her.

Millie is next in a matching gown, looking just as stunning as Remi and Thea.

My damn breath catches when I spot Eden step into the doorway, accompanied by her dad. The woman makes my heart pound heavily in my chest with her beauty. There are several things about this day I've been waiting on for months. Seeing her in her wedding dress, giving her my last name, cutting the cake and shoving it in each other's faces, our first dance, the wedding night.

Nothing could have prepared me for the feelings currently slamming into me as I watch her take the first step toward me. Her sleeveless dress is white and hugs her chest, while the waist down flows out in soft waves against her legs. I can't see how her hair is from the back, but it's up with a few loose pieces around her face.

Some days I still can't believe she picked me to spend the rest of her life with. I'm the luckiest bastard in the world.

Our eyes don't leave the other's as Charles leads his daughter down the aisle. My chest swells with pride as she gives me a small smile. When they're standing in front of me, Charles hands me Eden's hand with his shaky one. I couldn't tell you how the man feels in this moment because I only have eyes for the woman in front of me.

I frown when I notice the paleness on her face.

"I'm sorry I'm late," she whispers. "I got sick on the way here."

My frown deepens. "What's wrong? Are you okay?"

Her smile is gorgeous as she gazes at me with the same love I feel for her. Her next words just about knock me on my ass.

"Morning sickness," she giggles. "Well, more like afternoon sickness." She leans toward me, lowering her voice even more. "I'm pregnant."

I stand there stunned for a moment, probably looking like a complete idiot, before her words register.

"You're pregnant?" I ask, wanting to make sure I heard her right.

"Yes."

I'm doing it ass backwards, but I'm fresh out of fucks to give. I wrap my arms around her waist, lean down, and press my lips to hers. She opens willingly, like she needs the intimate touch just as much as I do.

A throat clearing has us pulling apart way too soon.

"Shall we begin?" Pastor Phillips asks, amusement lacing his tone.

I lean down for one more quick kiss and when I pull back, Eden's eyes are sparkling with euphoria.

I turn to the Pastor. "Yes, but make it quick, please."

Eden's giggles can be heard all over the room.

AS I LOOK DOWN INTO A SET of beautiful blue eyes, I understand why it's so easy for Eden to change her favorite color depending on her mood and surroundings. My favorite color just changed to baby blue.

It's still strange to think I have a little sister, but I love the feeling it gives me. It brings out the protective side in me. Thea has quickly been added to my list of people I would die for. And I know my brothers feel the same way. She's not only my little sister, but theirs as well.

"Are you enjoying yourself?" I ask Thea as we gently sway to the music.

She tips her head back, and although she smiles at me, I still see pain lurking behind her eyes. The look is always there.

"Yes. Eden looked so pretty today."

"That she did. So did you."

"Thanks."

I twirl us around, and I'm happy to hear the laugh escape her lips. This girl has been through hell and back. I love knowing I can bring some light into her life.

I stop us after a couple of spins and look down at her, my expression sobering. "I know all these changes are hard on you, Thea. I know the pain Mom and Trey put you through, because I've felt that pain too. It's hard to believe now, but it gets easier. Especially because of all the people here who care for you. You aren't alone anymore. You'll never be alone again."

Her lip trembles, tears gathering in her eyes, before she's launching her small body against mine, her face pressed to my stomach. I close my eyes and wrap my arms tight around her shoulders.

When she pulls back and looks up at me, I wipe away her tears.

"Thank you, JW. I'm glad I have a big brother."

I clear my throat and hope like hell I don't start crying like a fucking baby.

"I'll always be here to protect you," I promise her.

She doesn't know what I did to our parents and she won't know for many years to come. I won't keep it from her forever, she has a right to know, but only when I think she's ready.

When I took her all those months ago and brought her back to Malus, I did some digging. Apparently, Mom and Trey stayed true to Sweet Haven form and never registered her. Through my contacts in San Antonio, I was able to obtain a birth certificate for her, along with starting the adoption process. As of three weeks ago, Eden and I are officially her parents. That day was very emotional for the three of us. Eden and Thea have become very close since she came to live with us in Malus.

When the song ends, I escort her off the dance floor. Brittney, another eleven-year old, is waiting for her to go get another piece of cake. Within a week of Thea arriving, they were friends. Brittney's been handed her own shitty hand in life. I think because of that, they've formed a sort of bond.

As I watch the two girls walk off, fingers lace themselves between mine. I turn and look down at my wife, putting our laced hands behind her back and tugging her close.

"Hey, wife," I whisper.

"Hello, husband," she whispers back with a smile.

"Or should I say, hey, Mama?"

She laughs and the sound goes straight to my heart, just like it always does.

"How's your mom holding up? I saw your dad trying to take away her wine glass."

It's usually the father you have to worry about threatening the groom during the speeches. Not Eden's though. It was her mom who threatened to chop off my nuts and wear them as earrings if I ever dared to hurt her daughter. Of course, she did this stiltedly with the amount of wine she'd consumed. Eden was embarrassed while I barely choked back my laughter. Melanie Delmont loves her daughter fiercely and without reservation. I can't fault the woman for looking out for her only child.

"She's fine, but she'll be regretting it tomorrow. Dad just left to take her home."

Laughter has both of our heads turning. Thea, Brittney, and Hannah are sitting at one of the tables, their heads down as they look at something on Hannah's phone. Eden's friend, Millie, surprised Eden by showing up for the wedding with the two kids they watched over from the shelter they volunteered at. Apparently, the children's mother was caught trying to sell her kids for an eight ball of cocaine. When Millie found out the kids would be put in foster care, she spoke with her husband and they decided to apply for an adoption. It's not official, but their lawyer said there's no reason they would be denied. Eden was ecstatic when Millie gave her the news.

I look back at Eden. "Do you have any idea how happy you make me?"

"Hopefully as happy as you make me," she answers and slides her hands up over my shoulders.

I tighten my arms around her waist and pull her until our stomachs meet. I can't wait to feel hers once it starts to grow with our child tucked inside.

"More."

The soft tendrils of loose hair sways when she shakes her head. "Impossible."

I smile and lean down to press my lips against hers. "We'll have to agree to disagree."

Even though we're not on the dance floor, I begin to move us to the rhythm of the soft music.

"I love you, JW," she says, staring up at me with love shining in her eyes.

"I love you too, Gypsy. More than you'll ever know."

This woman is my life. She completes me in a way I never knew I needed, but I know I won't ever be able to live without.

other books by alex

Malicious

about the author

Alex Grayson is a USA Today bestselling author of heart pounding, emotionally gripping contemporary romances including the Jaded Series, the Consumed Series, The Hell Night Series, and several standalone novels. Her passion for books was reignited by a gift from her sister-in-law. After spending several years as a devoted reader and blogger, Alex decided to write and independently publish her first novel in 2014 (an endeavor that took a little longer than expected). The rest, as they say, is history.

Originally a southern girl, Alex now lives in Ohio with her husband, two children, two cats and dog. She loves the color blue, homemade lasagna, casually browsing real estate, and interacting with her readers. Visit her website, www.alexgraysonbooks.com, or find her on social media!

Made in the USA
Middletown, DE
13 October 2022